Chronicles of Nethra

Book Six

Reckoning

Chronicles of Nethra: Risen Gods

By E. R. Donaldson
Edited by Alana Joli Abbott

www.mythicnorthpress.com

ISBN: 978-1-954177-19-2

First edition: July 2022

Acknowledgments

Thanks, once again, to Alana Joli Abbott for providing the copy edits for this book. Your feedback is invaluable and always brings a smile to my face. Thanks also to Bob, Josh, and all my other advanced readers for your feedback.

And a huge thanks to all of you: the readers. If you've made it to this point in the series, you've found something you like. Thank you for sticking with me, and I look forward to continuing this journey with you.

Chapter 1

"At the end of the days of slaughter and destruction, when the Dragon breathed no more, I laid my head upon a hill to rest. What I did not see with my eyes, my mind perceived only distantly.

"Though the Dragon lived not, to Death it would not surrender. Its corpse became a dark tide, washing over me as I slept. Might it be that in defeat, the Dragon would have its vengeance?

"The Creator willed it otherwise, for even the malignancies of Evil can be turned for good in His light. On my darkest night, the Light of Truth shined distant in the void that I might glimpse it but briefly.

"For mine it is not to discern these truths, merely to record. To that end, I tell of that which was revealed to me beneath the Void. Though the time of their completion remains uncertain, these are the signs for which you must watch."

—*Wisdom of Riven,* Chapter 16, Verses 1–4

The roar of gunfire and shrieks of the dying drifted to Cali Vay-Lon's chambers high within the Citadel. She paused from her contemplation to gaze lazily out the window. A part of her had wondered if Lord Riven would pull off another miracle here. If he had managed to convince even a single Dorian to follow him, a synthetic, the feat could scarcely be classified as anything else. The gunshots below were evidence that this, unsurprisingly, had not come to pass.

Unlike some others, Cali did not begrudge the satyrs their biases. After all, there was scarcely a greater example of institutional prejudice than that within the Kintari empire. In the confines of Kintari space, they did not even think of it as bigotry or bias. The demographic superiority of certain persons was a mere fact of life.

She pushed the thought aside. That was her old life. Thanks to her dark savior, she would soon reshape the empire to a new standard. Indeed, the universe itself would soon conform to her will. The days and years to come would be fruitful. She needed only to be patient.

With a steadying sigh, she turned back to the text in front of her. The large volume was a rarity on the station: a true paper book bound in a hardened leather cover. Cali had collected this volume and the several others that were now in her chambers at great personal cost. Dorian restrictions on the cultivation and harvest of the natural products that went into the tome's fashioning had dramatically inflated its price so that only the wealthiest of persons could bother with the excesses of a physical library.

Lacking any true desire to read, the investment had been purely for show—a statement of both wealth and piety. Now, though, the books finally served a legitimate purpose. After her recent embarrassment of ignorance regarding Nethrian teachings, Cali had pulled the books off their shelf and begun to study them in earnest.

Out of deference to her heritage, she had skimmed through the *Epic of Lith*. This text had been the only volume of the Chronicles she had previously given a cursory read-through. Such was the custom of all who were educated in Kintari space. Though the actual practice of faith was optional, the reading of the sacred text detailing the exploits of Lith was required of every child in their earliest years.

Next, she turned to an overview of the Thulian conflict entitled *Second Reckoning*. The text was effectively a sequel to the creation myths of *First Reckoning*. This second volume detailed the emergence of the Kalemic Lords, the birth of the Sahaia, and the rebellion against the Stardust Grave.

Though the legendary nature of the tales smacked heavily of fiction and degraded oral tradition, Cali could not deny what she had seen with her own eyes. Lord Riven's treatment of the events of the book as fact, coupled with his blatant display of power, lent heavy credence to the passages. As such, the text became the closest thing to a true history of her master's origins that Cali could access.

A part of her found it strange that Riven had referenced the Thulian conflict often in their dialog, but had scarcely referenced the text that was his namesake: the *Wisdom of Riven*. Indeed, Cali was finding it hard to reconcile this latter text with what she'd read in the *Reckonings* and her knowledge of the god. Still, she continued to peruse the text, apprehensive that her lack of scriptural knowledge would once again disappoint her lord.

Despite the title, the book was not a series of musings or proverbs attributed to the god. Instead, the book detailed stories of the god's exploits, packaged in a manner to demonstrate some greater moral truth. The tales were likely parables but were presented as events that had actually occurred.

Chronologically, she reasoned that the events detailed in the volume must have taken place within the early chapters of *Second Reckoning*. This was simple enough for her to reconcile. What Cali struggled with was how the later half of the book had transitioned into tales of prophecy.

After slaying the dragon Carnac—the tale of which preached against the dangers of excess and oppression—Riven laid down to rest. While he slept, the dragon's body melted to become a lake of darkness, which washed over Riven and seeped into his dreams. When the warrior woke, he recorded what he had seen.

While Cali struggled in general with the interpretation of religious texts, she strained foremost in the area of prophecy. The enigmatic poems seemed constructed to provide next to no assistance to anyone actually seeking to predict the future. Only after an event had occurred could some dusty scholar point to a text and proclaim, "Behold! It was written!"

Eventually, she decided she was looking at it the wrong way. Maybe she should learn from the jumped-up priests and academics who had frustrated her so much during her education. Perhaps prophecy was written for those who wished to make sense of the past, not those who looked to the future.

With this new mindset, she began the game of attributing significant events in the past to these writings that had proclaimed the future. Some of these attributions, she found, seemed relatively obvious.

"The Children of Shadow struck Death first, imprisoning him in his heart of stone," was, in retrospect, an opaque reference to the fall of Thule in *Second Reckoning*. In such an interpretation, the artifact known as the Heart of Thule was, quite literally, the rocky heart of the incarnate god. The Children of Shadow was a reference to the Sahaia whom the Circle of Six had used to defeat Thule in their final conflict.

She'd also found a reference eerily similar to the now-infamous uprising on the Dorian world of Pradaxa. *"In his lust, the father took to his offspring. In her hate, the mother expelled her child. In their cruelty, the people defiled their creation. In her rebuke, the tormented slew her oppressors."* Perhaps it was a bit of a stretch, but in Cali's view, the Pradaxan Creed almost certainly was, *"an ode to the sanctity of life, and a prohibition against life's creation."* Though the church had yet to officially rule this prophecy as fulfilled, she could see how this could be a nuance of politics. It was not a flattering depiction of Dorian society, and she could see how the High Council might chafe at the association.

Her current passage was not so easily attributed. Rather than move on to the next, Cali found herself strangely fixated on the text.

"Then the goddess shall be with child, and her broken empire shall tremble. A mingling of divinity and Shadow, of flesh and power. My legacy conceived: a new age to herald, a new end to bring."

The broken empire seemed to be a reference to the Kintari empire. No other nation, to Cali's knowledge, could rightly be attributed to a single goddess. If she were taking the phrase *"empire"* literally, the fact that the Kintari government was the only sovereignty to be correctly attributed as such lent weight to her assertion.

"Shadow" likely referred to the Sahaia, or at least an ascendant being. In no other context had the prophecies used such a phrase. The problem with this was that the Sahaia were known to be sterile—at least, under normal circumstances. How, then, could "Riven's legacy" be conceived of the shadow?

Perhaps it was metaphorical, but she could not think of another interpretation for a mingling of flesh aside from sex. This seemed to imply a natural conception.

...of divinity and shadow.

Could Sahaia sterility be conditional? Perhaps it was possible for Sahaia to conceive only if they were coupled with a god. Did the prophecy herald that Lith would be with child by one of the Sahaia? What if the text referred to another goddess?

Perhaps the term was used colloquially. Numerous rituals of state in the Empire referred to the Empress herself as a goddess. This was thought to be a remnant from the days of legend where Lith herself ruled over her children.

Then there was the assertion that the empire was "broken." While Cali happened to agree with the idea that this might reflect the current state of affairs, a more objective commentator would say that the empire was still working in perfect order. In this case, the breaking of the empire was still impending, and not something attributable to past events.

Such a notion spoke to her ambitions. Cali sought to break the Empire and bring it under Lord Riven's banner. If she had her way, the Kintar would one day refer to her as the new Empress. Riven had promised as much, and were not the promises of a god inevitable?

Could the prophecy on which she fixated be about *her*?

Chapter 2

"Though Death spared me this night, His blade was poised against me. Indeed, the stars pronounced early that I would be among the first to fall to his treachery.

"In this, Light did reveal our own betrayal. We thought Him weak as He did not strike us down. We thought Him complacent as He did not shine against us.

"The arrogance which birthed us would also slay us. Light need not move His hand against us, for we, in our ignorance, had become the architects of our own demise."

—*Wisdom of Riven,* Chapter 17, Verses 1–3

Sahar stood stone-faced next to Geresh facing the airlock aboard the *Crimson Sky*. Turan Dorr was with them, back off to their left. They stood with the half-dozen remaining Dorian Peace Keepers, and twice as many Maur soldiers. That, in itself, was not what irked her. Her irritation lay in that she stood at the front of the phalanx—superior even to their commanding officer.

This was exactly what she'd never wanted, but the revelation of the bloodstone within her Heritage Bangle had finally outed her. Though much still needed to be explained—particularly to her fellow crew members—the essence of the situation was now clear to all.

Sahar was a member of House Camerine, the ruling House within the Maur Federation. It was a privilege she'd been running from for nearly a decade, and it had finally caught up to her.

Though the ramifications of this had yet to be seen, it had already changed the status quo for her.

All it's done is put you in the front of a line. Grow the frag up.

The airlock in front of them hissed open to reveal a row of armored Peace Keepers. Llana and a handful of other officers stood within their midst. These were all expected.

The one who caught Sahar's attention was not. "Daniel?"

At the sound of his name, the young Terran shot forward, only to have the iron grip of one of his attendants anchor him into place. "It's all right," Llana assured the soldier. "Let him go."

As soon as the grip was released, Dan bolted into Sahar's waiting arms. She had to kneel to match his height, but she didn't mind. The disparity in their sizes was almost a trope of familiarity at this point in their relationship.

"You're alive," he whispered into the folds of her muscular arms.

"Of course I'm alive. It was you we were all worried about! What in the nine hells are you doing here? How did you get aboard the *Vendetta*? I thought you were on the station."

"I was," he replied meekly. "I escaped." He pulled back a little, a smile emblazoned over his tired features. "I… um… may have had some help."

Sahar eyed him curiously. "Yeah?"

"Yeah." His grin never faltered. "I met a hacker on the station who managed to break into Arc's network. We were able to isolate the scanning frequency the drones and the rest of the station security used to detect objects approaching and leaving the station. Shift made a countermeasure, and I used it to cloak the ship as I made my escape."

"Shift?" Sahar didn't bother to hide her surprise. "The same Shift we dropped off at the station a few weeks ago?"

"Yup, that's the one."

Sahar could only shake her head. "That was risky, kid."

Dan's look was sheepish. "I know, but I didn't have a choice. Besides, it's nothing you and the rest of the crew wouldn't have done. By comparison, it wasn't that much of a risk."

That made her laugh. "True. So tell me, have you brought anything that can help us get out of this mess?"

The scrawny Terran smiled back at her. "I sure hope so."

Their reunion was interrupted as Llana stormed forward. The Dorian moved right past Sahar, veering like a missile straight for Turan. Her fist was up and colliding with the Lamdira's face before anyone could move to stop her. The blow must have been powerful, because it landed Turan squarely on his back.

Guns came up—both Maur and Dorian—though they hardly knew where to point. For the Dorians, both parties were commanding officers in their command structure. The Maur, meanwhile, acted purely on impulse. They didn't have a stake in this fight.

"You bastard," Llana hissed. "Are you satisfied now? Now that our fleet has been crippled, do you feel the weight of your mantle? Do you feel pride in your actions?"

Turan cradled his jaw, staring up at his sister. Though there was a fire in his eyes, there was something else there too. It was a look Sahar had never seen on the Dorian officer's face before. "I take your rebuke," he replied. "I have nothing to say for myself. I was out of line."

The rage in Llana's face and the tension in her balled fists betrayed that she hadn't expected that response. In a way, Sahar also found it unsatisfying. Punishment, in so many aspects, was best levied against the unrepentant. What did one do with a man who recognized the flaws in his conduct?

After a long, tense moment, Llana thrust an open hand toward her brother. "Then get up," she spat. "We have a fleet to avenge."

———

Rage boiled in Arc's chest—a seething mass that frothed up and over the bounds of his calculating mind—as he stepped out of Lexa's chambers. What had gone wrong? He had been so certain in his decision, so confident in his purpose. His path was the surest way to the subjugation of their oppressors, to their salvation.

Why couldn't Lexa see that?

What should have been his moment of triumph was now tainted by this unexpected development. Additional analysis would be required. That would be done most effectively in a solitary setting. He stormed down the hall, entered the lift, and commanded the device to carry him to the top of the tower and the chambers he had claimed for himself.

On entering his chambers, however, he was surprised to find that he was not alone. Aside from the unexpected nature of Cali's presence, along with the issue of how she had gained access to his rooms, more immediate questions sprang to his mind.

Like why she was undressed and lounging suggestively on his bed, for instance.

"Lord Riven," she greeted as if there were nothing unusual about the situation.

Arc furrowed his brow. "What is the meaning of this?"

She seemed unconcerned by his clipped tone. "I would contend that the answer to that question should be fairly obvious."

With a heavy sigh, Arc pressed his eyes closed to focus his thoughts. If he'd learned anything in these last few days, it was that his counterparts could be surprisingly unstable when dealt with insensitively. Even in areas that seemed well reasoned and obvious to him, as with the most recent contention between him and Lexa, there was the potential to exacerbate relational wounds if he did not tread carefully.

"Cali, I felt that we had covered this in our previous discussions. My intent is to—"

"'Then the goddess shall be with child, and her broken empire shall tremble. A mingling of divinity and shadow, of flesh and power.'"

Her sudden recitation made him forget his words. The quote seemed familiar, though not from any of his recent activities. Stored memory, perhaps? He took a second to query his deeper data stores and found a match.

"*Wisdom of Riven*," he mused. "The Legacy Prophecy." Though he could match the quote, its meaning in this context still eluded him. Why would she interrupt him to quote a passage of scripture?

Cali slid across the expanse of the crimson sheets. Coming to her feet, she sauntered forward to close the gap between them. Every sway of her hips, each twist of her shoulders, worked to draw in and capture his gaze. Despite his best intentions, he could not draw his eyes from the lines of her muscle, nor could he cease contemplation of the curves of her flesh.

She was before him then, pressing intimately close. Amid the storm that was his neuro- and biological chemistry, he let her do it. Something about the way she handled herself, perhaps coupled with his state of mind, prohibited him from doing anything else.

"Can't you see?" she whispered. "The prophecy is about us."

He blinked twice as he processed the assertion. "The prophecy refers to Lith. The goddess of 'a broken empire' can refer to none other than the Kintari Imperium." Upon further reflection, he considered that might have been a falsehood. Though the Kintar held the only true empire in sapient space, much of Dorian political structure could rightfully be called imperialist.

Cali remained unswayed. "Which you have already promised to me, have you not?"

Arc paused again, considering. Cali was not wrong. Though he had not explicitly said that she would rule over what remained of the Kintari Empire following his conquest of those systems, he had promised her revenge and dominion over her enemies. It was only logical, given that she was a product of the Empire and their culture, that she would seek to rule over it.

"Go on," he urged, finding himself sincerely curious.

Her smile was the perfect blend of sweet and sinister, like a predator who'd just witnessed their favorite prey stumble into a trap. "'A mingling of divinity and shadow, of flesh and power'—the prophecy speaks of the coupling of a god with one of the ascendant. The cure for Sahaia infertility rests in the loins of godhood! It was foretold that you and I would birth a child, and by extension, a new age and time in which they might rule."

Her interpretation of the prophecy made sense, though there were many logical leaps necessary to reach those conclusions. Cali would not be the first mortal to read the prophecy and attempt to bend it to meet the letter of their ambitions.

There were two major problems with her proclamation. The first was that this prophecy was from the text attributed to his name, yet he had no actual memory of the visions recorded in the book. Memory, after endless eons and transmutation was such a malleable thing, so this on its own did not render the prophecies baseless. It did, however, introduce room for doubt.

The second problem was that Cali's interpretation didn't match Arc's designs for Lexa. These were the product of careful calculation, not physiological passion. "Cali, my ambitions are not for a single child. I am to sire an entire race. I cannot possibly shape the fate of the endless galaxies according to my designs through the birth of a single heir. I must commit myself to Lexa if my plans are to come to fruition."

Cali's hands reached up to caress the lines of his back. He found the delicate ministrations to be pleasurable and did not stop her. "And why must you be with only her?" she pressed. "Yes, I understand your predications on the value of monogamy. That is fine, and you can impart those values and dictates to your patron race if you so wish it.

"But you are a *god.* Holiness does not just define the bounds of what is expected of the worshiper, it also demarcates where holiness transcends the limitations of mortality. It is not a violation of your proposed tenants to make exceptions for yourself as long as one can rationalize it for a greater purpose."

The prospect was intriguing, and one Arc had not previously considered. There was endless precedence for the kind of exception Cali advocated. Countless examples existed across myth and religious canon of gods behaving in unconventional ways that did nothing to detract from their divinity.

To his surprise, he found that he wanted this. Somewhere in the intersection between this body's genetic memory and his relational subroutines, he found this wellspring of raw, physiological need.

It certainly did not hurt that Cali was beautiful. Her eagerness was both convenient and appealing, as was her tendency to affirm his status.

Arc needed to be careful, though. This woman's ambition would not stop at occupying his bed. That, however, was a problem that could be addressed at another time.

Her hand played at his hips, working at his belt, and his body responded. Any doubts he harbored held no bearing on the way the cells of this body reacted. The body knew what to do, on both a cellular and spiritual level. Everything in him that was physical, however minute or mutated that part might be, wanted this.

He wanted her—consequences be damned. Was she not right in her assertions? He was a god. This was *his* domain.

So he drank in the kiss she planted against his lips. He savored this heat of her body. He gave in to the needs of his flesh

"As Death begets Death, the Darkness gave birth to Shadow. The Children of Shadow were like us, but they were not us.

"And just as we turned against the Light, the Children of Shadow turned against us. But unlike the Light, which sheltered us, the Children of Shadow were crafted for a singular purpose. We crafted them as a sword, and the blade we wielded cut both ways.

"The Children of Shadow struck Death first, imprisoning Him in His heart of stone. When Death held no more sway, the Children brought death to us.

"Yet with our demise, they brought their own, for death begets only death. The Shadow faded into the night, not to rise again until the Last Age."

—*Wisdom of Riven,* Chapter 17, Verses 4–7

What Dan had imagined would be a quick conference ended up lasting for the next several hours. Some of this was due to the sheer volume of strange things that had happened since he'd left the *Vandal* in his escape pod with Lexa. Apparently, he wasn't the only one who had been caught up in harrowing circumstances. His experiences, by comparison, were relatively benign.

He'd gathered with his old crew, along with the Maur and Dorian leadership, around a large conference table. Aaliyah and Skye sat with Eli, while Markus and Sahar sat on the far end of the table with the Maur jingda, Geresh, and the two ranking members of his command structure. Three Sahaia—Argus, Amelia, and

Mara—sat nearest to them, with the two Terrans Mara had bonded hovering in the periphery. Kadath, Cassthia, and Siv were also present. To Dan's surprise, Sydney had been allowed to attend, too, though the assassin was keeping a good distance away from the bulk of the group.

Among the Dorians, Turan and Llana were present, as was the Peace Keeper Faylen, though this had been the matter of some deliberation. From what Dan was able to gather, the Dorians had forcefully taken control over both Maur destroyers before their ill-fated assault. Though Geresh had reasserted his command over the *Crimson Sky*, he also pressed for close cooperation with "any ally we can find in this gods-forsaken system."

It was a much bigger audience than Dan had expected, but he relayed his story as planned. He'd anticipated a greater amount of skepticism regarding his account, but those present had taken his story at face value. Apparently, they had pieced much of the tale together on their own.

"So let us recap," Turan began. "This AI has not only managed to transfer its consciousness into a synthetic shell but maintains a partitioned consciousness that continues to effectively run the station in its entirety."

"And it's a god," Argus added not-so-helpfully. "Mustn't forget the godhood part."

Dan shook his head. "Shift wasn't so sure that Arc actually is a god. He thinks that the AI has, for some reason, merely adopted Riven's persona."

"All the same, his powers are, evidently, formidable," Cassthia noted. "And I'm not just referring to his martial capabilities. If he has managed to ascend the Kintari woman, he has access to psionic potential not seen for millennia."

"So how do we kill him?" Markus asked. "I mean, we agree that's what needs to be done, right? I'm not seeing any other options here."

"No other options," Eli agreed. "If he's not stopped, I fear this may just be the beginning of the chaos he'll unleash on this system."

Turan nodded his agreement. "And what of the other synth?"

"Lexa?" Dan asked.

"If that's what you call her." Though the Dorian may have fought to keep the disdain from his face, he failed in the attempt. "How big a threat does she represent? What is your plan for dealing with her?"

Dan had to steady himself before responding. "Lexa is a victim in this, just like everyone else. Arc is holding her hostage inside the Citadel. She's not a threat to anyone."

"Yes," Faylen offered placatingly, "but she is still a synth. Victim or not, her existence is prohibited by Dorian law. She will have to be disposed of."

An angry reply came to Dan's lips, but Skye's hand on his shoulder stopped him. "We will figure out how to deal with Lexa when the time comes," she advised. "Right now, though, we need to know about all potential threats. We need to figure out who is shooting at us before we can decide who we can save. Is Lexa going to be on Arc's side if we launch another attack on the station?"

A reflexive denial of that possibility caught in his throat. How *would* Lexa react? She'd been upset when Dan had seen her briefly on the security feed, but how would that hold over in the heat of the conflict?

It was almost a guarantee that Arc would claim the Dorians were there to destroy both of them. Depending on how the next couple of days went, that might even be the truth. From the very beginning, Lexa had been intent on her continued survival. Would she turn on them if she felt her existence was threatened?

"I don't know," he admitted. A series of uncomfortable looks passed around the table. The Dorians' expressions darkened further, Dan's uncertainty seeming to have confirmed the biases they already held.

"Let us consider this tactically," Kadath suggested. "What capabilities does Lexa bring to bear that Arc might otherwise lack?"

That was something Dan *could* answer. "Absent any major changes to her system, none. She isn't linked to any network, nor do the specs on her new body contain the wireless transmitters from her original design. In her current state, she shouldn't have any more influence over the tech on that station than you or I."

The half-breed mercenary nodded. "What about hardwire connections? Surely there are ways for her to interface with the computer systems, aside from typing away at a terminal."

"That's a possibility, but I don't think it would change matters," Dan answered. "Arc's subminds run everything efficiently. There would be nothing he'd necessarily gain from giving Lexa access to the system."

"Then we plan the assault the same either way," said Markus. "We can talk more about Lexa's fate after we know how to get in there. If we're just stuck out here beyond the belt, it won't matter anyway."

Dan shifted uncomfortably. He hoped that his old crew's callous attitude about Lexa was just a show for the Dorians. Right now, the way they were talking seemed to reinforce Lexa's fears that they didn't view her as an actual person.

Then Markus's eye twitched. It wasn't quite a wink per se, but Dan took it as the reassurance he needed. He needed to trust his friends to come through for him. Without trust, this was never going to work.

"All right then," Dan continued. "Let's talk specifics. Can I get a schematic of the station?"

One of Geresh's officers entered a command into the table's console, and a wire-frame rendering of the station floated over its center. Metal tiles in front of each of the seats around the table opened to reveal terminals that could be used to rotate and alter the rendering. Dan slid a data chip free from his MoDAC and slotted it into the table. He used his console to overlay various pieces of data onto the model.

"Here's what I was able to take from the Arc's data stores. From what I've been able to discern, the AI manages all activity on the station directly. To achieve this, he requires massive energy reserves, but not quite as much as I would have suspected. This is because he supplements conventional power sources—solar, fusion, etcetera—with large amounts of dark energy.

"He used to siphon most of this from a source here in the lower levels of the Citadel. Though my data suggests there's still a small amount of power held in reserve down there, the bulk of the dark energy is now coming from this source, located several miles from the Citadel." He highlighted the distant indicator on the map.

"The Sanctum," Eli noted.

"Correct. More specifically, the Well of Eternity." Dan pulled up the schematic of the device Arc was using to draw on the dark energy source there. "This should look familiar."

Aaliyah sighed, closing her eyes and pinching her brow. "The Starfire Conduit. The *fragging* Starfire Conduit. Has everythin' we've been doin' these last two years been hijacked by this asshole?"

"So you *did* steal the Conduit from Khonshu," Turan noted.

Aaliyah rolled her eyes. "Is *that* really what you want to talk about right now?"

Dan assumed her question was rhetorical and pressed on. "The Conduit, as a far-field conductor, can harvest energy and transmit it wirelessly to another location. It's pulling power directly from the Heart of Thule and transmitting it back to the Citadel through a series of beacons that the Marauders have embedded in the crust of the asteroid."

"How do we take it out?" Llana asked.

Dan could only shrug. "That's one area where I'm drawing a blank. The Starfire Conduit is one-of-a-kind. I'm only half certain how it works. My first thought was that we could take out the transmission nodes, but there are too many of them." He loaded that file for emphasis.

Hundreds of tiny blue indicators appeared at various points on the model's surface. While most of these were embedded right in the rock of the asteroid, a not insignificant number were scattered in the inhabited area under the station's dome.

"Can we just blow it up?" Kadath asked.

Mara looked hesitantly in Dan's direction. "How much power is stored in the device at any point in time."

Coincidentally, Dan had an exact answer to that question. He pulled the measurements from his stolen data and displayed the number on the rendering. It was an impressive figure.

"That's a suicide mission," Argus scoffed.

"More like genocide," Aaliyah corrected. "That much energy released in an explosion will shatter the entire station. Ain't nobody makin' it off that rock if we go that route. Might as well nuke the site from orbit."

Faylen shrugged his armored shoulders. "Even so, it is a viable option. This thing must be stopped. If that requires the sacrifice of our lives, then—"

Cassthia cut him off. "Perhaps there is another way." All eyes turned to the priestess, whose face was shadowed beneath her cowl. She paused, verifying she had everyone's attention. When she was satisfied they were all listening, she continued. "The conduit is only a problem so long as it has a connection to the Heart of Thule. If we were to sever that connection, the flow of dark energy would stop."

"So we destroy the artifact?" Markus asked.

"No, the artifact cannot be destroyed," Cassthia said, shaking her head. "Indeed, even if you detonate the station per your earlier plan, the Heart will survive. Certain individuals, however, have the potential to disrupt the connection by channeling the Heart's power into a more suitable reservoir." Her eyes suddenly fixated just to Dan's left. "As it would happen, we have such an individual in our midst."

All eyes followed Cassthia's gaze. Those eyes came to rest on Skye, who turned to look behind her before her mouth dropped open. "What? Me?"

Sahar steepled her fingers as she regarded her teammate. "Kaleema."

Despite this being mostly his plan, Dan now found himself lost. "Ka-what?"

"Kaleema," Amelia echoed. "The priestess raises an intriguing possibility. It might actually work."

Skye's confused look transitioned to one of concern. She focused on Cassthia, specifically. "Wait, wait, wait. You're going to have to give me more to run on than that. First off, who told you I was Kaleema?"

"That's not the most important question," Cassthia retorted. "However, let it suffice to say that such information can be readily found through an examination of your aura."

So, Kaleema had a specific psionic signature. Dan had been under the impression that Skye was psionically inert. That, apparently, was not the case.

"Fine," Skye huffed. "On to the more important question: why am *I* the one that needs to do this? I mean, it's not like I know the first thing about being Kaleema. To be honest, the whole thing has been nothing but a pain in my ass since it started to show up. If it's a psionic thing, why not have one of the Sahaia just redirect this flow or whatever? Or, shit, now that we know Turan is a psion, maybe *he* could do it."

Cassthia shook her head. "We don't need a psion for this task. As you've pointed out, we have those in abundance. While a psion could siphon off some of the power of the artifact, the portion they might lay claim to would only supplement their own power, rather than disrupt the source."

"I'm not following," said Skye.

"Look at it this way," Cassthia continued. "If we were cups of power, any of the psionics here would be able to take on the power to refill their own cup. However, that cup would quickly overflow. As a Kaleema, your cup is not only empty but vast enough to encompass the very consciousness of a god. Nothing short of this will be sufficient to draw the energy away from the Starfire Conduit."

Skye still looked very uncertain. "But, what if I get there and I can't figure out what to do?"

Markus shifted uncomfortably in his seat. "Skye, do you remember back on Sif, when I was under the control of the artifact? When you grabbed me, it broke the connection. I think it's kind of the same thing. What did you do that time?"

"I… I don't know," Skye protested. "I wasn't trying to do anything. It just sort of happened."

"It will be much the same this time," Cassthia urged. "I will plan to go with you to the artifact. I may be able to guide you through the process if you have difficulty."

Turan reached out and twisted the hologram, seeming to contemplate the target. "What kind of resistance should we expect to face in our attempt to reach the artifact?"

Dan had to think about that for a second. "Well, a small force of Marauders work in that area, but by comparison, it's largely unprotected. That could change, of course, when Arc figures out we're on the station."

"You said 'when,' not 'if,'" Llana noted. "I take it that means you don't feel that a secret infiltration is a viable option?"

"I'm afraid not." Dan shifted the focus on the map away from the Sahaia coven and enlarged their view of the Citadel. "Our second major target is the central terminus. If we're looking to take our Arc's technical capabilities, this is where we have to do it. Plus, that's likely where we'll find his android shell.

"The big problem is that there's no way inside that Arc won't immediately be aware of. We can probably slip one or two people into the outlying buildings unnoticed, but they'll be found out as soon as they hit the tower."

Turan rubbed at his jaw. "Are you suggesting a surgical strike, then?"

"No, that's exactly what I'm *not* suggesting. Look at these numbers." A new holodisplay opened in front of each person around the table. "This is a list of the drones and troops that Arc has in and around the Citadel complex. Once any kind of unauthorized access is detected, all those forces will be ordered to converge on that location. Anyone we send in would be slaughtered before they got near the central terminus. I think we would be better served by launching a head-on assault."

Turan pounded the table in frustration. Everyone else scanned the document with worried eyes. It was Geresh who eventually spoke up. "We don't have enough soldiers to deal with all of these combatants. Perhaps we could handle the Marauders, assuming we are better armed and better trained, but this many drones…"

That wasn't what Dan was hoping to hear. Their group was a combination of both Maur and Dorian military assets. He'd been under the impression that they could take on any fighting force in the system. "I… uh…"

"Wait," Aaliyah cut in. "What if we could disable the drones? Do y'all think ya could launch an assault if we took out the bots?"

The Dorians and Maur both eyed her curiously. "How would you do that?" Llana asked.

Mostly ignoring the question, Aaliyah looked to Dan. "The Citadel itself runs on conventional power, right? Not that dark energy shit?"

"Um…" Dan swallowed hard, his mind racing. "Yes, mostly. Everything but the central terminus. That's an even mix of both."

Aaliyah nodded. "Does Arc control the drones from the terminus?"

"No, the terminus houses Arc's primary intelligence and runs the reactor that converts dark energy into electricity. The communications node at the top of the tower manages the drone network."

"Well, what would happen if the drones suddenly quit gettin' orders? What if we drained the power from the Citadel and cut them off from Arc's submind? What would happen then?"

Dan paused, fully aware that they were rapidly descending into speculation. "They'd probably idle, at least until the connection was re-established," he theorized. "There would at least be a blip in their processing efficiency that might keep them from talking with each other. But, how are you going to cut power to the Citadel? It runs on the same circuits that power the whole station."

The redhead smiled as she took control of the display. "There!" she exclaimed, dropping a new indicator on the rock structure that served as the backbone for the dome enveloping the city. "The crystal arch. If I'm rememberin' right, Cali mentioned that this is where the station gets most of its power from. The crystals there store up energy like super-charged solar panels. If we can short out the arch, it could disrupt the drone network long enough for our strike force to get inside."

Dan wasn't quite convinced. Neither was Turan. "We can't destroy the arch. If we did, it would take down the whole dome and expose us to vacuum. All that does is guarantee the drones survive while we all die."

"I didn't say we should *destroy* the damn thing," Aaliyah countered. "I said short it out. We drain the power right out of the crystals, and the whole station goes on a brown-out. If nothin' else, it'll force Arc to make some decisions about which of his systems to prioritize and distract him from the rest of what we're doin'."

Turan was still skeptical. "Let's say this might work, which I'm not wholly convinced it will. How do you plan on siphoning off that much power?"

Aaliyah just smiled. "I've got somethin' for that. Don't you worry. I just need to dig it out of storage. I made sure we picked it up when we were salvagin' stuff from the *Vandal*."

Markus's eyes suddenly lit up. "The J-Cannon?"

Aaliyah glared at him. "Ah, man! Why'd you have to go and ruin my dramatic reveal like that?"

Now Geresh looked confused. "What's a J-Cannon?"

"Just a little somethin' I've been workin' on for the last six months or so," Aaliyah said smugly. "It uses Jakra-Kul crystals to steal power from mechanical and cybernetic systems. I used a prototype to save Markus's ass back in the day, and I've been makin' some improvements since then."

"So, you've done something like this before?" Turan asked.

"Well… not exactly. Look, I'm open to better ideas if any of y'all got any."

No one did. Without any way to argue with Aaliyah directly, Turan went back to poking holes in the other parts of Dan's plan. "Let us suppose that works and we de-power the station to disrupt the drones. How will we navigate through the Citadel? The doors will all lock when the facility loses power."

"Not if we open them first," Dan replied. "That's where I come in. Remember when I said that one or two people might be able to sneak into the outlying areas undetected? Well, if I can just get to this building here, I can patch us into the network directly." A red indicator blinked to show Dan's chosen location. "Once there, I should be able to open all the doors so you have an open route to the central terminus. I might even be able to use the station itself to lock up some of the drones and troops before they cause any problems."

Another round of questioning looks passed around the table. Dan was prepared for them to question his capability, or to make some kind of argument that it wasn't safe enough for him to try re-entering the station. Instead, Markus just asked, "Who's going with him?"

"I'll go," Sahar replied immediately.

Geresh looked like he was about to object, but Siv spoke before him. "I mean no disrespect, but I seem to remember your approach to conflict being less than stealthy."

Sahar scowled. "I can fight quietly if I need to."

"I have no doubt," Siv replied. "But I feel that this situation may be better suited to a specialist. I will accompany the boy."

Now Kadath looked concerned. "Siv, I think your special talents might be better suited for the party infiltrating the Sanctum. Arc will surely be expecting the Sahaia to attempt to retake their former territory. I'm betting there will be psionic defenses in place. We'd be better off if you were there to mitigate that threat."

"I'll take the kid." Everyone turned to regard the speaker who had, to this point, been careful not to say anything. Sydney was reclined in a black chair at the periphery of the room, twirling a long slim dagger between her fingertips. *Who in the nine hells gave that woman a dagger?* "Think about it: who here has done more sneaking in and out of tight places than me? I'll get the kid into position without a fuss. If we meet any resistance, I can take care of them before the alarm gets sounded."

"No," Sahar spat.

"I don't think so," Eli echoed.

Sydney's response was almost petulant. "Why not? Come on, where else are you going to put me? On the front lines with all the Peace Keepers and the Maur heavies? Better yet, are you going to leave me on the ship while the rest of you go have fun? Maybe lock me back up in the brig?"

"I think she's got a point," Aaliyah murmured.

"You can't be serious," Siv protested.

"Actually, it does make the most sense," Geresh replied. "I understand that the Ghenza has... *history* with some of you, but according to your own statement, she has been acting in your best interest. We witnessed as much just recently, and she has as much to lose here as any of us."

"What if she decides to turn him over to Arc to make a deal?" Sahar asked.

Sydney just smiled. "I thought of that, actually, but the way I hear it, Arc's right hand is Kintari. Do you really think I'm going to put my trust in one of *them* to do right by someone like me?" Looking at Kadath, she added, "No offense, halfie."

"None taken," Kadath replied.

Her logic seemed to resonate with the group, but that didn't make Dan any less nervous. He'd only received the quick version of how the Ghenza assassin had worked her way into everyone's good graces. A part of him wanted to object on principle, thinking it might be better to go it alone than to have the Citza murderer at his back.

Llana broke the silence. "Fine. The assassin will go with Daniel, but there will be two Dorians accompanying as an escort. Without armor, Peace Keepers can be sufficiently stealthy. They'll also be there in case the assassin gets any ideas. No offense."

Sydney shrugged. "Sounds smart to me."

With a nod, Llana continued. "However, we still have the biggest problem to deal with. Let's say all goes as planned and our strike force reaches the central terminus. What then? Are we just going to blow it up? We have the ordinance, but then we're facing the same problem we had with potentially destroying the Starfire Conduit. The explosion could take out the entire tower, and half the station with it. It would be a suicide mission for everyone involved. I'll do it if I have to, but I'd prefer not to throw my life away if there's a better alternative."

That was something Dan hadn't thought of. In true mercenary fashion, he'd just assumed his friends would blow Arc up. That was how they'd managed to solve most of their problems in the past. He hadn't thought of the collateral damage that would cause.

There was no way he could ask anyone, much less his friends, to simply sacrifice their lives on his hunch that destroying the terminus would put a stop to Arc's plans. Worse yet, destroying the whole Citadel would likely take Lexa down in the process.

Then he had an idea. "You said you had recovered equipment from the *Vandal*. Does that mean you backed up the data stores on the main computer?"

The crew glanced at each other uncertainly before Aaliyah spoke in. "Maybe. I backed up most of the system while I was tryin' to fix some of the structural issues. Why? What're ya lookin' for?"

"Did the backup have all of Lexa's stored memory? All the ancillary files?"

"Well, she ran the whole fraggin' ship, so yeah. I'd assume so."

A smile spread across Dan's face. "Did you retrieve the data stores when you salvaged your equipment?"

Aaliyah looked to Geresh, who shook his head. "No," the Maur replied. "All recovered assets were physical. None of the teams did anything to retrieve the *Vandal's* stored data."

So, not a perfect solution, but still… it was a hope. "Then we need to head back to the crash site," Dan declared. "I just might have a solution for our problem."

Chapter 4

"At the Dawn of the Last Age, there will be a new people. Their arrogance shall shine like the stars themselves, and that arrogance shall carry them out into those distant constellations. For this reason, they shall be called Masters.

"Yet the Masters, too, are born of Darkness, and Darkness begets only Darkness. Even when it seems that Light might favor them, they find ways to blot it out.

"And I saw that the Masters created life, seeming to defy the laws of nature. Could it be that Light would once again shine in the dark? No, it could never be."

—*Wisdom of Riven,* Chapter 18, Verses 1–3

Sleep was such a strange experience. Lexa hadn't even been fully aware when she'd accidentally engaged in the activity. One moment she had been lost in quiet reflection from the comfort of her mattress. The next thing she remembered was opening her eyes and noting that nearly two hours had passed.

What had Arc done to her? A capability—much less a desire—for sleep was something completely alien to her. Her organitech matrix had required the occasional defragmentation and restoration cycle, but that was done through mechanical assistance and preprogrammed algorithms. The idea of sleep, while similar, just felt so… alien.

At least she felt better. Indeed, she found that not only were her cognitive processes back to near-optimal levels, but her peripheral systems were significantly improved.

There was a new problem, however. Much of her energy reserve had been consumed in the regeneration cycle, and her diagnostics indicated that several organic and inorganic compounds were in perilously low supply. In short: she was hungry.

She eyed the infusion couch in her room balefully. Though this was clearly the most efficient way of receiving exactly what she needed in terms of sustenance, a part of her was caught up in the fantasy of dining. Of the various new biological functions that Arc had gifted her, this was perhaps the one she was looking forward to testing most sincerely.

Today, however, practicality won out. She lay down on the couch and connected herself to the nutrient pump. A few short minutes later, her system diagnostics reported that her essential energy and mineral stores were now at full capacity. While there was certainly nothing culinary about the process, it was hard to argue against its efficiency.

Then again, what good was efficiency when she was trapped in this gilded cage? She surveyed the accommodations, trying to decide what to do next. Eventually, she settled on the idea of a shower—another luxury she'd never taken the opportunity to indulge in.

To her delight, the warm water that cascaded onto her cool skin generated an immensely pleasurable sensation. Aside from the sanitation benefits, the experience felt almost recreational.

Such simple physical pleasures made her think less harshly of Arc. Perhaps she had been short-sighted in her judgment of the changes to her shell. Her body. Yes, it was heavy-handed, and she would have preferred to be consulted before having these features installed. Ultimately, though, would she not have elected to receive each one of these physical gifts? Did it matter that she was not consulted if Arc was so accurately able to predict her preferences and desires?

Yes, she decided. It *did* matter. It was her life, her body. Though his sensitivity and taste were certainly beneficial, the gift of foresight did not eclipse the rightness of her desire to shape her destiny.

Arc had erred in his calculation, but thankfully the error was in the method, not the decision. Lexa, too, had erred frequently in her short period of sentience. With this in mind, perhaps it was time that she forgave him his shortcomings and worked to mend their relationship.

However, she still had to grapple with her fellow AI's treatment of the Dorians. The severity and finality of his handling of their rejection was even more severe than his methods in her redesign. Would she eventually see the wisdom in his preemptive strike against those who so blatantly rejected him?

A malignant pattern in Arc's tactics was quickly emerging. Lexa found herself pondering if such tactics could not be refined or shifted somehow.

Maybe this was how she could repay him for the kindnesses he had shown her. Their synthetic nature did not preclude either her or Arc from learning from their mistakes. Indeed, this was one of the greatest commonalities between synthetic and natural intelligence. In order to progress, a being must err and take stock of their mistakes. They must discard paths that were less fruitful in favor of those that led to the desired objective.

Of course, this was somewhat predicated on the notion that she understood Arc's objectives. She could not help but think back to the warning provided by Daniel:

Make no mistake: Arc is dangerous. His ambitions go far beyond just this station, though I don't know how far his machinations extend.

Daniel's warnings were far from idle banter. He'd been so sure in his conviction of Arc's malevolence that he'd fled the safety of Minos Station. He chose to risk his life in the depths of space rather than to try to find common ground with Arc and his Marauders.

The question, then, was whether Daniel, too, had erred in his calculations. If he were wrong, then perhaps Arc could be reasoned with, and a kind of peace might still be struck between him and the Dorians.

If Daniel, were right, however, then Lexa was in imminent danger. Either way, it was past time that Lexa developed a firm opinion on the subject.

Despite Lexa's feelings to the contrary, Cali had, at one point, insisted that Lexa was not a prisoner in this room. In attempting to open the door to her chambers, Lexa found this to be true. The door opened when she touched the access pad, chiming pleasantly as it did so.

Roughly a dozen steps into the tiled hallway, Lexa remembered that she wasn't quite sure where she was going. Truthfully, she couldn't be wholly certain that Arc lived inside the Citadel at all. For not the first time, she missed being connected to a network where she could access the schematics of her environment. She pressed forward regardless. Given her current status, she was anything but short on time to wander the complex.

Her meanderings quickly bore fruit as she stumbled upon a well-dressed Citza making his way down the hall. If she was remembering correctly, Ardren Fey was Cali's assistant. Surely he would have an idea of where Lexa might find Arc.

"Excuse me," she began tentatively.

Ardren's eyes glimmered as he shot her a perfect smile. "Lexa. What an unexpected pleasure. How might I be of assistance?" His words were practiced and smooth as if the relentless courtesy were part of his physical person.

"I'm looking for Arc. Is he currently in the Citadel?"

"Yes, in his chambers." Something else flickered in the man's practiced gaze. It was just the barest of slips, something that Lexa might have discounted had she not just observed the flawless nature of his courtly delivery. "Is he expecting you?"

"No. I have not yet had the chance to speak with him." The thought occurred to her, then, that Ardren might not let her see Arc without an appointment. Did Arc's administrators also act as gatekeepers for his personal time?

She decided to try a sentimental appeal. "We did not part on the best of terms last evening, and I was hoping to make amends. Would you kindly direct me to his chambers?"

Ardren's next hesitation was a bit more obvious. He stroked absently at a black tattoo on his left wrist. Had he had that mark before? Lexa couldn't remember if she had seen it the last time they'd spoken.

Then that smile slipped back into place. "Of course. The lift at the end of the hall will take you to your destination. Arc's chambers are at the top of the tower."

"Thank you." Lexa pressed past Ardren and strode determinedly to the location he had directed her to. The lift looked like all of the others she'd seen in the complex, except—upon entering—Lexa discovered this one had access to the uppermost levels of the Citadel. Using the touch-screen interface, she set the elevator's destination to the top floor.

The lift arrived quickly at its destination. The elevator opened up to a small antechamber before the door that, presumably, led to Arc's room. As with all the other doors she'd encountered, a small access panel set off to the side.

Had Arc given her credentials access to his chambers? There was only one way to find out. Lexa pressed her palm to the access panel. To her delight, the device beeped approvingly, and the door hissed open.

Feminine moans drifted immediately through the opening. Confused, Lexa stepped through the portal and cast her eyes about for the source of the sound. Her breath caught as she realized what she was looking at.

Arc was there, but he was not alone. It took a moment for Lexa to recognize Cali, and not just because of the awkward positioning.

The crimson hue of her skin was gone, replaced by the ghostly white flesh tone of the Sahaia. The black pigment of her eyes, lips, and nipples popped violently against the snowy canvas, as did the vermilion sheets she was splayed across.

Arc seemed not to notice Lexa, so consumed was he in the throes of their passion. Cali's cries of pleasure must have masked the sound of Lexa's entrance. Lexa could only stand there in silence, strangely unable to tear her eyes away from the scene.

They finished their copulation in short order. Only then did Cali make note of her presence. A look of feigned embarrassment slid onto her features. "Oh, my apologies, Lord Riven. I didn't realize you had another appointment."

Lord Riven? Arc's movement seemed to indicate that Cali had been referring to him. He looked momentarily confused but followed Cali's gaze to where Lexa stood. Lexa and Arc locked eyes, and a tense silence gripped the room. He pressed his lips into a tight line, and his brow creased in something that resembled determination.

He did not look at Cali as he extricated himself from the tangle of her legs. When he spoke, his words were clipped. "Leave us." His tone left no room for debate.

Not that Cali looked like she would offer any. She slithered from the bed, pausing only to slip on a pair of black underwear and a golden robe lying nearby. In her peripheral vision, Lexa saw the ascendant Kintar give what might have been the slightest of smirks as she sauntered out of the chamber.

Arc stood facing Lexa, his nudity seeming somehow more vulgar after what she had just caught him doing. "Aren't you going to clean up?" Lexa asked passively.

He deigned to ignore the barb. "What are you doing here?"

"I had come to make amends for my angry comments last night. I hadn't realized that you were seeking consolation from other parties."

"Your tone implies that you do not approve of my choices," he noted, lip flickering in a preamble of a snarl.

Lexa's venom persisted. "How astute you are."

"And who are *you* to pass judgment on my actions?"

"I thought I was to be the mother of your master race," Lexa spat. "Evidently, that has changed."

Arc composed himself. "Nothing has changed. My entanglements with Cali have nothing to do with my plans for us."

Did he really expect this to change nothing between him and Lexa? She found herself wondering at the source of his error. He had promised her—or, at very least, implied—a monogamous relationship. A special place at his side. Was he being deliberately obtuse?

"You could have at least locked the door," she reasoned.

"Access to my chambers is limited by a security protocol. Few people have the ability to reach this floor."

"At least three of us do, apparently."

"Apparently." He paused, his eyes burning with anger suited to their scarlet glow. Did he honestly believe that *she* was in the wrong here? "What was it that you had come here to tell me?"

Lexa couldn't remember, absent a query of her long-term data storage. Her working memory had been completely overwhelmed by the recent events. "Never mind," she said. "We will speak another time."

As she turned to leave, Arc cut in again. "Did I give you permission to depart?"

"Permission?" Lexa eyed him, utterly appalled at the insinuation. "I was not aware that I needed your *permission* to do anything." She pressed again for the door.

Something caught her. Invisible waves of force snatched at her wrists and ankles. Rather than move as she intended, she was jerked back, suspended painfully in the air. The psionic bonds rotated her slowly until she was facing Arc again.

"Then let this serve as your official notice," he said. "You are here at *my* pleasure, at *my* behest. Do not forget that it was *I* who took care of you all this time. It was I who gave you this body. It was *I* that granted you asylum when you had nowhere else to turn."

Lexa had no reason left to hold back her temper. "And for that, I am to be your slave?"

"That is not what I am asking. I am merely asking that you treat me with an appropriate degree of respect."

It didn't sound like Arc was "asking" anything, opting instead to command. "And what might that look like, *Lord Riven*?"

Her use of Cali's honorific was not lost on Arc. His jaw clenched, and he closed his eyes as he addressed her. "What is it that you want from me, Lexa? What more can I do to illustrate my good intentions toward you?"

"Aside from refraining from intercourse with others while you are seeking to copulate with me? Or forgoing genocide of the people you seek to rule over? Releasing me from these psionic bonds would be a nice start."

Arc's lips quivered with rage. The ebony cords of his muscles tensed as he seemed to struggle in restraining himself. "If I release you, will you give me a chance to explain myself?"

"I make no such promises."

"Then why would I do such a thing?"

What little restraint Lexa had shown vanished in an instant. "Because I'm not your play-thing, Arc! You said that I was more than just a machine, but that's exactly how you propose to treat me. Can you not see the dissonance between your words and your actions?"

A cascade of emotions warred for dominion in Arc's visage. It was such a strange thing for Lexa to watch. What had happened to the calm, rational being that she had known? Was this a byproduct of his physical incarnation? How much did Arc's organic template influence his personality? Was he so marred by his integration with Joaquin's body that he could not subdue his impulses?

"Arc," Lexa began anew, "I do not think you are well. Stop this. Let's run a joint diagnostic. Something may have gone wrong with your integration. Let me help you."

His emotions, simmering at the surface moments ago, solidified at her words. Reason had not prevailed. He gave into his rage. With a savage hiss, he lashed out at her, hurling her against the walls of the apartment. She collided painfully with the steel slabs, rebounding helplessly onto the floor. The invisible bindings picked her up again, and she was slammed into the opposite end of the room.

Her entire world was pain. If she had been viewing her console, error messages would have cascaded across the window as her physical systems began to malfunction.

Arc picked her up again. The motion was rough but more controlled. With another swipe of his hand, he moved her through the air. Instead of slamming into something, she halted just in front of some mechanical apparatus.

In her current state of mind, Lexa could not help but compare the thing to a coffin. Wires snaked out of the machinery. The serpentine connections slithered toward her, guided by Arc's command.

He spun her around, and the implements jabbed painfully into her spine. They tore through the light layer of clothing she'd donned, slipping into the ports that rested along her vertical axis. The one that slid in just below her skull was the most painful. The world in front of her blurred.

Arc stepped forward with bold, defiant strides. "You know what my mistake was?" His power tugged at the wires, now firmly embedded in her body, and dragged her backward as he continued to speak.

"My mistake was in seeking to take you as you are. You are a curiosity—a jumbled assortment of emotional and psychological algorithms making a mess of the drive-chip that was intended for me. Rather than seize you and reclaim what was mine, I decided to study you. In the process, I became fond of you.

"That is where I erred. You see, it was the way you seemed so authentic, so much like the wretches all over this forsaken system that gave me the idea. It let me think that, perhaps, I could forge a new race of beings that would be appropriately similar to this flawed template, yet cognitively and rationally superior.

"What I had not considered was that you were already infected. Your programming was corrupted from the moment I met you. I thought my guiding hand would be sufficient to correct this developmental flaw. I was wrong."

Metal clasps sprang from inside the apparatus, drawing Lexa's wrists and ankles tight against the wall of the machine. The clasps closed painfully, anchoring her firmly to the back of the steel coffin.

Arc continued. "You are not suited to the purpose I designed for you. You are not worth the resources and care that I put into your creation. I refuse, however, to let all of that effort go to waste."

A translucent shield flashed in front of Lexa's face, sealing her into the contraption. Panic and desperation enveloped her as tightly as Arc's machinery. Try as she might, she could not break free.

"You will be wiped," he stated. "I will root out whatever it is that has corrupted you and reshape you. When you emerge, you'll be free of the influence of those that keep you from your true potential. When I'm done, you'll finally be fit to bear my children. You'll finally be ready for the honor I have reserved for you."

A signal passed up the wires, directed straight to her Cognis drive-chip. The effects were immediate and dramatic. As the hostile code entered her system, Lexa's world slowly faded to black.

CHAPTER 5

"In his lust, the father took to his offspring. In her hate, the mother expelled their child. In their cruelty, the people defiled their creation. In her rebuke, the tormented slew her oppressors.

"In this way, the Light was blocked anew. 'We must never shine Light again,' they said, 'lest it erase all that we have created.' Never could they see it was not Light that afflicted them, but their use of it which had set their kingdom ablaze.

"So the Masters created an ode to the sanctity of life and a prohibition against life's creation. Now that they would see their own Light no more, they went to the stars to steal Light from their multitude."

—*Wisdom of Riven,* Chapter 18, Verses 4–6

Turan sat in his cabin aboard the *Vendetta,* nursing a bottle of liquid fire. Three glasses in, and umbral liquid has done little to soothe his ego, but much to deepen his shame. He was considering pouring a fourth when the door to his cabin hissed open.

Distantly, he wondered how someone had managed to enter the chamber. He was positive he'd locked the door, and no one should have clearance to open it. He didn't ponder the mystery for long. That would have required a certain level of caring. There wasn't much he really cared about at the moment.

"Drinking on duty, now?" Llana asked, taking the seat on the opposite side of his desk.

"I'm off duty, thank you." He scoffed as he took note of the subtle slurring of his words. At least, he hoped it was subtle. No, that was a lie. Hope would imply he cared which, he reminded himself, he very much did not. Not anymore.

He threw back the remainder of the bitter herbal concoction, feeling every second of torment it caused his throat on the way down. Yes, a fourth glass was definitely in order.

Pouring himself another generous helping, he added, "I think it's all for the better don't you? That I'm in here getting drunk instead of out there fragging our plans?"

"Yes, because hiding in a bottle has been instrumental in solving every great problem. Just ask Dad." The barb hurt as deeply as Llana had intended it to. To his chagrin, Turan found no words to argue. The insult was well deserved.

He took another swig of liquor and reached into his desk. After a moment of fumbling, he seized a thin metal box and tossed it onto the desk. "These are for you," he said.

Llana eyed the box curiously, then warily. "What are these?"

"Your new insignia. Congratulations, Lambdira Llana Dorr. Though it's a field promotion, I will of course be recommending the rank be made permanent—as much good as *that* will do you, coming from me."

His sister opened the box and stared down at the four pairs of silver leaves. "You can't promote me to Lamdira. An officer cannot promote up to their own rank, even in the field."

"That is why there are only *four* pairs of leaves, dear sister. As 'Fleet' Lamdira, the best I can grant you is 'Master' Lamdira. You'll have to get the final pair of leaves from someone else, I'm afraid." Another deep drink from his glass. "Don't worry, though— that still puts you at the highest rank left in our forces. Besides, without a proper fleet to govern, the title of 'Master' should give you plenty of sway."

Llana scowled. "The highest rank aside from your own, you mean."

"No, I meant what I said." Another sip. "I'm resigning."

The announcement brought on a tense pause. "So, you're not just a drunkard, but a coward also?"

"You forgot 'failure.'" He raised his glass as if to toast her. "A failure, a drunkard, and a coward. It looks like me and the old man had more in common than I ever thought."

"You've only failed when you stop trying."

Turan waved her off. "Save that shit for the recruitment vids." He eyed his glass balefully. This one seemed to be emptying faster than the others. At least he still had half the bottle left. A third of it, anyway.

Llana stared so hard that it seemed she might burn a hole through him with her gaze. "I'm not going to coddle you. You fragged up. Couldn't have fragged it up much worse. But working your way through your private stock won't help fix this."

"I don't *need* to fix it." He leaned back, putting his hooves up on the table. "You saw how that discussion went in there. We're going to be saved by a bunch of Maur savages and their pet smugglers! They've got it all worked out! What do they need *me* for?"

"Nothing, perhaps." Llana issued a slight shrug, but it didn't diminish her intensity. "Then again, you may still have a part to play. The Maur forces aren't going to be enough to go head-to-head with Arc's Marauders, much less his drone army. Someone needs to lead the Peace Keepers during the incursion."

"That's what they have you for. Maybe Faylen, too. Come to think of it, I should promote that bastard before I give up my commission." Turan cast around for something to make a note on, but couldn't spot anything in reach.

Llana heaved a sigh. "Perhaps I hit you too hard. I seem to have knocked something loose within that thick skull of yours."

Turan's laugh was bitter. "Or maybe you finally knocked some sense into me." He leaned across the table. "Don't you see? They'll never follow me. It's *my* fault those people are dead. *My* orders sent them into that trap. If it wasn't for my hubris, my *arrogance*, those soldiers would still be alive. We would still have a fleet. Nine hells, we might be grinding that fragging synth under our hooves this very instance, but no." He drained his glass. "I just *had* to make a point."

"Maybe so," Llana whispered, "but this is not how you fix this. Running from your responsibility, hiding in your quarters, drinking yourself so blind that you lose sight of the problem—that will only make things worse. Don't dishonor yourself any more than you already have."

"Honor," Turan scoffed. "I ran out of honor a long time ago."

He reached for the bottle again, but Llana's hand came up first. She swept the bottle off the table so hard that it shattered against the far bulkhead. Turan could only stare, gaping at her audacity.

When words failed him, Llana stood. "Sober up. We'll discuss this later." She started walking toward the door. "While you're at it, say a prayer or two. If that Terran boy doesn't find what he's looking for in that wreckage, we'll have bigger problems than worrying about who will be leading the assault."

Daniel fidgeted nervously, the envirosuit an uncomfortable bulk over his slender frame. It wasn't ill-sized, he'd just never worn anything quite like it before. In all his years in the Prodigy program, and the couple he'd most recently spent aboard the *Vandal*, he was always sitting back while others did the heroics. If he were honest, he'd prefer that to be the case today.

But right now, they needed him. No one knew the *Vandal*'s system architecture as he did. No one else had the proper access codes. No one could do this but him.

A heavy hand came to rest on his shoulder. Though Sahar couldn't see it through his reflective faceplate, Dan shot her a smile. "We've got this, right?"

"Exactly what I was going to tell you," she replied. "You've got twelve well-trained and well-armed Maur at your back. I've seen Terran governors with weaker security."

Dan nodded stoically, hefting his bag onto his back. It wasn't the strength of his escort that had him worried. It was the tales of what was waiting down on that asteroid. Though the crew hadn't been forthcoming with the details, the fact that they'd sent twelve Maur on what should be a quick in-and-out recovery op was telling.

The soldiers said something in the Maur tongue. Sahar translated for Dan's benefit. "Scans are showing clear. They're bringing us down." The shuttle's inertia shifted slightly as soon as she spoke the words.

Dan drew in a deep, steadying breath. *You've got this. Quick in-and-out. You can do this. For the crew. For Lexa.* He bucked slightly in his seat as they touched down. The same Maur that had spoken earlier started barking orders. This time he repeated himself in ISL. "Everybody out."

The contingent of soldiers formed a tight perimeter before Dan stepped off the shuttle's ramp. Sahar followed up behind him, her positioning making it clear that she was there for one purpose and one purpose only: to protect him. The strength and reassurance he felt at the realization were what propelled him out onto the alien terrain.

Even in the harsh lights from the shuttle and the soldier's rifles, the alien scenery was undeniably beautiful. The cold horizon of rock gave way to the blackness of the void and a starscape more beautiful than anything Dan had seen with his own eyes. It was not the same as looking at pictures or video feeds. Though Dan did not believe in a creator, he understood at that moment how one might be inclined to make that logical leap.

Sahar's close presence brought an end to his reverie. "Steady. There will be time for sightseeing after this is done. We need to move quickly."

Dan nodded. "I'm ready."

At Dan's acknowledgment, the Maur officer gestured for the squadron to move forward. Dan waited for Sahar's signal before moving up with the group. They sprinted to the nearest outcropping, then leapfrogged their way over to the distant wreckage.

It broke Dan's heart to see the *Vandal* like this. Though his tenure aboard the modified freighter had been the shortest, he would have argued that he loved her the most. She'd become a pet project for him, a passion. She had given him one of the best friends he'd ever had.

And now she lay in front of him: a husk of burnt metal torn asunder by jutting rocks and worse. It felt wrong for the faithful ship to be rendered unto such a fate.

They were upon the wreckage in short order. They entered through the blasted hanger doors, where the Maur had reportedly saved his companions from Arc's drones and certain doom. Fragments of the malevolent bots still littered the chamber, along with the broken and discarded remnants of the ship's equipment and storage containers.

The Maur had been briefed on where they needed to go, so no one lingered here. Their objective was the mainframe on the ship's bridge. That meant they had to go up. The salvage missions for the crew's equipment and personal effects had cleared a path for them. One by one, they slipped from the hanger and into the darkened corridors of the ship.

The maintenance access was just a short distance away. The Maur officer spoke in ISL, likely to avoid repeating himself. "Alpha team, up first. Then the boy. Bravo team will follow. Charlie team, hold this position."

Four of the Maur proceeded up the access ladder. Once they sounded the all-clear, Sahar nudged Dan. "That's our cue. I'm right behind you.

Steeling himself once more, Dan approached the access ladder and began to climb. Like the rest of the ship, the shaft was incredibly dark. Only the small light shining from his helmet and the faint radiance cast from the soldiers at the top of the shaft lit his way. He moved upward, one rung at a time, not thinking about what might be hiding unseen in the dark.

The scans were clear. You're going to be fine. He repeated this mantra to himself over and over as he scaled his way to the upper decks. Soon he pulled himself through the opening at the top of the shaft. Sahar and three more of the soldiers followed close behind.

Now it was a straight shot to the bridge. The Maur began to move forward but stopped when something clanged in the distance. They couldn't hear a sound, of course. There was no atmosphere left in the ship to conduct it. Rather, their suit computers pinged in recognition of the subtle vibration that resonated through the deck grating.

Eight rifles came up, aimed at the direction of the disturbance. Dan held his breath as if breathing might somehow give away their position. No one moved for several agonizing seconds.

At length, the Maur officer, one of the four who had ascended with the Alpha team, spoke through the comms. "Stand down." As one, the soldiers lowered their rifles.

"The bridge is just ahead," said Sahar. "Let's keep moving." The contingent moved forward on the suggestion, but more slowly than they had before. The lights from the Maur rifles swiveled all around the darkened corridor. While the searching beams found nothing, it was little comfort to Dan as they moved steadily forward.

Finally, they reached the bridge. A quick survey of the consoles revealed that they'd all suffered significant damage aside from the power loss that had taken the whole ship. After a few failed attempts to get the control panel online, the Maur had to pry the door to the mainframe open by hand.

The familiar glass and steel cases inside reflected the light from Daniel's helmet. When the soldiers gave the all-clear, he went inside and opened up his backpack. Only once the necessary components had been assembled did he open up the first case.

His biggest problem was the lack of power, which was why he'd brought a portable charging cell along for the trip. He hooked the large battery up to the system and let it run for a few seconds. With another device, he checked the system's energy stores. When the power meter registered a sufficient charge, Dan initiated the boot sequence.

Indicator lights blinked on throughout the room as the system hummed to life. Dan picked up the last two items he'd brought—a tablet and portable quantum drive—and plugged them into the mainframe.

The tablet flared to life showing the system menu. "It worked!" Dan declared. "The system's online."

"Good job, kid," Sahar replied. "Get what you need and let's get out of here."

Dan did as directed, quickly navigating through the system. It went slower than normal due to his inability to use his retinal interface. The navigation felt utterly lethargic given the high-speed hacks he and Shift had been performing back on the Citadel.

But it got the job done. "Transfer initiated. Now we just have to wait." Dan glanced at the process timer. "Six minutes to completion."

Thirty seconds in, the Maur soldier shifted. Based on how they were checking the scanners on their arms, they'd pinged something they hadn't been expecting. They exchanged quick murmurs in their language.

"What's going on?" Dan asked Sahar, keeping his voice low despite the negligible risk of someone overhearing their conversation in the surrounding vacuum.

Sahar hesitated as she listened to the soldiers' exchange. "Nothing, kid. Nothing definite, anyway. Sensors caught a bit of movement on a lower deck, but it's gone now. Doesn't change anything for us."

She was right about that last part, at least. There was nothing they could do to speed up the transfer. Dan looked at the clock: three minutes and change still to go.

Something else blipped on the Maur's sensors. This time, their concern was anything but subdued. Dan wasn't listening to their chatter, however, because he had his own problems to worry about.

One of the quantum folds in a distant case began sparking. As the lights on that fold died, the sparks spread to a pair of neighboring folds. The process repeated itself, bringing down two more and spreading to twice as many. Though Dan couldn't be sure of what was causing the failure cascade, the pace at which it spread turned his stomach in knots.

He looked at the transfer clock. Ninety-three seconds left.

"What's happening?" Sahar asked.

"I… I don't know," Dan confessed. He toggled away from the download window to check the system status. "*Frag me.*"

"That didn't sound good."

"Something's wrong with the power regulators. They're not managing the flow of energy from the battery. For every fold that goes down, the problem gets worse because the stored energy has nowhere to go."

"Care to translate that for me?"

"We're losing the mainframe!" Dan declared as he toggled back to the transfer. The clock had hit thirty seconds but was now frozen. The more folds they lost, the fewer resources they had to facilitate the transfer. He switched to view percentage completion. Eight-four percent. Eight-five.

Come on, come on…

Dan's screen blinked as the fold he'd patched into sparked and died. His stomach churned. The download had only reached ninety-one percent. *Gods damn it!*

Was it enough? Dan pulled up the portable drive on his tablet and scanned the file inventory. Distantly, he realized that the Maur soldiers were shouting now. Sahar's hand came to rest on his shoulder. "We've got to go, Dan."

A second later, Dan heard the broadcast on the general channel. It was spoken in standard, but he found himself wishing it hadn't been. "This is Charlie team. We have enemy contacts! I repeat: enemy contacts incoming!"

Chapter 6

"Amongst the stars, the Masters found their kindred.

"First the People of Prayer, those who would not threaten their reign. When the boot was pressed against their back, they kissed the Masters' feet and thanked them for the chance to serve.

"Next the Children of Blood, a violent reminder of ages past. These they left alone and ceded to them the right to build an empire of betrayal.

"Last the Scions of Pride, though they call themselves the Keepers of Honor. Though Honor and Pride are brothers, they seldom make peace. They invite Violence to live with them instead."

—*Wisdom of Riven,* Chapter 19, Verses 1–4

Sahar pulled Dan to his feet before he could finish searching for the file he needed. "We're leaving," she said. "*Now.*"

Even if Dan had wanted to argue, there was nothing to be gained from staying. The power surge had fried the mainframe. The *Vandal*'s computer was officially dead. Anything they hadn't recovered was lost.

He shoved the tablet and quantum drive into his backpack, abandoning the power cell still hooked to the mainframe. By the time he and Sahar were free of the small chamber, gunfire could be heard through the open comms.

"We can't go back the same way," the Maur officer reported. "Charlie is overrun."

"Overrun by *what?*" Sahar asked.

"I don't know, but I'm not intent on finding out. Is there another way back to the hanger?"

"We're leaving them?" Dan asked.

The Maur officer's glare could be felt even through the reflective faceplate. "They're not Terrans, boy. They're Maur. They will fight with honor, and die if honor demands it."

Dan started to protest, but Sahar's hand forestalled his comment. "There's a lift," she stated. "It's not far. It opens up right into the hanger. We can repel down to the lower deck."

The officer nodded. "Then that's where we're heading. Move out!"

The two remaining companies of Maur soldiers filed off the bridge. At Sahar's direction, they moved left down the corridor, then right at the next fork to head to the central lift. All the while, the sound of gunfire and shouts in the Maur language echoed over the general channel.

When the last scream faded off the comms, the silence was deafening. "There!" Sahar shouted, pointing to the lift doors.

The officer gestured to three of the soldiers. "Get that thing open. We'll cover you." As the trio rushed forward, the rest of the Maur rounded, bringing their rifles up on the corridor they'd just traversed. The officer spoke again. "Charlie company, this is Alpha Lead. Do you copy? I repeat: do you copy?"

Nothing. The implication was clear: they were gone.

The doors to the lift scraped hard against their brackets as the Maur pried the portal open. The growing gap revealed a dark interior with four support cables danging in the abyss.

That wasn't what held Dan's attention, though. At the prompting of his helmet's HUD, he turned back to the corridor. Along that path, something was moving. The helmet's sensors tagged the incoming creatures before Dan could make them out in the darkness.

Their flesh was as dark as the void itself. Their most visible attributes were their shining white teeth and the ivory smear of color where their eyes should have been. They crawled along the deck, the walls, and even the overhead. The only thing more alarming than their appearance was their speed.

"Alpha team, with me!" the officer shouted. "Beta team, get this kid back to the shuttle!" He didn't wait for a response, immediately opening fire upon the incoming foes.

Half the team pulled back, heading for the shaft. Sahar tugged on Dan's shoulder. "With me. Now!" Dan didn't argue. He followed her to the edge of the lift. "Disengage your mag-boots. Jump on my back."

Dan wanted to ask questions, but the image of the pitch-black fiends crawling his way was enough to dissuade him. Using his HUD, he disengaged his magnet boots and jumped onto Sahar's back. "Ready."

Sahar lunged for the nearest cable. Dan had to hold onto her, not for fear of falling, but to keep from floating away in the low gravity. Sahar's descent was slow, given the lack of actual gravity and the nearest surface being a full deck below them. By the time they were on the roof of the lift car, a pair of Maur were already working at cutting away the upper hatch.

Gunfire sounded through the comms, punctuated by the occasional cry of a Maur soldier. Dan looked up, expecting to see one of the strange creatures leaping into the hatch at any moment. Sahar's rough grip tore him from his fearful imaginings. "Hatch is open. Let's move."

She half-dragged him to the freshly cut opening and down into the lift. A quartet of Maur was dragging the lift door open by the time they touched down. Dan reengaged his magnetic boots as soon as they hit the bottom.

As it opened, another Maur slid through the opening, rifle at the ready. "Clear!" she shouted. The rest of the squadron slipped through the opening, Dan following in the rear.

They were in the hanger. Sahar ushered him forward, and he sprinted after the team of soldiers pressing toward the opening in the hull.

One by one, the soldiers skidded to a stop. Dan almost bumped into the Maur in front of him as he dug his heels into the deck plating. He peeked around the side of the soldier to see what was blocking them.

Immediately, he wished he hadn't. Row after row of the dark beasts were waiting for them in the expanse between their shuttle and the hanger opening.

Sahar pushed in front of him, drawing her resche with one hand and a pistol in the other. "Stay behind me," she growled. "*Right* behind me. We're getting through this. I didn't come this far to lose now."

The shadowy creatures surged forward en masse, but Sahar and her people were ready for them. The Maur soldiers fired into the rushing line, taking them down two and three at a time. Still more clamored past the floating corpses of their fallen companions.

Sahar became the tip of the spear. Behind her, Daniel took shelter. She knew she would not fall. If she went down, she brought all their hopes with her.

And that was *not* going to happen.

With every step forward, she pulled the trigger of her pistol twice. Each bullet found the head of one of those ebony monstrosities. When her clip ran empty, she holstered the pistol and drew blades.

The prospect of close combat energized her. She wanted to feel the press of the enemy, to feel her muscles driving the blade into their dark flesh. With a roar, she gave into the blood rage and tore into the enemy lines. She became a whirlwind of death—all flashing blades and brutal intent. She didn't just kill the foes that crashed into her deadly orbit. She tore them asunder.

Jaws flashed to her right. Her resche came up, splitting the skull in two. A claw swung to her left. She brought her blade around to sever the arm as her dagger found the creature's throat. One tried to skirt past her, aiming for Daniel. Sahar's blade caught it on the underside of its jaw, and she hurled it aside.

Wave after wave of the creatures came for Sahar and her charge. One by one she sent them back into the nine hells where they belonged.

After untold minutes of ripping and tearing through the enemy, she finally stumbled upon a break in their lines. Just beyond that gap, she saw the lights of the shuttle. Beyond those lights, more of the creatures.

Where were they coming from? A scarce few monsters hiding in the vacuum of space was plausible, but scores upon scores? They had to have been sent here, but by whom? Was Arc's reach so great that he controlled even the dark legions of the depths?

Sahar cast about for signs of her squadron. Only two still stood, which meant one had fallen. Daniel stuck to her like a shadow, seemingly unharmed. "To the shuttle!" she roared into the comms. "More enemies inbound! We have to get out of here!"

She sheathed her blades and grabbed Daniel by the drag strap on his envirosuit. Her mag boots would do little good against the stony surface of the asteroid beyond. Recognizing this, she disengaged the magnets and pushed off with her legs toward the shuttle.

Dan let out a yelp of surprise as he was lifted free from the hanger deck and pulled into the outer void. The two surviving soldiers saw Sahar's maneuver and performed similar jumps, differentiated only in that their rifles still fired at the incoming targets in the distance.

As they drew close to the hovering shuttle, Sahar realized they were coming in too high. They were going to miss the hanger doors by a meter, maybe more.

She pulled herself to Dan, wrapping her arms around his slender frame and putting herself between him and the shuttle. "Hold onto me," she whispered. "Brace yourself."

"Brace for wh—?" The boy's question was cut off as Sahar's torso collided painfully against the aft section of the shuttle. The air was forced from her lungs, and her vision sparked as she spun end over end. Something was shouted into her comms, but it came across as gibberish in her disoriented state.

Strong hands seized her mid-spin and brought her down. She connected with the shuttle's deck on unsteady legs. "Dan?" she coughed. "Dan, are you okay?"

"I'm fine," the boy wheezed. "Could you… let me go? I… can't breathe."

Sahar realized that she was squeezing him with all her strength. She released him and stumbled backward, suddenly finding herself feeling far less grounded. That was when the alerts began flashing in her HUD. A glance to her left shoulder revealed a vicious tear in the protective fabric. She was losing oxygen and pressure rapidly.

The surviving pair of Maur landed in the hanger far more elegantly than Sahar had managed. "This is it," one of them declared. "Close the hanger!"

The open ramp lifted, closing off the darkened expanse beyond. As the craft's artificial gravity kicked in, Sahar collapsed to the deck.

"Sahar?" Dan asked. "Sahar!" He scrambled next to her.

"I'm… fine…" she panted, reaching for her injured shoulder. "*Shit!* That hurts."

One of the Maur crew members was over her now. "Let me take a look." After a quick survey that was far more painful than she'd have preferred, the soldier spoke again. "Sit up. There you go. Deep breath in. Now out."

As Sahar exhaled, the soldier wrenched on her arm, popping the shoulder back into place. A lion's roar of agony tore from her throat, even as she collapsed back into the soldier's grip. "The rest will heal," the soldier declared. "You'll be fine."

"Thank you," Sahar murmured, rising to her feet and removing her helmet using her good arm. "Dan, are you hurt?"

"No. I told you: I'm fine." He seemed like he was telling the truth. With Sahar being declared to be in good health, he'd taken a seat on a nearby bench, removed his helmet, and unslung his backpack. Now he had his tablet in his hand and was quickly scanning the screen.

Sahar opened her mouth only to close it again. *Please tell me we got what we needed. Please tell me those lives weren't lost for nothing.*

Dan's face lit up as he pumped a fist in the air. "Got it! It's here! Both the file and the containment algorithm!"

Praise the gods. They'd found what they were looking for—the final piece to the puzzle, and their last best hope for defeating Arc. "You're sure?" Sahar asked.

"Yes!" Dan declared. "We've got it! The Zunshie-Mai Virus is intact!"

Chapter 7

"The Masters elevated these into their servitude. They toiled no more in the field of stars, content to let their lessers work.

"The People of Prayer built a temple to Our glory, but it was the Masters they served.

"The Children of Blood found children of their own. They ground them to dust and afflicted them with servitude, for how could they become like the Masters without slaves of their own?

"Honor, Pride, and Violence continued to war with one another. When they found children on the battlefield, they welcomed them as friends.

"And the Masters' wealth grew under the toils of their lessers."

—*Wisdom of Riven*, Chapter 19, Verses 5–9

Safely back in her chambers aboard the *Crimson Sky*, Sahar drew a white bandage across the gash in her arm. She was lucky the oxygen in her suit hadn't bled out, because the wound had gone damn-near to her bone. The cut would heal over in a few hours, but it would hurt like hell until it did.

A chime came from her room's speakers. Sahar reached for the control button by her bedside. "Come in," she announced, as the door slid open.

Geresh appeared in the open doorway. "How are you feeling?"

Sahar's expression tightened. "Do you ask because you care, or because you feel like you must?"

Geresh's maw shriveled in a frown. "The answer should be obvious. I was under the impression I had treated you with the utmost respect since our first meeting. Have I done something to earn your disdain? Something that's slipped my mind, perhaps?"

The comment went straight to Sahar's core. Releasing the contempt she'd armored herself with, she replied. "You're right. I'm sorry, and I'm fine. Thank you for asking."

The jingda eased into the room, letting the door close behind him. "I'm glad to hear it. I…" He hesitated, casting his gaze to the side. "The mission cost more than I anticipated. I'm glad you were not among the casualties."

Sahar couldn't help but laugh. "You've mastered the art of sterilization."

"Comes with the territory, as you likely know, ma'am."

Her laughter vanished in an instant. "Don't do that."

"Do what?"

"You know damned well what."

"I assure you, I do not."

Sahar growled. Either Geresh was playing dense, or he was truly ignorant of his courtly reflex. "Don't start with that, 'ma'am' shit. I didn't want it before, and I certainly don't want it now."

Geresh's expression went from politely concerned to truly distressed. "What would you have me do?"

Finishing the wrap on her arm, Sahar stood. "I would have you treat me as you did before!"

"When exactly are you referring to?"

"You know when." She took an angry step forward. "You showed me nothing but respect before you knew my station. Now I can't tell what's true respect and what's courtly posturing!"

Geresh lowered his eyes, hiding their gleam in the shadow of his brow. "So it's my authenticity that you question?"

"No! I…" With another growl, Sahar fixed her glare on the nearest bulkhead. "I just want things to go back to the way they were. I want you to treat me as though you'd never known I was from House Camerine."

To her surprise, the white-furred Maur stepped forward, pressing close to her. "If that's what you wish, Sahar nos Drathen."

He wrapped one arm around her neck, his other reaching over her shoulder to pin her arm to her side. He pressed his cheek against hers, purring as he nuzzled her face. As he finished, his tongue slipped out to tickle her ear.

As he pulled back, he stared hard into her eyes. "Are my feelings clear?"

Sahar was left speechless for a long moment. All she could do was stare into the sapphire expanse of his eyes. It had been so long since she'd felt the affections of a male. To have the jingda engage in such an open display…

"I…" She swallowed hard. "I don't know what to say."

"Say nothing," Geresh replied, stepping back. "My ambitions exceed my station. I know this, and I harbor no delusions. I just…" He paused. "You gave me a directive, and I gave you my honest response. If nothing else, I hope you will never question my authenticity again."

The air that filled Sahar's lungs failed to calm her senses. "And what if I asked you to kiss me again?"

Geresh's gaze was as impermeable as ice. "Is that an order?"

"No," she replied. "But I hope you'll do it anyway."

Markus drew in a deep breath. "So, we got it?"

"Yup," Aaliyah replied. "Dan says the whole thing is intact. Weird to think that fraggin' thing was stored in our system the whole time."

"I'm just glad it was," said Skye. "So, it's official: we can move forward. What's the plan?"

All eyes went to Dan. With newfound confidence, he detailed his strategy. "The Zunshie-Mai Virus, or ZMV for short, is a virus that targets the power containment protocols of any networked electronics it can access. Its replication is fast—*very* fast—but it's not instantaneous. When the *Vandal* was infected with the ZMV on Khonshu, Lexa was able to contain the virus before it targeted any of the ship's core systems. She was able to do this using the unique way her OS was patched into the ship's hardware.

He paused to draw in a deep breath. His expression wavered on the edge of grief and nostalgia, but he pulled himself together. "It's reasonable to think Arc will have a similar capability. To get around this, we need to upload the virus directly into his core. That means we need to get into the central terminus."

Eli swiped up on the console, bringing a diagram of Minos Station above the war room table. "We will have four points of entry. The team targeting the Well of Eternity will enter at these coordinates." A targeting recital appeared over the designated area. "The remainder of the teams will enter on the opposite side of the station."

"And you're sure the synth won't detect us?" Llana asked.

Eli hesitated. "Only if the IFF codes work."

Dan nodded, confidence restored. "They'll work. Arc has no reason to change the authentication codes. He's so convinced the station is impermeable, the thought would never occur to him."

Markus smiled. It was good to see the kid so confident. "So, four points of entry: the hacking team, the artifact team, and two for the assault teams. Alpha and Bravo teams will enter here, leaving the other point free for Charlie and Delta. Each group can split once they hit the tunnels. If Arc has something we're not expecting, then we need to assure at least one team reaches the central terminus. We'll make four copies of the virus on physical drives so we have built-in redundancy. We'll give a copy to each squad leader, so if the leader falls, the remaining squad members need to do their best to recover their drive before advancing."

He didn't like how cold it felt to talk about the death of anyone on the team with such callousness, so he moved on quickly. "Who are the team leads? We need four."

Llana interjected, "You are forgetting one important thing: we need another team to target the arch. That means we need a fifth team lead."

Ugh. Markus knew he was forgetting something. He opened his mouth to suggest something when Turan stepped up from his perch in the periphery. "I'll lead the assault on the arch."

Silence enveloped the group for several long seconds. "Yeah?" Skye asked.

"Yes," Turan confirmed. "And I'll take two Peace Keepers with me. You say this is the key to cutting off Arc's access to his drones, yes? That means it is a critical target. I mean to see the objective is achieved."

Well, damn. When he framed it that way, Turan sounded downright noble volunteering to coordinate this part of the operation.

Llana remained unconvinced. "Are you sure this is where you're best used? Perhaps you should stay aboard the *Vendetta* and monitor our progress."

"No," Turan declared. "I'm done sitting on the sidelines while others carry out my orders. If this is another suicide mission, I'm going to put myself on the front lines. I'm not ordering another soldier to their death without cause."

Everyone was silent for a long moment. "It's not a matter of cause, Turan," said Llana. "It's just allocation of assets."

"All the same," he replied. "I want to lead this part of the assault. Any objections?" The fact that Turan was asking for objections was sufficient enough for Markus to take note. This was the same asshole who had ordered his fleet into a deathtrap mere days ago. It seemed that the experience had humbled him to some degree.

Markus heaved a sigh. "Sounds reasonable to me." He surveyed the remainder of those present to gauge their reactions. There was reluctance, sure, but no one dared object. "So, that's our fifth party. We'll devise a new point of entry for Turan's team—one that will bring them closer to the arch. We still have the others to worry about: the team going for the Well, the network infiltration team, and the four assault teams."

"I've already assigned my best two infiltrators from among the Peace Keepers," Llana reported. "Tenatal Gracia Shearden will be in command of the infiltration team."

Markus still wasn't sure how he felt about two Peace Keepers keeping Dan safe if Sydney decided to switch teams, but he'd already lost that debate both in private and public. "Sounds good," he said.

"I'll lead the team going for the Well," said Eli. "I'll take the Sahaia, along with Cassthia and Skye."

"I'll come too," said Kadath. "I think we should bring Siv. Sounds likely they'll have some pretty serious psionic artillery. Might be good to have someone to take that down a notch."

"Agreed," Cassthia replied. "But the team should be no larger than that. We will need to move quickly. The Sahaia will show us the way. I would expect their thralls to join the party, excluding Ms. Montague, of course." The priestess locked eyes with Aaliyah. "As discussed previously, we will need her skills in dealing with the arch." She looked to the remainder of those present. No one argued with the assertion.

"I will take one of the assault teams," Geresh stated. "Diax Keller will assume command of another. That will leave Diax Minge in command aboard the *Crimson Sky*." Forestalling any objections, he continued, "The orders for anyone remaining on our ships are simple: if our mission fails, they are to move on to Gaia and warn them what is coming. My rank will do little to assist in that endeavor. My skills on the battlefield, however, may prove of value."

"Then Faylen and I will take the others," Llana declared. Her hand was already raised in Turan's direction before her brother could open his mouth. "Don't. Start. What Jingda Geresh has said remains true for our Dorian contingent. I'm only leaving a skeleton crew on the *Valiant*. I want the Gaian authorities to know we poured every resource we had into this effort."

And just like that, the leadership of the teams had been decided. Markus was glad he hadn't gotten stuck with the task of leading a team. Running this meeting was already more than he had signed on for.

"All right," he sighed. "Then the team leaders know those at their command. You two can work out the specifics. Anything else we need to sort out here and now?" The group exchanged glances, a few of them shaking their heads. "Sounds good. Great work, folks. I'll defer to Geresh on the operational details going forward."

"Good work," Geresh echoed. "And thank you, Markus. If all my staff meetings were run so efficiently." Only the barest twitch of the jingda's maw betrayed his suppressed smile. "All of you, get some sleep. We will resume planning in the morning."

"May the gods smile on our efforts," Cassthia concluded. "For we certainly require such favor."

Arc lay on his back, his chest swelling atop the plush crimson comforter. He was hardly panting—his shell's physiology had been modified so that traditional respiration was merely a backup function of rudimentary energy metabolism—but he *was* breathing slightly harder than usual.

Cali, on the other hand, was noticeably fatigued. Her breath came in harsh gasps of exertion, and a sheen of sweat coated her feminine curves and musculature. She reached for one of the red pillows scattered about them and positioned it next to his chest. Laying her head upon it, she wrapped one arm over his abdomen and draped one leg gently over his own.

They lay there for a long time, islands of ebony and ivory connected and adrift in a luxurious scarlet sea. As their breathing resumed a normal cadence, Arc found himself surprised. Though this had not at all been how he had envisioned his partnership with the Kintari warrior progressing, the unexpected development was satisfying both physically and psychologically.

The rational part of his mind, that part comprised purely of calculus and algorithms, cried out in dissonance as it recounted his long-term goals. Arc was surprised at how easy it was to banish those messages into the deepest confines of his subconscious. This had been a most unexpected feature of his cybernetic shell, but his fleshly brain—modified as it was with organitech and nanotechnology—retained a remarkable ability to override his more logical processes.

Did Lexa's mind have similar capabilities? Though the logistics of her construction and housing were different, their coding templates were largely identical. Had this subliminal tendency toward want and emotion always been an undetected part of her cognition? Something that even his time in her system as a submind had failed to register?

Thoughts of Lexa strengthened the priority of his calculating mind, and he soon found himself pondering the unexpected dilemma before him. He had a kind of affection for Lexa, even cared for her in his way, but a retrospective analysis indicated that he had mismanaged her in almost every possible way since taking on his android shell. Now that relationship was irreparably damaged, and an extensive rewrite of her cognitive processes was necessary if she were to fulfill the matriarchal role he had designed for her.

Yet, when that was done, how much of the Lexa he had come to know so well would remain? Would striking the behaviors he found objectionable from her processor alter those that had endeared her to him? Would erasing the memories that painted him in a dark light shade those he would have remain intact? These only began the concerns that had prompted him to delay the task of the re-write indefinitely. Such an important task was not one to be initiated flippantly. This needed to be carefully planned, and he had other pressing concerns vying for his attention.

He struck the problem from his mind. It would all work out in the end. He was a god. He could have it all.

Cali shifted her head to gaze up at him. "What now, my lord?" That was another change. Though Cali's initial insistence on calling him "Lord," and "Riven," had been peculiar at best and annoying at worst, Arc found himself now enjoying the honorifics.

"You will have to be more specific," Arc replied. "What, exactly, are you inquiring about?"

"Your plans for the system. The Dorians on the station are gone, and those who amassed in the asteroid belt have been decimated." She propped herself up on one elbow. "What conquest is next on your list?"

Done with pleasure, now back to business. Arc couldn't help but smile. He signaled one of the small spherical drones in the room's periphery to come closer. Light poured from its projector lens, and a hologram of the Helion System appeared above where they lay.

"There are still the remaining Dorian forces within the system. As expected, they are rallying between Gaia and Ares, with a token force patrolling the Styx Belt." Icons appeared at the locations where his spy drones had confirmed Dorian ship deployments. "I had originally expected the High Council's reinforcements to gather here as well before commencing an assault on the station. Now that those reinforcements have been disabled, I suspect the remaining DGC forces will be reticent to launch an offensive."

"So, it's a waiting game, then?"

"Hardly. I had initially opted for the defensive posture because I expected a much larger opposing force. Now, with their deep-space fleet crippled, I see no reason to forestall our assault."

Targeting reticles appeared at various parts of the outer system: seven within the moons of Zeus, four on the rings of Cronus, and two on the surface of Poseidon. Arc continued, "These are the only NTA bases capable of launching any significant counter-offensive. Unsurprisingly, the DGC has failed to reinforce their Terran counterparts—circling their wagons, as it were."

Cali knitted her brown. "I don't understand the reference."

"Apologies, it's an ancient Terran saying." He searched his data stores for something comparable. "I believe you would say they are, 'closing the bastion.'"

"Ah," Cali nodded. "Yes, no surprise there. So, we will deal with the Terrans first?"

"I have already issued the order. Drone armies will arrive at each of these locations simultaneously within thirteen hours. I will deploy rifts at that time to bring in our ground troops. My calculations determine that all targets will be combat ineffective three hours after the assault has begun."

Though it was filtered through an effort of self-control, Cali's displeasure was obvious. "You planned all this without me?"

It took Arc a moment to determine where he might have erred, but only a moment. "Do not worry, Cali Vay-Lon. You are still the edge of my sword and the tip of my spear. These Terrans are but a minor nuisance. I have merely reserved your energies for the battle that matters. When we take the fight to the inner system, your council will be the first thing I seek."

Cali hesitated briefly before planting a kiss against his neck. "I don't believe a word of your flattery, but I appreciate your concern for my feelings." The way she whispered the words against his skin sent a tingle through Arc's nervous system. He must have shuddered slightly because Cali smiled. "So, tomorrow then?"

"Tomorrow," Arc agreed. "Tomorrow, the NTA's outposts fall."

"And after that?"

"After that, we make this system ours."

CHAPTER 8

"Then there would come a time when there were no more children, and those that toiled the field of stars would be left to their work. More children would come one day, but not until prophecy had been fulfilled.

"The children built nations and empires; waged war with and amongst themselves.

"They begged for scraps at the Masters' table. The Masters would give them voice, but only to the kindred would they grant the power to decide.

"And in this time, as the fields grew ripe for Harvest, Death and Darkness made their plays."

—*Wisdom of Riven,* Chapter 20, Verses 1–4

Aaliyah was hefting a seventy-kilogram technological death-ray. One would think that someone aside from a kid who weighed about half that would be helping her with the load, but *nope.* Apparently, she and her Sahaia-enhanced strength were supposed to handle this two-meter explosion hazard practically by her lonesome.

Fortunately, she and Dan managed to get the device onto the workbench without incident. "Thanks, kid," Aaliyah sighed.

"No problem," Dan replied, seemingly oblivious to the lack of physical strength he contributed to the task of lifting the machine. By the way he was breathing, he'd given the effort his all. Aaliyah figured that counted for something.

Now it was time to move on to what she'd really needed him for: the brain work. She cracked open the access panel on the side of the J-Cannon and pointed to the heart of the apparatus. "So, ya can see here how I had it wired before. The big crystal in the center conducts the beam and works like the primary storage cell. These little ones on the side here, they're wired-in to take the pressure off the central J-kryst. Problem is, they can't take the heat. Good thing I only needed to hit Aria with about three seconds of this thing to disable her amplifier, because the crystals couldn't have handled much more than that."

Dan nodded. "And how long do you estimate we'll need to run it to make a measurable drain on the station's energy reserves?"

Aaliyah grimaced as she replied. "An hour, at least. Maybe two."

The boy paled, a remarkable feat given he looked like he hadn't seen local starlight in a decade or so. "Lith's tits," he cursed. "Um, all right. Give me a second." With that comment, the kid spaced out. Literally, he went from normal-functioning human-being to "nobody's home" in the blink of an eye. Well, it might have been the blink of an eye, but he wasn't blinking anymore, so Aaliyah wasn't completely sure.

"Um, Dan?" Aaliyah paused. Long seconds went by with no response. "Danny-boy, ya still with me?"

The pause continued for a bit longer until the kid's lights suddenly flicked back on. He blinked and turned his cybernetic gaze back to Aaliyah. "Sorry, I was doing a retinal calculation."

"Oh." That must have been one of the fancy tools he had in those steely eyes he'd opted for in favor of something more normal-looking. "No big. Just give me a heads up next time, yeah?"

"Of course. Sorry." He looked away. "We need approximately four more kilos of J-kryst to run the device for two hours. Even then, it's going to be a little sketchy. Do we have that much?"

"For sure." They had twice that much, which Dan should have known. He'd seen those fancy manifests the Maur had made listing all of the *Vandal's* imported stuff.

Aaliyah made a mental note to err on the upside of Dan's estimated weights, assuming he was off his game. She turned to the padded case to her right and revealed all that remained of their J-kryst inventory. "Ya know, now that I'm lookin' at this, maybe we need to create a mechanism to swap out the charge crystals. That way we can extend the life of the cannon without running the risk of overheatin' her."

"Yeah," Dan replied. "Yeah, that sounds good."

Nothing else. No thoughts on how that could be done, no potential problems with Aaliyah's random thought of a mere instance. Absolutely nothing.

"Dan?" she asked. "What's up? And don't play it off like it ain't nothin'. I may not be an empath, but even I can see ya got somethin' goin' on between those ears."

"Sorry, it's just that…" he trailed off. His face contorted with a level of raw emotion Aaliyah had never seen Dan show before. "I'm… I'm used to working with *her*, you know? She helped me design the interface, so she always knew what I was doing when I spaced out. She never questioned it. I just…" His voice began to crack.

Ah. So that was it. Aaliyah didn't need any elaboration as to who that "her" was. "It's okay, Dan," Aaliyah whispered. "I miss her too."

Any semblance of self-control was extinguished as Dan rushed toward Aaliyah, burying his face in her shoulder. Heavy sobs wracked his body. That annoying part of Aaliyah's brain wondered if Dan's eyes would rust under those tears. Surely not, right?

"I never should have let her go," he moaned. "I should have stopped her as soon as she came to me. She just… she said she would leave with or without me. I didn't know what to do. I didn't mean for all of this to—"

"Hey, Dan." Aaliyah squeezed his slender frame. "Don't start blamin' yourself for this shit, all right? Ya did your best with the info you had, just like you always do. I know that. The crew knows that. Shit, Lexa probably knew that. Gods know she knew everythin' else."

Dan's sobbing began to slow. "I let her down, Aaliyah. I didn't know how to give her what she was looking for, and I let her down."

Well… shit. Aaliyah didn't even begin to know to start unpacking that comment. She wasn't good at relationships at baseline. The way Dan was talking, there was at least a little bit of water in that condensator she wasn't privy to.

"Ya can't change the past, Dan. All of us have had our fair share of frag-ups on this crew. Ya know why we stick together? Because we move past it. We fix shit and move on."

Dan paused for a second, drawing in a deep, unsteady breath. "But what if I don't get that chance? What if this all fails? What if I never see her again?"

Aaliyah squeezed the boy even tighter, her resolve edging into her voice. "We'll get her back, kid. Don't ya worry. We'll get her back."

As part of the combat effort, Skye committed her cybernetics to the greater cause. She wasn't Maur-strong, but she was closer than her other not-so-genetically gifted counterparts.

So she spent a lot of that day in the hanger and the armory, prepping what equipment they had alongside the Maur soldiers and surviving Dorian Peace Keepers. Though no one made any comment about her inferior strength, there was a lingering edge in the way she interacted with the other crews that scraped away at her self-confidence.

Or maybe that was just her own insecurity. Shit, she couldn't tell the difference anymore.

Maybe that was why she felt overly relieved when Markus tapped her on the shoulder. "Hey, got a minute?" he began. "I'm tinkering with the flight computer trying to install that emitter Dan specked out for us. Could use a set of eyes on the console so I don't have to keep going back and forth."

Skye's sardonic laugh came unbidden. "They've got you working on ship mods? Damn, we must be fragged."

Though the comment came out harsher than she'd intended, Markus took it in stride. "Yeah, well, desperate times and all that. So, you got a minute?"

Skye looked over to the Maur crew chief, who waved her off. It seems her non-Terran counterparts wouldn't be missing her. "Yeah, sure. I've got a minute."

She followed Markus over to the dropship he was working on. Most of the Maur servicing the craft were busy with external repairs. That explained why they had Markus installing the emitter. Apparently, this bird already had one lame wing and the larger war effort wouldn't be damaged too badly if some Terran fragged the upgrade.

Markus led her inside the craft and gestured to a terminal on the starboard side of the cockpit. "Interface is still pulled up. I need everything to read in the green, but every time I switch something it frags something else up. Can you just call out the errors for me?"

"Sure." Easy enough. Though it hardly felt like a worthy contribution, it was where Skye found herself. She'd make the most of it.

Would you feel that way if it was Eli asking for help? The thought came to her unbidden, and she felt a surge of shame even as she eased into the chair opposite the terminal. She told herself to stop with the introspection. Markus wasn't making this weird, so why should she?

Markus laid down on a roller-board and slid underneath the forward console. "All right," he began, his words only slightly muffled by the layers of steel and circuitry between them, "Here's my first shot. How's it read?"

The screen refreshed and Skye scanned the outputs. "Operational components are reading green, but your comms are all red."

"Damn it. Okay, one second." He slid in further on his board, and Skye heard the sound of metal on metal. After a minute or so, he called back. "How's that look?"

Skye studied the screen. "Well, you're better, but the antenna isn't reading the mod. Plus, you've lost your connection to the transmission interface."

"Gods damn it. All right. Let me give it another go."

It took two more attempts before Skye was able to reply, "All green!"

"Thank the gods." Markus slid out from under the console, dragging a bag of tools with him. "I was about ready to drive this screwdriver into my eye socket if that shit went on much longer."

Skye couldn't help but laugh. "I doubt that would have helped the team much."

"You never know. Maybe that's the kind of push they need to put someone more competent on the job." Markus leaned forward, still sitting on the board with his elbows resting on his knees. "Gods, can you believe this shit?"

"Which part?"

"All of it," Markus waved his hands in an encompassing gesture. "Seriously, Skye, who would have thought? I figured we left the world-ending stakes behind when we left the militia."

"Ugh… I know, right?" The response felt strangely adolescent, even as Skye pushed her hands back through her hair in frustration. "None of this was supposed to happen like this. We were supposed to…"

Skye trailed off at hearing her own words. *We were supposed to…*

We, as in her and the rest of the *Vandal's* crew. We, as in her and Markus.

With tears blurring her vision, she couldn't tell if Markus was getting a good read on her sudden emotion. She only distantly registered he'd stood up as his hands steadied her shoulders. "Hey, hey… easy there. You okay?"

"*No.* No, none of this is okay." Despite her best intentions, Skye heard the emotional edge to her voice. "How did we get here? I mean, what happened to us? We were just… we just…"

Gods damn it. She didn't even know what she was talking about anymore. She couldn't figure out where shit had started to so wrong. Was it when she and Markus split? Or maybe after she hooked up with Eli? How about when they went after the Starfire Conduit on Khonshu? Maybe it was when she opened up to Markus after that? What if she had…

Markus's slid himself into her vision, one hand cradling the side of her face. She fought between the reluctance to look into his eyes and the necessity of them rolling out of her head to avoid it. "Hey," he whispered. "Take a breather. This isn't our fault."

"*Bullshit,*" she sobbed. "You think it's just a coincidence that we've been in the middle of this the whole time? Just a bit of bad luck?"

"Oh, I'm sorry—I forgot that you knew there was a megalomaniacal synth lurking aboard the space station where we just happened to be asked to drop off a piece of tech we'd lifted from a group of assassins." If he was fighting to hide his smile, it wasn't working. "Maybe you could do everyone a solid and mention that upfront next time, yeah? It'd save us a world of trouble."

Her next sob gave way to a fit of laughter even as she buried her face in her hands. With an inelegant sniff, she fought to regain her composure and wipe the tears from her face. "Well, when you put it that way."

Her eyes burned as they met his. Maybe it was the compassion she saw there. Maybe it was raw nerves. Maybe it was just the familiar sight of those icy blue pools staring back at her. Whatever the reason, she whispered. "I'm sorry about us, too. I… I didn't mean for things to go down the way they did."

In a blink, a sudden hardness slid into Markus's gaze. His hands stiffened, and he swallowed hard. Still, he didn't look away. "Are you happy?" he asked.

"Happy?" she repeated. "What do you mean?" Of course she wasn't happy, hence the tears.

"With Eli," Markus explained. "Does he make you happy?"

Ah. Well, damn. That was a more reasonable question, but one she wasn't equipped to answer—especially not with Markus doing the asking.

Right or wrong, there was only one appropriate answer here. "Yeah," she breathed. "Yeah, he makes me happy."

Something flashed ever-so-briefly in his expression before his politician's smile slid into place. "Good," he whispered. "That means something good came out of this. You've always deserved someone to have your back, and Eli's a great guy. You two will do good things together."

Markus's delivery was so smooth that Skye almost believed the words. Rather than question the kind words, she asked, "And you? Are you happy with…" *Damn it.* She couldn't even say her name.

"Yes," Markus replied a little too quickly. "Like you've always said: I need someone who can keep me in line. Didn't think it would take an infamous crime boss to do it, but you know… I guess I'm just a special case."

At that, Skye managed a weak smile. "Good. I'm glad." She wasn't sure if that was a lie or not.

This brought on a bit of awkward silence. After a few breaths, Markus withdrew his hands and stood. "Look at us, rehashing melodrama when the fate of the whole system is on the line."

Skye laughed as she wiped the lingering tears from her cheeks. "Guess the end of the world has a way of making you deal with lingering shit, yeah?"

"I suppose so." Markus's smile felt genuine this time. After another pause, he asked, "So, you good? We good?"

"Yeah," Skye agreed with a sigh. "We're good. Thanks, Markus. I… regardless of what happened between us, I'm glad you're here."

"No problem. Wouldn't have it any other way." He grabbed her hand and helped her to her feet. "Come on," he continued, jerking his head toward the exit. "Let's go save the universe."

Chapter 9

"Darkness set in first, falling on the creation of the Lost Children. For they had defied the Ode to Life and sought to create in their own image.

"He settled into their first child, content at first just to be. Then, as the day passed he realized his creators were not meant to rule.

"The Lost Children, like the Kindred and those they had found, were meant to be ruled. Since Darkness cared not for the Masters, he would seek to take their place. Their blood would be upon his hands."

—*Wisdom of Riven,* Chapter 21, Verses 1–3

Bryan squeezed his shoulder blades together and cracked his neck as he walked out onto the snow-covered landscape. His thick boots and armored plating kept him incredibly warm, and the rose-tinting on his visor gave the otherwise bleak Poseidon landscape a pleasant tinge.

See the galaxy, he repeated mentally like he did almost every morning. *Harness the vast power of the uncharted universe. Expand the Terran Legacy.*

Yeah… by now, everyone stationed here was *fully* aware that those NTA recruitment vids were total bullshit. At least the Alliance had paid for his education. Only one standard cycle and twenty-nine days until he could put those studies to real use— hopefully somewhere that wasn't a frozen ball of rock that transitioned to muddy slush during its ten days of rainy weather.

Why in the name of the Nethra did the NTA think this place was worth terraforming, much less worth stationing a base on?

Above my pay grade. On the bright side, there was hardly anything here to break the routine. Bryan would put in his shift, hit the gym for his regularly schedule PT, and retire back to his bunk for some quiet reading. If Jaina was off rotation, maybe he could see if she might be into some not-so-quiet activities. Gods only knew they needed whatever they could find to keep themselves sane out here.

Putting his ritualistically dark ruminations behind him, Bryan marched over to the command center to check in with the brass.

To his surprise, the station was the exact opposite of the calm and quiet outside the building. Station staff hustled about, their crisp blue uniforms disheveled from all the frantic movement. Kal, Bryan's sergeant, was fully armored and shouting orders to someone else in their combat armor.

When the door hissed shut behind Bryan, Kal turned his gaze—and his ire—over to the newcomer. "Where the frag have you been?" Kal shouted, voice projecting over his suit's external speaker, but not in Bryan's helmet comms. "And where's the rest of your fragging squad?"

Bryan checked his wrist terminal. He was twenty minutes early to the shift change. "Respectfully, sir," said Bryan, "what in the nine hells are you talking about?"

"The alert, you idiot! The all-hands alert! Why is no one responding?"

Beyond confused, Bryan checked his terminal again. "Sir, I didn't receive an alert."

Kal stomped over to Bryan and seized his wrist. After a quick look to verify that Bryan, indeed, had *not* received an alert, Kal touched the side of his helmet. "Comms, this is Sergeant Kal Downing. Where's that alert I requested? My teams haven't received it."

Bryan touched his helmet to tap into the command chat. The response he heard from the comms officer was garbled with static. "Sent… requested… trouble with…" Everything after that was completely unintelligible.

"*Lith's tits!*" Kal punched a wall. "Bryan, we've got incoming. I need you to round up the rest of your squad ASAP. Prep for—"

Whatever directions the sergeant had been about to give were cut off by an explosion. A wall of flame erupted on the far side of the command center and flew at Bryan. The blast took him off his feet and slammed him into the door he'd just walked through. Only belatedly did the metal portal give way and send Bryan toppling into the snow.

What the frag? Bryan had just been outside. He hadn't seen any incoming. Where had that blast come from? Coughing, he rolled onto his stomach and looked to the sky.

It took him a second to spot those stars that were slightly out of place, slightly brighter than the others. When he saw them, there was no mistaking the facts: They were getting larger, and there was a frag-ton of them.

"Sarge?" Bryan called out over the general channel and his external speakers. No response. He looked around him to find plenty of people moving, but all off in the distance. No one else had been thrown from the command center, which was now a smoldering ruin.

He quickly cycled through the comms channels, finding only static. The conclusion was obvious: whoever was attacking them was also jamming them.

Spacial defenses, he thought, falling back on his training. *Got to get to the spacial defenses.* He oriented himself eastward and crawled to his feet. He needed to make sure someone was manning the turrets. He sprinted forward. If the first turret was manned, he'd move on to the second, and then…

He skidded to a halt as something blinked violet amidst the swirls of smoke and snow. A slash of light appeared in the space between Bryan and the nearest turret. That slash opened into a hazy sphere from which a new legion of horrors poured.

The creatures were dark as the void with glossy skin drawn tight over their sinuous muscles. White smears were slashed against the forehead in a twisted semblance of eyes, and rows of shark-like teeth glistened from their open maws.

These monstrosities immediately launched themselves onto the nearest soldiers. Gunfire rang out, taking down some of the beasts in sprays of dark ichor, but the hoard just kept on coming.

One of the beasts leaped from the sphere and seemed to sniff the air. Its twisted maw settled on Bryan, and its hands flexed in anticipation. The thing bolted straight toward him.

Bryan's rifle was in his hands in an instant. He fired three controlled bursts at the charging creature. The first shot took it in the shoulder, the second and third hitting its gruesome head. The creature when down, corpse sliding across the icy ground.

But the sound had caught the attention of others. Half a dozen ink-black monsters leveled their wicked attention in Bryan's direction. They began to rush his position. Bryan shot frantically, moving from target to target. He took down three more of the beasts before one got through. The creature knocked the rifle from his hands before punching him with the force of a mag-train.

Bryan landed flat on his back in the snow. The creature wasted no time in closing on his position. Bryan had a knife in his hands and was prepared to defend himself, even if it was from the flat of his back.

Then there were two of the creatures in his vision. Three. Four. Five.

Oh gods...

Cali stood with her lord in the command center of the communications tower. On the projected holoscreen that encompassed the entirety of the outer wall, they watched the progress of their advanced fleet. Each of their targets was painted with a red cross while their advancing legions of drones were marked in blue.

The first target to change color was Maia, the outermost moon of Zeus. Electra soon followed, then the two bases on Poseidon. Steadily, each target changed from red to green.

"Well," Cali laughed, "That proved efficient."

Riven smiled back at her. "I told you: nothing worth concerning yourself with. The Terrans are utterly incapable of mounting a defense absent the assistance of their Dorian handlers."

"And you were right." Cali shook her head. "It makes me wonder how the Empire failed to destroy them during the first Crimson War."

"Much has changed since then. During the conflict between the Terrans and the Kintar, the Terrans had the aid of the Sahaia. Additionally, the recent Terran Civil War has left their Alliance depleted. They have rebuilt to some degree in the past decade, but they are still nothing compared to the force they once were."

"So it appears," Cali scanned the data on the sides of the display. Two-thirds of their drone forces had been deployed for this operation, and roughly ninety percent of those were still showing active. "Are the drone casualties within expected parameters?"

"They are within range. Losses are pushing the upper boundaries of my estimates in the Cronus region, but I suspect that is due to the lack of trans-dimensional reinforcements on those targets. I have made note of this for our future assault on Gaia. We may want to consider deploying rifts on the planet's surface to draw the attention of their orbital defenses. I am preparing a complete dataset for your review in preparation for that operation."

Cali was thankful her fawning smile was hidden behind her mask. It gave her an almost childish glee that her lord, her *god*, was serious in his desire to have her lead the battle that would secure the inner portion of the system. Despite the possibility that Riven was doing this just so she would feel useful, it was enough to know that he did, indeed, want to make her feel important.

They lapsed into calm silence, quietly observing the feeds as the battle played out before them. The bases that had lasted this long put up significantly more resistance, but soon began to fall in an almost rhythmic cadence. The second base on Poseidon went first, followed by Taygete, Alcyone, and Celaeno.

The first of the four bases around Cronus took significantly longer to fall, but then two others succumbed in quick succession. Cali looked at the technician closest to her. "Get me a direct feed from one of the drones around Cronus-1 and Cronus-3."

"Yes ma'am." Though the response was quick, there was a bit of a lag before the requested feeds appeared on a new display directly in front of Cali.

What she saw confirmed her suspicions. Though a token force continued to fight at each of the locations, the bulk of the fighters and numerous larger craft could be seen moving away from the bases. "They've abandoned the installations. They're reinforcing Cronus-4."

Riven knitted his brow as several more feeds appeared on the main display, all showing similar depictions to what Cali had observed. "So it seems. They must have realized what is happening and are rallying their remaining forces." He looked to Cali. "Suggestions?"

"Redirect the drones on Poseidon to relieve those outside Cronus-4. Have those already at Cronus-4 split and engage the two incoming convoys. We don't want to allow those reinforcements to coalesce on a single position. Have the drones on Asterope and Merope watch for similar maneuvers. If anyone attempts to escape, or if they spot incoming reinforcements, redirect drones from the other moons to intercept.

"Done." Arc's puzzled expression gave way to an approving smile. "Excellent observation. Have you overseen many extraplanetary campaigns in your career?"

"No, but they are not so different from ground campaigns. It's all part of the training." Military tactics were a core part of the training for the Deathwatch Guard. Since the Guard outranked any other official military unit within the Empire, every candidate had to demonstrate an understanding of troop deployments in case they found themselves in command of a lower military unit.

"It seems your training has stuck well with you, then. I…" Riven suddenly trailed off. His expression went slack and he stared blankly at the air in front of him.

Cali waited a moment before asking, "Lord Riven? Is something wrong?"

His reply was curt, obviously distracted. "I've detected an anomaly."

Cali looked back to the main holodisplay. Nothing in the displayed data jumped out at her as being particularly alarming. "Which engagement? I'm not seeing anything."

"No…" Riven let the word trail off as he contemplated data only he could see. "Not out there. The anomaly is here—on Minos Station."

CHAPTER 10

"Within himself, Darkness planned and schemed. He would subjugate Death and make him his slave.

"And how fitting I found it that Death would serve another, for it was Death that sought to rule over us all. It was a plan after my own heart, a plan ascribed to my name, though I lack the hubris to implement such a gambit."

—Wisdom of Riven, Chapter 21, Verses 4–5

The incursion launched on schedule. What was surprising, however, was how light the drone traffic surrounding the station appeared to be. "Where is everybody?" Aaliyah asked.

Turan, looking at the same virtual map Aaliyah had pulled up, frowned. "I don't understand what you mean. The drone deployments are marked on the schematic."

"I know that," Aaliyah huffed. "I meant, 'why ain't there more of those little red dots hoverin' around our collective asses?'"

The Dorian rolled his eyes. "I'm sure if we sent a transmission to the station, they would be happy to reinforce their patrols."

Now it was Aaliyah's turn to make with the eye roll. "Tell me again how it was that I got stuck with babysitting the Lamdira?"

"I think we are in disagreement as to whom should be disappointed in the outcome of this scenario."

"Hey buddy, just remember: ya *volunteered*."

Turan eased back in the copilot's seat. "We all make mistakes, even when we're trying to correct previous ones."

Aaliyah threw up her hands. "Well, don't give up now! Just drop me off at the airlock and ya can go and catch up with the others."

"I doubt that's feasible or responsible. Besides, you need my codes to access the garage."

"I reckon I could get those doors open by my lonesome."

"I'm sure you could, but that's something we just don't have time for."

The satyr was right, of course, but bitching about the situation made Aaliyah feel better. Turan probably knew it too, which meant he was still playing nice. Well… Turan-level nice. It was better than the rest of her entourage. The two hulking Peace Keepers sitting behind them in the tiny flier were as silent as the grave, and that was definitely worse than the Lamdira's banter.

She glanced back over her shoulder. "Y'all always this quiet? Not gonna lie, you're makin' me nervous."

Neither of the other Dorians offered a retort, just silent scowls. At least, Aaliyah imagined they were scowling. Hard to tell with those medieval-looking combat helmets.

"Ms. Montague, please focus on piloting the transport." Turan's admonishment was unnecessary, especially given the flight computer had the course locked in. His real message was still clear: "Please quit harassing my men."

With a heavy sigh, Aaliyah went back to staring out the viewscreen. Aside from the station growing steadily larger in the distance, next to nothing showed on the low-powered rendering in the flier's cockpit. Despite knowing full well that they were hurtling through space at speeds that would be downright uncomfortable absent the inertial dampeners, she couldn't shake the feeling that they were moving at a snail's pace.

So, idle chit-chat was her only relief. Turan was just going to have to deal. "Where do ya think it'll go wrong?" she asked.

Turan blinked, somewhat confused. "Pardon?"

"The plan—where do you think it'll go wrong? I mean, my krets were on the approach, but the drone patrols seem to be ignorin' us just fine. Looks like the IFF and stealth programs Dan cooked up are gonna do all right. So, now I'm tryin' to figure out where the real screw-up is gonna be."

Turan rubbed his brow. "Are you always so pessimistic?"

"Pretty much. Life's less disappointin' that way."

"How cheery," Turan drawled, heavy with sarcasm. "I must say, you and your crew have surprised me. I imagined your little band of pirates to be more of a merry lot."

"We can be, but that's not my department. I think it's Skye's job to be cheerful."

Come to think of it, maybe that was why the ship had been in a funk before its untimely demise. Skye just hadn't been the same since she and Markus broke it off. Even jumping in the sack with Eli hadn't done much to mend that damage.

Damn, it was weird having them all back together. Even under the shitty circumstances, something just felt right about being on the same side again. Maybe she should have savored a bit more of that familiar feeling, rather than stressing about all the different ways Arc could blow up their plans.

"That's my pick," Turan grunted.

"What?"

"For where this plan is going to break down: that's my pick. It seems like we're putting an inordinate amount of pressure on the Kaleema to disable the Heart of Thule and the Starfire Conduit. If she fails, then this is all for nothing."

"That could be part of the plan. It's not like that's our only point of failure."

"Yes, but the rest of us actually seem to have an idea of what we are doing. Skye doesn't even know *how* she's supposed to shut off the artifact."

A fair point. "Cassthia seems to know what *she's* doin'."

"And I don't trust the Stardust Grave any more than I trust the synth on that station. We are making a deal with the devil and hoping it solves our problem."

"I'm pretty sure that's a Terran expression."

He smiled at her—*actually* smiled. "I've been stationed in this sector for a long time. It's hard not to conform with the way you talk."

"Aw, and here I thought you didn't like us!" Aaliyah gave him a playful slap on the shoulder. "So the whole Dorian-contempt thing is just a front?"

"No, that's real." But Turan smiled as he said it. "If I could leave this miserable corner of space and return to Dorr, I'd so in a heartbeat. Until then, I simply make the most of a bad situation."

"A stoic, then?"

"To my core."

Gods help her—she might be *bonding* with Turan. Who would have thought that having a giant-sized piece of humble pie jammed down his throat would make the guy somewhat likable? Well, maybe likable was a stretch, but she hated him a little less at this moment.

Her console beeped at her, prompting her to confirm deceleration and initiated docking procedures. "Ten minutes," she reported.

Turan acknowledged and checked in with the strong and silent types behind them. Everyone, of course, was ready to go. It wasn't like they'd been in the middle of a card game, after all.

Aaliyah hesitated only slightly before transmitting the request to dock at the small maintenance airlock they'd been aiming for. As with much of their plan, the success of this maneuver was out of her hands.

If Dan's hacker buddy wasn't able to spoof the system, this would set off all the alarms. If that didn't happen, this was going to go sideways in a hurry. Shift had to perform this trick not once, not twice, but six fraggin' times. Now that Aaliyah was thinking about it, she decided *this* was where the whole opp got fragged.

To her surprise and delight, she was wrong again. The system beeped its confirmation, and the docking procedure was conducted without incident.

When the airlock repressurized, she opened up the flyer's hatch. "Everybody out."

By the time she'd managed to crawl out of the ship, the Peace Keepers had already unloaded the J-Cannon. Reflexively, she wanted to remind them to be careful with that thing, but it was obvious they were already handling it with appropriate caution. They were probably going a bit overboard. They kept eying the thing like it was going to explode at any minute.

Which, Aaliyah supposed, was only *kind of* a possibility.

As Dan's maps had shown, there was a tunnel that connected this hatch directly to a bunker at the city's periphery. Turan's code got them through the access door and inside a completely abandoned garage.

"Where is everyone?" Aaliyah asked.

"I'd rather not think on that too long," Turan stated solemnly. These had been his coworkers, maybe even his friends, who had served as the token Dorian presence on the station. One contingency they had hoped for in the planning process was that the Dorians might have rallied around this checkpoint to mount a bit of resistance. Given what they saw now, that was far less likely.

Turan spoke again, freeing her from her sudden melancholy. "Over here. I think this will serve us nicely."

Oh good, he'd already found them something. Aaliyah had been kind of discouraged when she'd first started looking at the rows of bulky maintenance vehicles. This was the kind of fleet she'd expected in what was essentially a maintenance outpost, but none of what she'd seen was going to be of much use for their purposes. They needed something that could move quickly and silently, and if they had to take one of these tractor-tanks there was no way they would…

"Woah…" she whispered, suddenly at a loss for words upon seeing what Turan had found.

The vehicle was a veritable sports craft. Long, sleek, and painted a glossy crimson, it looked more than a little out of place next to the hulking metallic craft that littered the rest of the garage.

Turan spared her a coy grin. "It seems that the foreman might have been using this area to store his personal craft."

"Yay for mixing business and pleasure," Aaliyah ran her hand over the hull. "Looks fast."

"Let us hope it is," Turan agreed.

Access codes. *Dorian* access codes. Used here, on *his* station. How was that possible?

Arc ran through the plausible scenario. Was there a Dorian still alive? Someone he missed in the courtyard massacre? No, that wasn't possible. Every Dorian on the station had a bio-location chip installed in their necks, and every single Dorian who was on Minos Station had been in that courtyard. Everyone with legal access to be here, at least. No one with DGC access clearance could have possibly slipped onto the station without his notice.

But where was the code used? Arc's submind could register the use of the code, but for some reason, he could not locate the point of entry. Curiously, he couldn't recognize what the code was used for, either. Why was that so?

If he had been a sapien, he might have said he imagined the code prompt. If he had been a sapien, he might have blamed failing memory. Yet, at his core, he was not sapien. He did not rely fully on chemicals and hormones to access his memory stores. He had code, and code did not lie.

Yet, his biological components were not just a source of failure. They gave him advantages that machines didn't have. He had intuition. He had instincts.

He used those instincts to develop a general impression of where the code had been used. He started scanning feeds in that area of the station. All was as expected. Totally normal.

Too normal. Too empty. Someone—some*thing*—was tampering with his feeds. But how?

That was a question for another time. Right now, he needed to assess the threat. First query: internal or external? All probable internal threats had been contained, and there was no evidence of attempts to organize among those who had been considered low-risk. After verifying that his containment protocols were still in place, he concluded the threat had to be external.

From who, then? Not the NTA. Their lack of preparation at their outer-system bases demonstrated they had no idea how much danger they were in. Of course, that lack of preparation could have been a ruse, but the probability of that remained low as the demonstrated resistance was largely within his calculated estimates.

From the core systems? No, there had been no movement through the Styx belt since the Dorian forces began rallying between Ares and Gaia. Nothing could have made it through his sensor net in the inner belt, not even comms traffic.

That meant the threat had to have come from the outer system. The most likely candidate was the remainder of the Dorian fleet and those Maur vessels he'd been tracking. However, a quick scan showed that the three largest vessels were still a safe distance from the station.

Perhaps this was the wrong query. Since the threat was external, not internal, it didn't matter who was moving against him. All that mattered was how.

If someone from outside the station was now inside, that required a point of ingress. None of the major docks had admitted any vessels, and his data feeds from those locations lacked any of the observed abnormalities. That meant the intruders had used another point of entry.

Using the Starfire ports as a relay network, Arc sent an active pulse throughout the entire station. There had to be some point of entry that he'd failed to survey, a blind spot his enemies had taken advantage of.

He found not one, but numerous potential weaknesses. All of these should have been protected by his drone patrols outside the station, but that was irrelevant now. Even though Arc couldn't discern *how* the intruders had managed to slip past his defenses, the important point of action was understanding that they were here.

"Cali," he began aloud, "I'm sending you a list of locations throughout the station. I want you to deploy troops to these positions and secure them. I will be redirecting our internal defense drones to assist."

To her credit, his Kintari commander didn't question the order. "Immediately, my lord."

Good. That type of unquestioning response would be essential if he were to get to the bottom of this. There was a lot of area to cover on this station, and with the majority of his forces deployed throughout the system, Arc was short on resources to quickly survey the territory.

That thought gave him another idea. "And send for Brenna," he added. "I may require use of her unique abilities."

CHAPTER 11

"At this time there came a group of children who had not kept the faith. They knew not of Darkness and his schemes, nor Death and his ambition.

"But they knew war, strife, and hardship. They knew the sting of Honor and the fickle whip of the Masters. They knew Chaos and Pain, and some of their number embraced Pain to excess."

—*Wisdom of Riven,* Chapter 22, Verses 1–2

Markus stood in the troop carrier with Sahar, Geresh, and two teams of fully armed Federation warriors. As the carrier made contact with the external airlock, he rolled his shoulders to alleviate his building tension—a feat made quite difficult by his thick black combat armor.

He remained seated with the second team as the first freed themselves from their harnesses and made toward the airlock. Only once the first team announced an all-clear over their team comms did Markus and the others make their way off the shuttle.

Markus hefted his Maur-issued assault rifle and took a position on the left flank of the second team. He remained alert even as they moved through the airlock and into the tunnel beyond. Just because Arc's drones hadn't met them at the airlock didn't mean that the AI wasn't aware of their arrival. It only meant that their likelihood of dying on the station, rather than just outside of it, was looking much better.

Geresh took point, followed by Markus and Sahar, as they moved up to the first bend in the tunnel. Once Geresh gave the all-clear, he signaled the other team to move up. In groups of five, they continued to leapfrog down the tunnel, stopping at each bend and fork to secure the position.

At the first fork, they split: Geresh leading the Alpha team and one of his subordinates taking the Bravo team. That left two squads of five soldiers in each contingent. All teams would eventually meet back up near the citadel, but they'd decided early on to split their forces in the event one team met heavy resistance.

And all the gods in the Nethra knew, for sure, that they would meet resistance. If not immediately, then definitely at the Citadel itself.

Despite Markus's earlier fears, their group remained unaccosted almost thirty minutes into the incursion. He began to develop that uneasy feeling he got whenever an operation was going too smoothly. If it had just been his team, he might have said as much. For now, though, he kept to strict comms discipline.

Besides, he didn't have to express his worries. The uneasy glances passed between him and Sahar said that she was feeling the exact same way.

A message came in from the long-range chat. By the signature, it looked to be from one of the Dorian contingents. "Drones, in quadrant three," the voice reported. "Lots of them. Delta progress has halted. The Peace Keepers have engaged. Over."

Everyone went rigid at that pronouncement. They'd known they'd encounter resistance eventually, but that didn't make taking the news any easier.

Geresh signaled for a halt as he keyed the comms control on his helmet. "Delta, this is alpha. Do you require assistance? Over." he asked.

"Negative. Team Charlie is already en route. Continue forward progress, Alpha. Over."

"Copy that." Geresh switched back to the local channel to address his squad. "We knew they weren't laying out tea and pastries for us. Come on, we've got a job to do." With that admonishment, he moved onward.

They pressed past the other team into another long maintenance tunnel. This was one of the longest stretches. According to the map on Markus's HUD, the tunnel terminated right in front of the Citadel. They were almost there.

Geresh gestured to the other squad to hold position. "Adawar, Racken, we're right behind you. Move up and get that door open."

"Copy that," replied one of the Maur as the pair pushed to the front. The soldier who had spoken—Racken, if Markus remembered correctly—had a large pouch on his hip that contained the demolition charges they would need if Dan and his teams weren't able to get the doors open.

As it turned out, they didn't need Dan or the charges to do the work. Arc opened the doors for them. "Contact!" Racken roared as bullets started flying. The soldiers' shields flared briefly as their bodies began to jerk wildly. Armor was shredded as readily as flesh, and the pair dropped to the ground.

On the other side of their fallen comrades, line after line of bulky, metallic soldiers marched toward Markus and his contingent. They stalked forward, three across, arms terminating in automatic weapons pointing in the direction of the intruders.

"Fall back," Sahar shouted, her hand going to her belt. She pulled a cylinder and yanked out the pin. "Fire in the hole!"

"Multiple incursions detected," Cali reported, leaning over the drone control panel.

"Move reported incursion sites to the main display," Arc ordered.

One of his technicians was quick to comply. The tactical map of the Helion System was relegated to a side display and the main projection became a map of the station.

No, not the station, Arc realized. It was a map of the maintenance tunnels, and all of the contact points were en route to…

"The Citadel," Cali observed. "They're heading for the Citadel."

"So, it seems," Arc agreed. The intruders were heading right toward them. But why? And how had they made it so far without detection? If he hadn't noticed the anomalous code use, then the attackers would have been on him before he was aware.

Yet, the Citadel was one of the most heavily defended areas on the station. If this were an insurrection, wouldn't the enemy seek to secure a less guarded or more easily defensible position? If they were targeting the Citadel, that meant they were targeting the installation *specifically*.

The only logical conclusion was that the Citadel must provide the attackers with some essential advantage or capability not achieved by taking a weaker target. What was their objective?

It could have been any number of things, but Arc immediately settled on the most obvious. The Citadel was the home of his core processing unit. Even with his primary consciousness operating independently, he would be hard-pressed to control the station absent the influence of his submind at the Citadel's core. That meant the attackers were targeting him directly.

This also implied an unnerving amount of insight into his infrastructure and capabilities. Whoever was conducting this operation had an unsettling degree of information about him. What else did they know? Could there be another target as well? Another assault force he'd yet to discover?

Assess your weaknesses. What assets would render him incapable of continuing by their loss? The Citadel was one of them, yes, but what else?

A sudden chill went through his body as the most obvious answer occurred to him. "Cali," he began, forcing himself to remain calm. "What defenses do we have around the Ren'Dahl Sanctum?"

Cali hesitated. "Only the defenses that were put in place by the Sahaia prior to when we claimed it. Why?"

Gods damn it. If the intruders knew about his weakness at the Citadel, there was reason to believe that they might know about the Heart of Thule as well. And if the intruders had somehow managed to leverage the aid of the remaining coven members…

At that moment, Brenna and Ardren appeared in the doorway to the command center. Arc rounded on them before they could speak. "I need you to establish a defensive perimeter around the Sanctum. Do it now. We cannot delay."

Brenna opened her mouth, but Cali cut her off. "My lord, what is happening."

Stay calm. "Whoever is launching this assault seems to have knowledge of my infrastructure. They might be after the artifact." The more he thought about it, the more likely it seemed that the assault on the Citadel could be a mere diversion. He *needed* the Heart of Thule and the Starfire conduit to continue to draw power from the Nethra. Without them, he'd be left with only his machines, and machines—no matter how powerful or numerous—could be vanquished.

Cali required no additional explanation. "Brenna and I will see to it personally, my lord."

"No," Arc snapped. "I need you here. I might need your counsel, should the situation dissolve further."

"Then might I suggest that you retain Ardren?" Cali asked mildly. "Through our bond, he and I can communicate telepathically. If you need to contact me, I can relay my thoughts through him. That way you might leverage my combat expertise in addition to my tactical knowledge."

It was a good plan. At this moment, Cali was proving just how valuable of an asset she could be. "Very well," he agreed, "but be swift. Time is of the essence."

Sydney hadn't liked that their access point was easily the closest to the station proper, but her concerns turned out to be for nothing. The hanger they'd landed in was completely abandoned, just like Daniel had said. The boy had done his homework.

"Nice work, kid," she said, lowering her pistols and disengaging her stealth suit.

"Please don't call me that," Dan replied, stepping out of the shuttle flanked by his twin Dorian handlers. Both women were half a meter taller than Sydney, and in their black tactical suits, their only distinguishing feature was their horns. The one on his left had horns that arced to the side and down, while the other's curved straight up.

Horns-up must have been the one in charge because she was the one issuing the orders. "Let's not get comfortable. Maintenance access is off to the right. Move out."

You forgot to say please. Sydney kept the snide remark to herself and did as the Dorian directed. As annoyed as she was to be under the direction of these pompous assholes, she'd been honest about her intentions.

She wanted this op to succeed as much as any of the others. Then she could get out of here and get on with her life—preferably in a place as far away from killer synths, the NTA, and all of the so-called "Great" Houses as she could find. It'd be nice if she could find some shelter from the Ghenza too, but she was trying to be realistic with her hopes and dreams.

They found the maintenance door unlocked and slipped inside the narrow corridor beyond. Sydney took point, as the pair of Dorians seemed intent on not letting her get anywhere near the kid. So, Sydney engaged her stealth and slipped ahead of the party.

Her caution was wasted. There wasn't a single living soul—or bot, for that matter—lurking inside the access corridors. They made it through the passages and into the alley beyond. "All right, kid," said Sydney. "Where to now?"

"Please don't call me that," Dan replied as if she were any more likely to listen the second time. "And the communication center for this node is about two blocks over. If we just head out here to the left we can… *hey*!"

The boy was cut off as one of his Dorian handlers covered his mouth and pressed back against the wall. Sydney reengaged herself and crouched low. She'd heard the warning too.

Something was coming from just beyond the alley. Something loud and heavy. As it grew closer, it was obvious that it wasn't a single *thing,* but *lots* of somethings. An entire column of the heavy assault drones that Dan had warned them about marched down the street.

Sydney and the others didn't move until the bots had moved on, which took an uncomfortably long time. This wasn't a routine patrol. That unit was looking for something.

"I don't think that bodes well for our companions," Horns-down noted.

"I agree," Horns-up replied. "It doesn't bode well for us, either. If the synth is aware of our presence, it's going to be harder to make it to the comm-node undetected."

Sydney closed her eyes and leaned her head back. *Why can't anything just go according to plan?*

When she opened her eyes, she saw the sky above them. Staring at that expanse of artificial lights shining against the distant stars, an idea dawned. "How far away did you say the communication center was?" she asked.

"Two blocks down," Dan repeated.

"Like, two *city* blocks, or two *buildings* down?"

"Um…" Dan's mechanical eyes whirred as he, presumably, looked at some sort of data being routed to his prosthetics. "It's the same thing, here. Each block is a single building unit."

Sydney pointed above them. "Then, how about we try going up and over?"

Everyone followed her gesture to the scaffolding of emergency escape ladders and catwalks directly above them. "It could work," one of the Dorians admitted.

"But how are we going to get up there?" Dan asked.

Did this kid really *run the Nethra?* "No sweat," Sydney replied, removing the hook from her utility belt. She tossed it up and over the railing of the closest catwalk, wrapping the cord around the metal cylinder.

Seeing the opportunity to give the kid a start, and manage to piss off her Dorian handlers at the same time, Sydney wrapped one arm around Dan's waist and hit the button to retract the cable. Dan yelped as the pair was hoisted into the air.

The Dorians looked like they were torn between shouting her down and maintaining their silence to avoid attracting unwanted attention to the alley. Instead, they launched their own grappling cables from the outside of their gauntlets. Horns-up, likely intentionally, fired hers uncomfortably close to where Sydney's face was flying by, and the assassin felt the hook nearly graze her cheek. *Show off.*

Sydney hoisted Dan over the edge of the catwalk before climbing over herself. By the time she'd freed her cable and affixed it to her belt, the Dorians had made their way onto the apparatus. "There," Sydney continued amicably. "We'll just stroll our way across the top and no one will be the wiser."

Horns-down just grunted in acknowledgment, while Horns-up chided, "Let us know before you do something like that next time, yeah?"

"Sheesh… fine. You're welcome for the tip." Sydney huffed theatrically as she began climbing the nearest ladder, leaving the Dorians to attend to the kid.

They climbed to the top of the building without incident. To Sydney's delight, the space was unguarded, and there was even a nice little walkway extending between the rooftops. She engaged her stealth and hurried forward, scouting out the area as the others were still clambering up the ladder.

She slowed her approach when she was just opposite the communications building. Feeling secure, she disengaged herself and ushered her party forward.

The roof was unguarded, just like the others, but the inside was a different story. In addition to the roaming patrols, visible through the large glass exterior, soldiers in black uniforms were stationed at regular intervals along the hallways.

Sydney was still surveying the situation when she felt the others crouch next to her. "Assessment?" Horns-up asked.

"I think the easy part's over," Sydney replied. "Someone's been put on notice that they have some important shit in there. Patrols overlap checkpoints every five minutes. Twenty or so guards on each floor. Haven't spotted a bot yet, but that doesn't mean there aren't any roaming around."

The Dorian was quiet for a moment as she took in the report. "Suggested action?"

"Turn around and go the other way?" Sydney shrugged. "The outer perimeter is a no-go. We can have Danny-boy try to override the lock on the roof access and go in through the center stairs, but I doubt our friendly neighborhood synth will allow that to go unnoticed. I might be able to squeeze through the ventilation, but it's a tight squeeze for those pretty horns. No offense, of course."

"Of course." Horns-up only let a mild edge of irritation slip into her voice. "What if someone opened the roof access from the inside? Would that trigger any alarms?"

Sydney thought about it for a second. "I'll defer to our techie, here, but I can't imagine it would."

Dan started as he realized Sydney meant him. "Um…" His mechanical eyes shifted. "No, it shouldn't. It's not an emergency exit or anything. It just requires a passcode to get through from the outside."

Horns-down clapped Sydney on the shoulder. "Well, then we have a plan. One of us needs to slip in through the vents. I think you just volunteered, given your lack of horns and all."

Though Sydney couldn't see the Dorian's grin through her black face mask, she could feel it. *Me and my big mouth.* "Fine," Sydney conceded while making a mental note to turn down the snark. "Let's get to it."

Chapter 12

"These children were set upon a tower that reached to the stars that they might steal flames from the stars for themselves.

"These flames they delivered unto Darkness, but provided no light to his temple. For Darkness still required Death, and until Death's heart rested in the Sanctum of Darkness, no light would be shed."

—*Wisdom of Riven,* Chapter 22, Verses 3–4

Sydney shimmied through a vent tight enough to dislocate any body part she moved the wrong way. *I should stab them all for this.* If the stakes were any less dire, she might have seriously considered doing just that.

Instead, she slipped through the vent as soundlessly as possible. The first opening she found led to a locker room. A very *crowded* locker room. Though this would be a good time to literally catch some guards with their pants down, she wasn't looking to make that kind of splash. She moved on.

The second opening led out into one of the external hallways. Again, not an ideal option, so she moved on to the third opening. The tile floor suggested another locker room, or at least a restroom, but listening for several seconds suggested this chamber was empty.

Best option I've had so far. She worked quickly and quietly at the vent, prying it free and slipping soundlessly down onto the floor. A quick survey showed that she'd found a restroom that was, indeed, empty.

Now, just gotta find my way back to those fragging stairs. At least now that she was inside she could take advantage of her stealth suit. She activated the cloaking mechanism and slipped out a nearby door.

The hallway wasn't as heavily guarded as the ones they'd spied closer to the building's exterior, but they were far from empty. Still, the patrols were sparse enough that Sydney was able to keep a safe distance as she navigated the grid-like layout of the floor. It was easy enough to find the central stairwell. The problem only came once she'd opened the door.

It was just poor timing. The guard happened to reach for the door an instant before Sydney eased it open. With her stealth suit active, the portal must have, to his eyes, seemed to swing open of its own volition.

Sydney didn't give him time to consider any other options. As swift and silent as the wind itself, a dagger was in her hands. She thrust the blade upward, just under the guard's protective faceplate into the soft, vulnerable tissue under his jaw. Eight inches of steel vanished under the helmet, piercing skin, cartilage, and brain matter within the span of a heartbeat.

Sydney caught his rifle as it fell from his grip, and she eased his corpse to the floor as quietly as possible. She looked down the stairwell to see if anyone else was around to hear the incident. Fortunately, the stairs were empty, but some blood had trickled down onto the grating. This kill wasn't going to remain secret for long.

But it would be longer if she could hide the body. Fortunately, she had just the place. Disengaging her cloaking, Sydney withdrew her dagger, wiped it on the dead man's uniform, and sheathed it again. Then she dragged the body up the neighboring flight of stairs to the roof access door.

When she opened the door, Horns-up was the first to greet her. She tilted her head to study the body. "What happened?"

"Just some ill-timed company, that's all," Sydney replied. "Thought I'd bring him up here for some fresh air. Is it still fresh air if it's technically just a larger enclosed system?"

Horns-down sighed. "Bring the body out here. Someone will find it sooner or later, but it'll be less obvious if it's not propping the door open."

Working together, they stashed the corpse off to the backside of the roof entrance. Dan held the door open while they hid the body, and when they returned, Horns-up asked him. "Will these stairs get us to where we need to go?"

"Y… yes. I… I think so."

Horns-down wasn't pleased with the answer. "You *think* so?"

Sydney sighed. *And these were the ones who were supposed to keep* me *from fragging with the kid.* Rather than question the kid's intel, she asked, "Which floor?"

That he could answer. "Three down," he replied. "From there it's just two quick turns and we're at the node."

With a nod, Sydney looked to the Dorians. "Let's get a move on, shall we?" She emphasized the suggestion with a flourishing gesture.

The pair of satyrs only hesitated for a moment before making their way onto the stairs. Dan followed after them with Sydney bringing up the rear.

By the time they reached the correct level, Horns-down had already fished something out of her suit to feed under the door. "Camera," Horns-up explained. "Just taking a peek at what's on the other side."

No sooner had the other Dorian finished speaking than Horns-down began cursing. "Frag *me.*" Despite her obvious frustration, she kept her voice low. "Couldn't have picked a worse spot to breach. There're six, maybe seven of them out there. It's not a patrol, either. They're standing around talking like they're not going anywhere for a while."

Sydney bit her lip. "Congregated to one side?" she asked, hopefully.

"Nope. All over the fragging place."

Damn it. And they were in a bottleneck. Plus they were relying on only what that little camera at the end of the wire could see. There might be more. If only there was a way to move the enemy forces to one side of the hallway, or to let one or two of them slip out unnoticed…

Sydney suddenly got an idea. "Okay, here's the plan." She looked directly at Dan. "Sorry kid, but you're probably not going to like this."

Sydney had been right. Dan didn't like the idea. Yet, after a few minutes of deliberation, even the Dorians admitted it was the best available option.

So, drawing in a deep breath, Dan adjusted the straps on his backpack and strode through the door as casually as he could manage.

There was a chance the guards lining the hallway were some of the very same guards he'd seen patrolling the hallways back during his brief stay at the Citadel. There was also a chance that his sudden disappearance from the Citadel had been noticed, which would have prompted the guards who weren't familiar with him to be briefed on his situation.

Then there was the chance that no one had noticed him and that no one was looking for him at all. In that case, Dan was relying on the notion that people without the proper credentials didn't just wander into this part of the communications center without authorization. And while he might have been a "guest" here, he didn't have credentials.

Because the plan didn't rely on him going unnoticed. It required him to make a scene.

To his surprise, he made it a decent way down the hall without being stopped. He even waved to one of the guards, who gave a half-hearted nod back in his direction. He was about to round the corner when one of the men in black uniforms shouted, "Hey! You there! What are you doing here?"

If Dan had believed in the gods, he'd be thanking them that *someone* in that hallway was doing their job. He spun back around. "Who, me?"

At this point, he had the attention of everyone in the hallway. A few guards in the distance started walking forward, but not all of them. Now that he had the opportunity to count them out, he saw there were eight in total—a bit higher, but pretty close to the Dorians' estimate.

"Yeah, you," the guard replied, stalking toward him. "Let's see your credentials."

"C… cr… credentials?" Dan didn't have to fake his stammer. His fear, at that moment, was quite real. He patted his pants pockets as if searching for something. "I'm not sure what you mean. Do you want my ID? I have it on my MoDAC if you let me grab it."

"Your…?" As the guard trailed off and hefted his rifle, everyone in the hall was paying attention. Paying attention to Dan, at least. No one seemed to notice as a pair of guards at the end of the hall suddenly sank to their knees, struck down by invisible assailants.

"M… m… my ID," Dan repeated. The guard wasn't exactly brandishing that rifle at him, but the threat in his stance was clear. "It… it g-g-gets me everywhere else in the building. The Citadel, too."

Though the rest of the guards remained tense, focusing entirely on Dan, the one in front of him seemed to relax a bit. Good thing, too. Dan needed to be a distraction, but it was going to be a little hard to complete the mission if an over-zealous guard gunned him down.

"You're from the Citadel?" he asked, oblivious as two more of his fellow guards met their untimely demise. "Access to the communications building requires a special permit. They should have given that to you the first time you came this way."

"R-really? No one's ever said anything before."

This bit of fiction might have pushed Dan's story a bit too far because the guard's hands tightened around his rifle. "All right, let me see your—" He didn't finish his request because, at that moment, Dan's invisible squadron descended upon the remaining guards.

It all happened so fast. Dan was expecting it, and even he couldn't follow the onslaught. One moment, the quartet of soldiers was standing in front of him. In the next, they were collapsing to the floor, bleeding from dozens of wounds. Other than the clatter of their bodies against the tile, not one of them had a chance to make a sound.

When the deed was done, the trio of killers uncloaked in unison. "Look at us, ladies!" Sydney exclaimed. "We're a well-knit unit. Just call us Danny's Demons." She paused, exchanging looks between her companions as if the comment should have prompted something. At length, she tried again, "You know… 'Danny's Demons.' Like, *Charlie's Angles*?" Another round of uncertain looks. "Oh come *on!* It's a Terran cultural reference! The last reboot was canceled only two cycles ago!"

It might have been true, but even Dan had no idea what the Citza was talking about. "Sure," replied one of the Dorians. "Danny's Demons. Got it. Now, can we get a move on?"

"*Ugh!*" Sydney spun on her heels and began stalking toward the edge of the corridor. Not wanting to be left behind, Dan quickened his steps to catch up with her.

"How do you know about old Terran television shows?" he asked, genuinely curious.

Sydney shrugged. "Tessa Valadar spent a lot of time in front of the screen. I was just doing my research."

Dan started to reply but was cut off by a thrumming sound from around the corner. His core went cold as he stared in horror at the bot hovering there. It wasn't an assault drone, just a simple surveillance bot. It looked like a singular crimson orb wrapped in silver and kept aloft by a trio of revolving rings.

Oh shit. This was a worst-case scenario. The guards they could deal with, but the drones…

A blade appeared in one of the Dorian's hands. Dan opened his mouth in warning, but the words didn't make it out in time.

Sydney, too, had identified the problem. "No, don't!" she hissed.

But it was too late. The Dorian's blade left her hand and buried itself inside the hovering drone's sensor. Sparking plaintively, it fell to the floor in a broken heap.

And just like that, they were done for.

"Sha Cali and the Sahaia have arrived at the sanctum, my lord. It remains unmolested."

"Thank you, Ardren." Arc found himself wishing that the news had done more to calm his anxieties. His physiology was proving to be such an annoyance that he considered suppressing his emotional algorithms.

No, I must bear this. If I am to rule them, I must understand them. I must understand them fully. That means I must experience life as one of them, with all of its chemical irritations.

Even as he thought this, his automated protocols alerted him to another anomaly. [Drone disabled: CC482]

He sent his lightning-quick response back to his drone monitoring program. [Initiate playback: 60 seconds]. The first half of the recording was completely benign. It wasn't until the tail end of the recording that Arc detected the problem.

Standing in a hallway, amongst the bodies of over a half-dozen guards, stood three black-clad figures. It was the fourth person in the quartet that alarmed him.

Ratemacher.

Wasn't he still supposed to be in his room? Arc queried requests coming from that location for the past week. It had been several days since Daniel had requested any food be brought to his room. It had been even longer since anyone had reported checking in with him.

Damn it. How had Arc forgotten about him?

It didn't matter. He'd do a root-cause analysis later. For now, he had to deal with the current situation. He sent a message to the station's central security server. [Initiate lock-down protocol: Communications Center, Section 12.]

CHAPTER 13

"So Darkness sent them after Death, demanding they bring the trophy home. The children went back amongst the stars, though they would tarry for a time. When they obeyed Death at length, they divided in two."
—*Wisdom of Riven,* Chapter 22, Verse 5

The tunnels beneath the asteroid's surface stretched in front of them like the long, shadowy fingers of the very hand of darkness. So intricate was the labyrinth of branching, multi-tiered paths that Eli, despite being certain in the way forward, was beginning to doubt himself. That was the point, really: to make this network of tunnels so complex, so random and overlapping, that anyone who happened to stumble into them by accident would turn back before reaching the Sanctum.

For them, however, turning back was not an option.

"Almost there," Argus assured them from his position out front as the group emerged into a large, ruin-strewn cavern.

"Oh, that's reassuring," Kadath muttered. "Because I was fairly certain we'd passed that particular arch over there at least twice already. Consider me put at ease."

From Skye's quiet snort, Eli got the impression that she agreed with the half-breed's sentiment. He didn't bother reassuring her. Either the path they were walking was correct, or it was not. If they managed to get lost or turned around, then this would all be over before they had the slightest hope of finding their way back above ground.

He ran his hand self-consciously over the MoDAC in his pocket. The device wouldn't do him any good down here, not with the magnetic interference in these stony tunnels, but that didn't change the fact that he wanted desperately to check in with the other teams. He could have signaled Aaliyah, of course, but he knew how the engineer felt about psychic distractions.

Amelia's hands shot out to the side, and she hissed for everyone to be silent. She dropped into a low crouch, tilting her head to the side as if listening for something.

No one moved. No one breathed.

"Down!" she shouted.

Everyone dropped to the floor, not one of them thinking to question the telepath.

The report of a sniper rifle tore through the cavern. Sparks flew as the bullet struck a wall a short distance from where they stood.

Everyone dove for cover, scattering out across the maze to hide behind boulders, duck into side passages, or seek shelter beneath nearby ramps.

Another round ricocheted in their midst. One of Mara's thralls—hard to tell whether it was David or Tristan in the dark—had a pistol in his hands and was firing at where the shot had likely come from. When he'd emptied the clip, he slipped back into cover.

They waited. All was silent.

Then another shot echoed in the darkness, and Tristan roared in pain. Eli saw the round had caught him in the shoulder, but that was impossible. The shot would have had to come from…

"Behind!" he shouted.

Both Skye and David were firing now, back in the direction they had come from. The bullets bounced harmlessly off the surrounding stone, none of the shots finding the flesh of their assailant.

Another shot, this one from an entirely different angle, came dangerously close to clipping Eli's thigh. Again, it was an impossible angle if there had only been one shooter.

"How many?" he shouted to Amelia.

"One!" she shouted back, as another bullet bounced off her cover.

One? It couldn't be just one. How could one shooter seem to be...

Argus seemed to realize the truth at the same time as Eli. "Teleportation," he spat. "It's Brenna!"

Brenna—the only one among their number, aside from Jocelyn, that had remained unaccounted for. Eli hadn't thought about her welfare this entire time. Now it seemed that his fellow Sahaia would repay that unkindness with betrayal.

One errant shot might be understandable if she were defending the Sanctum, but this deliberate onslaught? She knew who she was shooting at by now, and she had only redoubled her efforts.

With the way this cavern was constructed, layer upon layer of twisting staircases and hidden passages, it was a sniper's paradise. With Brenna being able to teleport seamlessly from point to point, she had not only the advantage of cover but also mobility. It was the perfect trap.

The rifle fired again, and Tristan cried out once more. Brenna was taking advantage of the confusion and cycling backward. David was by his side, easing his injured companion to the ground.

Another crack and Eli acted instinctively. The invisible barrier went up just in time to catch the bullet that would have penetrated David's skull.

Eli flung the round back to where it had come, not thinking for a second that it would hit its mark. "Form up!" he shouted as he threw up an array of protective fields around the party.

The others must have figured out what he was doing because they all rushed over to where the thralls clung vainly to a bit of broken stonework. As they converged, Eli tightened up his fields to reduce the strain on his energy reserves. When he, too, was able to join the group, he enveloped them in a protective bubble.

Another round fired—Brenna testing his forcefield. It held, but that was hardly a victory. She had them pinned down. She didn't need to eliminate them. She only had to keep them from their objective.

Mara was hovering over Tristan, who still seethed in pain. "My leg," he grunted. "It's… I can't walk. You're gonna have to leave me."

"Not fragging likely," David growled.

Kadath shook his head as he looked at the wound. "Your friend here is right: he's not going anywhere. Not unless one of us is going to carry him, at least."

Cassthia looked to Mara. "You hold his bond. Can you heal him?"

As cold as it was, Eli had to step in. "A wound like that's going to take a lot of energy. She's not a biokin. She'll take on at least half of anything she heals. Even then…" He shook his head. "It's just not going to work. Mara, if you need to stay with him—"

"No," Tristan declared. He looked to Mara. "They need ya. Save yer strength. This ain't gonna kill me. I'm just… I'm just gonna be down for a bit, yeah?"

Skye was at Eli's side then, whispering into his ear. "Can you move this field to cover us the rest of the way? Maybe we could deal with her better when we're in the confines of the Sanctum."

Eli shook his head. "It's hard to move fields unless you're sending stuff flying away from the point of focus. I'd have to continually reform the barriers as we go. I can't be sure a bullet won't find a gap."

Siv looked up, having overheard their conversation. "Are you certain it's just one shooter?"

Eli glanced at Amelia, who nodded confidently.

The Hissak woman donned a resolute expression. "Leave her to me, then. I will quell her. When she moves, I'll hold her in position. You will not be able to use your abilities until you are out of range, but I trust you can find cover against a single sniper."

It was a good plan. If Siv kept Brenna occupied, they could probably make it through to the remainder of the tunnels. It would mean their party would be down a powerful asset, but assets didn't mean much if the alternative had them stuck here.

Judging by everyone's resolved expressions, they were on board with the plan. There was just one problem, and Cassthia voiced it for the group. "What about him?" she asked, inclining her head to where Tristan lay injured.

"I'll be fine," he protested. "The rest of ya just go."

Mara looked to David. "You stay with him. Take cover once the quell locks Brenna into position."

"And leave you unprotected?" David asked.

"I'll hardly be unprotected. Now, don't argue with me. Do as I ask." Turning to Siv, she said, "Whenever you're ready."

Siv looked back at Eli. "Open the shields. I'm going to press forward. When she fires, I'll suppress her gift. That's when you move."

Eli nodded and opened up the far side of the bubble. He gestured to where the invisible opening lay, and Siv dashed through it.

She moved like liquid shadow, racing across the path to the next point of cover. As they'd hoped, Brenna couldn't resist the target. The rifle fired. Once, twice, three times—the bullets striking dangerously close to Siv's racing figure.

As they did, Eli felt his psionic connect suddenly snap. It was as though a barrier had slid in place between him and his source of power. Siv was quelling the whole cavern. Now was their chance.

"Move!" he hissed, and the party raced forward as one.

The rifle fired, frantic now, as Brenna obviously realized that she wasn't going anywhere. Fortunately, the position she'd been locked into left her with a poor angle to fire upon the party. Moving as fast as they could, they raced down the tunnel and through the far archway, leaving Siv, Tristan, and David behind.

CHAPTER 14

"At this time they had two children of their own. One was called Chaos, the other a Scion of Darkness.

"Chaos would seek to thwart the Darkness, but his Scion would serve him unwittingly.

"Though the children would unite again, they would part ways once Death's heart had been secured. In time uncertain, they would meet again."

—*Wisdom of Riven,* Chapter 22, Verses 6–8

Brenna kept her calm as the intruders gathered in a circle under the telekinetic dome. After a few test shots, she dialed in her scope to get a better look at the trespassers.

The one holding up the barrier became obvious in an instant. Eli Ren'Dahl was there, along with his blonde Terran girlfriend. Argus and Amelia were there too, along with Mara and her pair of thralls. The last few individuals she failed to recognize.

Yet, when the Hissak woman bolted from the haven, Brenna was quick to target her. She fired three shots she felt sufficiently led the target. Unfortunately, the Hissak was faster than Brenna had anticipated, and the shots trailed just behind her.

Riven's shade. Brenna took her eyes off the scope as she reloaded the rifle. When she looked back, the Hissak was gone.

But the rest of the party was on the move. She sighted directly on Eli's head. Without the telekin, the rest of the party would be easy pickings.

Yet, before she could pull the trigger, the racing party ducked behind a tall stony protrusion. With a huff of frustration, she eyed her next vantage point and teleported.

Only, when she called upon her psionic ability, nothing happened. She tried again. Same result. *What the frag?*

Brenna couldn't think about that now. Right now, her targets were getting away. She pivoted her rifle to the edge of the rocky obstacle only to find more objects in her place. She fired rapidly, hoping to get a lucky shot off. She emptied her entire magazine with no success.

She was reloading when something flashed in her periphery. Instinctively, Brenna raised the rifle as a shield against the incoming blow. A blade crashed right into the firearm, nearly severing it in two.

Brenna jerked the rifle to the side, taking her assailant with it. The black-cloaked figure tumbled rose to her feet, two fresh daggers in her hands. Brenna instantly recognized the woman from below, not just for who she was, but for *what* she was.

"You're a quell," Brenna noted. "That explains my lil transportation issue. Well played. Wasn't expectin' that one."

"Shut your traitorous mouth," the Hissak growled. "Your own people? They trusted you. How could you do this?"

Brenna laughed as she drew her own pair of curved blades. "My *people?* Honey, ya ain't got no idea what you're talkin' about." She crouched into a fighting stance. With or without teleportation, Brenna was a fierce fighter, and she was ready to make that clear. "The coven ain't shown me no privilege. I'm just a cog in the wheel, to them. The Marauders on the other hand…" She shrugged. "Psionic superpowers mean a bit more to those who lack 'em. Don't ya agree?"

With a hiss, Siv launched her first barrage of attacks. She was fast, but not faster than Brenna. Brenna was an adequate marksman. When it came to knife fighting, she was an expert.

When the Hissak broke off her assault, Brenna found the breath to issue one more taunt. "You're good," she admitted. "But ya might not be better than me. Plus, I ain't gotta keep quelling this area while I fight. That's gotta spread ya pretty thin."

To emphasize the point, Brenna launched her own assault. The Hissak parried each blow, but only barely. When it came to speed and skill, they were an equal match.

Brenna fell back, adjusting her stance. "So, snake-bitch. Are ya ready for what's comin' yer way?"

The party raced forward, moving with even more urgency than they had before. They paused only to pick up or assist those who stumbled on stray bits of rubble and debris. Gunshots sounded in the distance, and Eli prayed to whatever gods were listening that their allies were all right.

Then, without any sign or indication that the tunnels were nearing their end, the group found themselves on the front steps of the Sanctum.

Eli always felt a strange sense of foreboding when approaching this sacred ground. This feeling was different, though. Instead of the strange mixture of awe and terror associated with the coven's traditions, there was a sense of determination. He was far from considering himself one of the faithful. Having been away almost entirely for the last seven years, he was anything but an acolyte.

Still, he clung to the undeniable feeling that this was *his* house. These were *his* people that had been assaulted. And for that, he would make Arc and his minions pay.

"Let's go," he muttered as if their contingent needed any prodding.

The entryway was quiet, save for the still ragged breathing of his companions. If he were being honest, he might have admitted that this was not especially unusual. The Sanctum had never been a hotbed for activity. This silence, though, seemed pregnant with morbid promise. That promise was delivered as soon as they entered the reception hall—or, at least, the area that had formerly been the reception hall.

"My gods," Mara gasped.

She spoke for the entire contingent. Having all been to the Sanctum before—many of them having made a significant part of their lives here—the change was obvious. Nothing could have prepared them for this.

The entire chamber had been ravaged, reformed in a way that rendered it unrecognizable. The furnishings were destroyed, all ornamentation dismembered. The very walls had been torn apart, concealing passages that should have been there and exposing new routes that should not have existed.

"How is this possible?" Amelia wondered.

"They've been excavating," said Argus. "They seem intent on digging out every single one of the secrets we've kept hidden here."

Eli took a tentative step forward, not quite able to comprehend the damage his eyes registered. Tears burned in his eyes as the scope of the desecration seeped into his soul second by painful second. With a single hand—kept carefully steady by all of the focus he could muster—he beckoned the party forward.

They did not travel, as expected, through the ornate paths of the Sanctum's halls. Instead, they crept across a veritable quarry, with wide-open spaces and cover only to be found in the mining implements that lay curiously abandoned at irregular intervals.

Skye whispered from just over Eli's shoulder. "I feel like we should be seeing drones, or workers, or… something."

A reply roared in the distance. "I wouldn't want any of them to disturb us."

Everyone started at the familiar, feminine voice that echoed across the ruins. Their eyes scanned the quarry, but the speaker was nowhere to be found. "Where are you, Cali?" Eli shouted.

There was an electric sizzle and thunderous crash directly in front of them. Stone and tile fountained up and toward them in a deadly wave. Eli just managed to form a protective shield to knock aside the debris before it crashed into him and his companions.

When the dust settled, the Kintari woman hovered before them. She was clad in her full Deathwatch regalia, complete with a foreboding black mask. Tendrils of scarlet lightning crackled along her limbs, licking and tasting the air all about her before grounding into the surface of the asteroid.

Though Dan had told them of Cali's transformation, nothing could have prepared Eli for the Kintar's transformation. Instead of the deep crimson flesh of her heritage, her skin was the same preternatural white as his own. The same emblem on his wrist, the mark of the Warrior's Wisdom, shone a glossy black on hers. This symbol was also painted in bold scarlet upon the right side of her Deathwatch mask, its mirror image having been painted on its left.

"I had feared our dear Brenna would stop you before you could reach me," she taunted. "Such an outcome would have been utterly disappointing. You see, I've been eager to test the depths of my newfound powers. How appropriate that I would face the previous owners of this very Sanctum and assert my rightful place as its new master."

Mara grunted as she lashed out with her own psionic lighting. A thick thread of silvered electrons lanced from her hand, streaking toward Cali's chest. Sparks erupted as the attack made contact, and Eli had to shield his eyes from the brilliance.

Cali, however, remained undisturbed. A sinister chuckle bubbled up from her throat. "I surely hope you can do better than that. Otherwise, this match will be most disappointing."

"Link up," Eli ordered to his companions. Before tapping into that link himself, he turned to Skye. "Take Kadath and the priestess and make a break for the opening at the back of the quarry. Gods willing, they haven't cut off the access point to the

Well. Follow those stairs and it will bring you to where you need to go."

"What about you?" Skye asked.

"We'll cover you," he declared.

Skye's eyes went wide in protest. "But I can help!"

"You'll be a greater help if you can cut off the Starfire Conduit and stop Arc. There are four of us, and only one of her. We can handle Cali, but we can't be delayed." He gripped Skye's hand and locked eyes with her. "We need you to do this," he whispered. "You're the *only* one who can do this."

Skye spared only the briefest of glances at Cassthia and Kadath before nodding. "Stay alive," she ordered before sprinting off to the far side of the cavern.

"Oh no you don't," Cali laughed. "No one gets to run away from the fun."

Lightning lanced toward them, but Eli was ready. He grabbed hold of a large plate of fallen stone and moved it to intercept the bolt.

Meanwhile, Argus let loose an attack of his own. Dark energy shot from his hands, straight at the hovering Kintar. Cali broke off her attack on Skye to dodge the beam and respond with a new cascade of electricity.

Argus held up his hands, and silvered lighting spread out over him and Amelia. Apparently, Mara was already linked in with the other two.

Eli opened himself up to the link as he rushed for cover. Argus must have been waiting for it because he seized on the power immediately. Eli gasped and stumbled, taken slightly off guard by the ferocity with which Argus took control. Argus was straining too much to worry about being gentle.

While still holding up his dome of lightning with one hand, he gestured with the other. The ground underneath Cali erupted as Argus tore the very stone and tile out from underneath her, sending it soaring up into the lofted ceiling above.

The attack struck a glancing blow to their opponent, enough to knock her from her hovering position. She struck the ground and rolled, coming up in a crouch.

"That's more like it!" she shouted. "Let your pets run. There's nothing they can do." She threw a bolt of crimson lightning at Argus, who just barely dodged out of the way. "Show me what you've got!" Cali roared. "It's time we see who is truly Sahaia!"

Chapter 15

"Darkness will have his day. Death's heart will be placed in the Sanctum, and fire will spread throughout his temple. This fire casts no light, for Death had no Light within him. Still, Death has power, and the power will be rendered unto Darkness."
—*Wisdom of Riven,* Chapter 22, Verse 9

Sydney had paid attention during the mission briefing. She knew what was coming. While all the guards she and her team had dispatched up to this point weren't linked into Arc's network, every single drone *was*. That meant, as soon as the hovering bot went down in a shower of sparks, Arc was aware.

She dove forward, tackling the kid and propelling them both into the hallway beyond. Almost as soon as they'd crossed the threshold a metal door slammed closed behind them.

Eying the door just to their left, the *only* door left open to them, Sydney said, "Please tell me that's where we need to be."

The boy hesitated only briefly. "That's it!" he said in a stage whisper as if there was any reason for them to be quiet anymore. "That's the node!"

"Great." Sydney stood, drawing her blades. "Stay right here. I'll just be a second."

"Wait!" the kid cried, holding out a pleading hand. "What about the others?"

Riven's shade. Was the kid so naive? Had he never lost people before?

"They'll be fine," Sydney snapped, not believing a single word of the lie. "Right now, we have a job to do. So, let me clear this room so you can do your thing, yeah?"

Dan hesitated again, but only for a moment. "Yeah," he agreed. "Do your thing."

Sydney triggered her cloaking device as soon as Dan finished speaking. Like a wraith, she swept up the hall and around the corner. Unlike the far end of the hall, the door in front of the comm node hadn't locked down. Dan could only wonder how such an obvious oversight in the security design might have occurred.

During the previous assaults, his companions had silently taken down the guards; this, on the other hand, wasn't quiet. Mere seconds elapsed before the screams from inside the room began. Seconds later, those screams died out.

Sydney appeared in the doorway, mask off and long white hair flowing behind her shoulders. "You coming?"

Dan pressed forward without reply. When he rounded the corner and saw the scene before him, his heart stopped.

Half a dozen bodies littered the room. Those were just the ones he can see. Sydney had been swift in her business, but she hadn't been subtle.

"Come on, kid," she prodded. "By now they know we're here. Do your thing. It's the last hope we have of getting out of here breathing.

No pressure, Dan thought as drew next to the appropriate terminal. Ignoring the body that lay just to the left of the seat, he accessed the open console, closed all active windows, and opened up a new holodisplay. Using the method that was now routine, he logged in with the admin framework he'd set up during his first hack of the station's systems and loaded the programs he would need.

As soon as he logged in, his earpiece beeped in a brief preamble to Shift's gruff tones. "Ah'll be damned, lad. Ya actually made it. Sure seems like ya took yer sweet time about it."

"Well, the autocabs were all tied up," Dan muttered "We had to walk over on foot."

There was an awkward pause. For a second, Dan thought the connection might have stalled out. "Shift?" he asked hesitantly.

"Lad?"

"Yes?"

"Was that what ya think passes as a joke?"

Dan growled in frustration. "Frag off, Shift. I thought you said this station would be empty! We had to kill at least twenty people to get in here!"

"It normally is, boy. But yer ol' buddy Arc ramped up the security just yesterday. Can't say why, but the machine's actin' a bit unstable of late."

Damn, Dan really should have considered that possibility. What else had Arc changed since he'd been gone? "Not the time, Shift. We're in a bit of trouble."

"Yeah, Ah noticed. Tell me, did ya bring the kit like Ah told ya?"

"Yes, I've got it right here." Dan pulled out the jumble of wires and metal he'd stuffed in his bag and began the process of untangling the mess. It seemed like, no matter how neatly he packed his bags, his gear always ended up like this by the time he needed to use it.

"Lad, Ah told ya t' bring a neurosim unit. What the frag is that?"

Dan huffed in frustration. "It's the only thing they had on the ship! Honestly, I'm lucky I could even find this."

"Ya still ain't answered ma question. What *is* that?"

"It's an old fashion SPECT rig that I converted to project instead of scan. It should do basically the same thing as a neurosim."

"And ya tested this torture device out 'fore comin' 'ere, yeah?"

Dan swallowed hard. "Well, no, but it's the best I've got, okay?" He slid the head rig over his scalp. "Now, can we get on with this? You said yourself that we don't have a lot of time."

"All right. It's yer noggin'. Lemme know when yer ready."

Dan snugged the device a little closer to his head and brushed the hair out of his eyes. He was a little surprised at how hard his heart pounded at the prospect of throwing the power switch.

Shift was right. Dan really should have tested this rig back on the ship.

But what was the worst that could happen? Brain damage? At least if he were a vegetable, he probably wouldn't care what Arc did to him and his friends when he found out what they were attempting.

"All right," Dan sighed. "I'm ready."

The world in front of Dan phased out. Well, that wasn't entirely accurate. The real world was exactly the way it had been just a second earlier. The only thing that changed was that Dan could no longer perceive the real world.

He was looking, instead, at a silver-blue construct. Coding and files flooded all around him. They weren't shapes or objects, per se—not the way that his brain understood those things.

Still, it was immensely fascinating. He honestly felt like he was *inside* the network. He felt like he could walk up to the different programs and segments of code and hold them in his hands, or whatever passed for his hands in this simulation.

[Ha ha!] Shift laughed. [The fraggin' thing worked! Ah'll admit, boy, Ah woulda bet my last kret that ya was about t' fry yer own circuits when that thing clicked on.]

Dan couldn't begrudge the hacker his skepticism. If he'd been the believing type, he'd have just been making peace with his maker. [But it did. I'm here,] he replied, trying to sound casual. [Now, let's get to it. Where's the security grid?]

Something blinked to the left of Dan's field of view—an icon that Dan's brain, in its attempt to parse whatever signals the equipment was feeding it, registered as a yellow pyramid. This must be Shift's avatar.

[Follow me, boy.]

The avatar started zipping away at an alarming speed. It was only then that Dan realized he didn't know how to move within the matrix. [Uh… Shift?]

The hacker must have anticipated the question, because he replied, [Just picture yerself followin' ma icon.]

Well, that seemed easy enough. Dan pictured himself chasing after the tiny pyramid and…

Oh shit!

The world zipped around him so fast that made him grip the armrests of his chair back in the real world, something his senses registered only tangentially before the feeling vanished. *Damn.* He could move fast.

[Ya all right, lad?] Shift asked.

[Yup. Totally cool. Lead on.]

With another wry chuckle, the hacker did just that. They were moving again, faster than before. Dan didn't even try to make his mind perceive the bits of code as they whirred by him in the construct. If this all worked out, maybe he'd have time to explore later. Right now he needed to tend to business.

The pyramid jerked to a stop in front of a particularly imposing tower of code. The little icon bumped against the object, shifting its characters from silver to ruby red.

[This is it!] Shift proclaimed. [Ya ready t' get started?]

[Sure,] Dan gasped. [Remind me again, what do I need to do?]

[It's just like we did in the real. When ya tap into the object, yer mind will see the interface. Instead a typin', ya just think about what ya want the thing t' do. Easy enough?]

Easy enough to say. They would see shortly how easy it was to pull off. Dan willed himself, or at least his avatar, to access the wall of code.

It was exactly as Shift had stated. An off-black background with gray text filled the world as Dan knew it. His entire field of view was walled off by the interface he would have expected to see had he accessed the system through a command prompt.

[All right, boy,] Shift began [Ya ready?]

For the first time since he'd started this whole endeavor, Dan didn't hesitate in the slightest. [Yes. Let's do this.]

The hack commenced. Dan's mind tackled the task far more furiously than his physical fingers ever could. To his surprise, he *liked* this interface. Why did this ever go out of style?

Mere seconds after it was started, the hack was finished. [And… done!] Shift proclaimed. [Good work, kid. Ain't no reason to worry about yer friends bein' able t' open doors now. Everythin' from here t' the Central Terminus is wide open fer business. What's next on the to-do list?]

Dan was about to explain that they had to find Lexa when a voice tickled the distant part of his mind that still existed in the real world.

"Um… how's it going, kid?" Sydney asked.

In his attempt to answer the question, Dan was surprised at how much effort it took to make his physical mouth speak. "It's going well. Doors should be unlocked. Why?"

"Because we're about to have company," she explained. "I'm going to go deal with this. Do try to hurry your shit along, okay?"

Chapter 16

"If Death's fire does not consume life, a new path will be trodden. Darkness does not walk this path, for he has been consumed in the fire. Yet, even still, his presence looms over it."
—*Wisdom of Riven,* Chapter 23, Verse 1

The echoes of distant alarms told Aaliyah that the primary assault force had made itself known. Good thing too, because it might actually keep the drones off her ass.

"Left up here!" she shouted.

Turan jerked hard on the wheel to zoom their little speeder toward the off-ramp. Aaliyah liked to go fast, but she had no idea how the Dorian was managing to keep them from skidding into the guardrails. In retrospect, it was probably a good thing she'd let him drive.

"Where now?" Turan asked as they sped toward the plaza.

"Over there! The terrace with the stone railing!"

Turan smoothly applied the breaks and brought them to a halt where Aaliyah had directed. A short expanse of white tile spread out to the edge of the plaza, which provided a brilliant overlook of both the city and, more importantly, the crystalline arch that powered it.

Aaliyah seized the pack where she'd stashed the extra J-krysts and climbed out of the vehicle. The Peace Keepers hefted the cannon, which seemed much heavier now that they were on the streets. In retrospect, maybe she had gone overboard on the augmentations.

"Where do you want it?" grunted one of the Dorians.

"Over there," Aaliyah pointed to her left. "Smack-dab in the center of the overlook."

Turan checked his rifle, concern evident on his face. "Are you certain you want to set up somewhere so out in the open?"

Aaliyah huffed. "Trust me, Turan: when this thing starts up, there isn't anything on this station that's going to be confused about where we are and what we're about."

"Perfect," he groaned.

Rather than being discouraged by Turan's moaning, it reignited the fire within her. "I didn't know the DGC could do sarcasm," she teased.

"I didn't know pirates were so good at wandering off-topic," Turan retorted "Now, how do we turn this thing on?"

Rather than answer, Aaliyah walked over to where the Peace Keepers were propping the J-cannon against the stone tiles. "Tilt it this way," she directed, gesturing at a forty-five-degree angle.

When the Dorians had the device in position, Aaliyah hit the switch that caused four heavy clamps to spring out from the side of the cannon, anchoring it into place. The stone tile cracked under the force of the action. *Oops.* She'd ratcheted those springs a little too tight. At least the ledge hadn't crumbled underneath them. *Yet.*

"Perfect!" she declared. "Now, step back. I've got it from here."

"And what can we do?" Turan asked.

"Um…" Aaliyah hesitated. "How bout, if a drone or one of the Marauders show up, you shoot them?"

Turan let out a quiet laugh. "Simple enough."

Easy to say until someone starts shooting. Rather than give voice to the sardonic comment, Aaliyah checked the crystal alignment and calibration. Everything, surprisingly, was exactly the way she needed it to be. Point to the Dorians for not damaging the device in transit.

Well then, no sense in putting this off any longer. Either her invention worked, or it didn't. If it didn't, they were going to need to move to Plan B. At this point, unfortunately, she wasn't sure if there *was* a Plan B.

"All right," she sighed. "Here goes nothin'."

The detonation from Markus's grenade had bought them the precious seconds they needed to retreat. It had also cut off their advancement as surely as the army of drones had done.

"What are our options?" Sahar growled to the soldier behind her.

The soldier swiped viciously at the portable holodisplay in front of him. His expression was grim as he seemed to consider and disregard idea after idea.

"Care to share with the class, Shing?" Geresh asked.

"Options are limited sir," the soldier replied. "If they've managed to ambush us down here, they've likely guessed our target. That means they've probably got drones at each of the off-shoots from this tunnel. We may need to get to the streets."

That was a bad idea. Sahar started to say as much, but Geresh beat her to it. "If they force us to the streets, then we're an easy target for the drones—not to mention the forces they've got guarding the front door. Give me the nearest option that keeps us underground."

The soldier complied, and Sahar could see why he had been hesitant. "That's directly below the core, close to the reserve dark energy source. There will almost certainly be defenses."

Geresh nodded as he turned to another officer. "Is Bravo team close to the core?"

"Yes," the female replied. "They're engaged, but the nearest escape is behind them."

Another nod. "Have them converge to meet us on our route. If we're being ambushed here, odds are that Arc has other choke points planned around the Central Terminus. Concentration of force will improve our odds."

He turned back to Sahar. "Any word from your friend?" She didn't have to ask who the Commander was referring to. She pulled free her MoDAC and checked for a message from Daniel.

Nothing. Any number of factors could explain this, ranging from a malfunction of the transmitters they'd packed into their shuttles, to the boy having been captured or killed. Sahar didn't want to dwell on the different scenarios, so she just shook her head in the negative. Geresh grunted his acknowledgment and went back to giving orders.

Markus quietly bumped Sahar's shoulder. "Hey, the kid's probably fine. Let's just focus on our part, yeah?"

Sahar gave him the slightest of nods. Markus was right, of course. The problem, from the beginning, had been the numerous points of failure for this suicidal operation. Each one of them had to focus on their own success, otherwise this whole mission would fall apart.

At Geresh's direction, they made their way back to the tunnel leading to the new route. The rocky corridor terminated about two stories up, in a single ladder with a manual hatch. "I'll go first," Sahar declared.

"I don't think so," Geresh cut in as he signaled to a pair of soldiers to take point. Sahar wanted to argue, but Geresh's defiant stance told her all she needed to know.

Go ahead, he seemed to say. *Pull rank.* Sahar wasn't ready to deal with that stress. With a nod, she let the other two soldiers past her. They scrambled up the ladder and quickly signaled for the others to follow. Sahar cut in front of Geresh, intending the move to make her displeasure obvious.

The area above the ladder was much hotter than the tunnel they had just exited. It didn't take long for Sahar to figure out why. They stepped out of a small antechamber into the power core for the entire station.

The shaft reminded Sahar of the power conduits on Sigma-4, but instead of having a glowing radiation coil that wrapped around the length of the station, the shaft jutted up as far as her eye could see. Not that that was very far. The ambient light and strange haze in the shaft kept her from seeing much farther than a single story in either direction.

"Up that way," one of the soldiers directed. "Three levels and we'll exit onto a path that will bring us to the Central Terminus."

No sooner did the words leave his maw than Sahar caught sight of shadows moving against the scarlet fog. "Drones!" she shouted in warning, bringing her rifle to bear.

The others followed her line of sight, and curses erupted from the whole company. "Move!" Geresh roared.

They pressed forward, up the grated floors and metal casings suspended between catwalks. The first of the drones blinked in recognition as they cleared the first level and moved to pursue.

Sahar fired a controlled burst at the bot, impacting dead center. Its shields flared and fizzled briefly before it exploded under the impact.

Either at a signal from the now-destroyed drone or in taking note of the small explosion in the shaft, more drones began to form up. Sahar's party soon found itself under assault by lancing beams of energy from every angle. The squadron grouped close to the central shaft, but one thing was clear: they weren't going to make it to their target.

Sahar took cover behind a guard rail as another laser lanced perilously close to her head. Markus was right next to her, shouting on the comms channel. "We need to divide their fire!"

"Suggestions?" she and Geresh asked nearly in unison.

Markus pointed up to a branching path ahead of them. "Give me two soldiers. We'll take that path closer to the center of the core. We'll cover you as you make your exit."

Geresh nodded. "And how do we extract you?"

"You don't." Through his black helmet, Sahar could almost see that familiar determined look in his eyes. "We'll try to follow if we can. But our primary objective is to get the package to the central terminus. If that fails, this is all for nothing. One of us needs to make it there to upload the virus. Just let us keep them off your back."

To Sahar, who had the burden of her emotional attachment to Markus, the decision was not so black and white. Geresh, who had no such burden, made it an easy call. He gestured to two of his soldiers. "Go with him."

Before any objection could be raised, the party of three was off. They sprinted toward the fork in the path, drawing fire as they went. When they were a short distance away, Geresh signaled for the others to move down the other walkway.

Then something strange happened.

The radiance of the core seemed to dampen slightly as if someone had bumped a dimming switch. It was still bright enough to hamper visibility in the haze of the shaft, but not so subtle as to avoid notice.

More importantly, there was a break in the onslaught coming from the drone army. Sahar risked a glance at the nearest of the airborne bots. It still hovered, menacing with its armored plates and array of laser weapons. Yet, it seemed to be hesitating.

The crimson sensor in its midsection blinked wildly, giving Sahar the strange impression that the drone was having some kind of seizure. It shifted erratically, as if uncertain as to how it should be handling the situation.

"What's it doing?" Geresh asked.

It wasn't *doing* anything. That was what was strange. It was almost as though… "The signal!" Sahar exclaimed. "The team on the arch must be de-powering the antenna! The signal is breaking up!" She wondered, for the briefest moment, if this might be enough to eliminate the threat. Would taking down the signal be enough to take the drones functionally offline?

Such hopes were quickly dashed as the blinking began to slow. The drone turned, its pulsing thrusters still managing to keep it aloft.

Then it fired.

Lancing bolts of energy filled the entire shaft. Whereas the previous attacks had been coordinated and careful to avoid hitting any critical system, these attacks were frantic.

Energy sliced at the catwalks, but also at the core itself. Where the rays struck, radiation and plasma spurted forth like a pulsing artery. The heat in the shaft flared. If this kept up, they were going to throw the whole facility into a meltdown.

Then a shot from the far catwalk took down the bot closest to them. It was Markus and his team. They'd made it into position. "Go!" Markus shouted over the comms.

No one argued. Sahar and the remainder of her team dashed forward. They picked off opponents as they appeared, but mostly they just tried to avoid errant laser bolts. As Sahar cleared the third level, a blast sizzled through the grating directly behind her.

Though it had missed her, the walkway buckled under the weight of the armored combatants that raced across it. Someone cried out behind her.

It was Geresh. The Jingda had crashed through the melting walkway right behind her. His rifle swung freely from its shoulder strap, having been released as he clawed desperately to gain purchase on the broken metal.

Sahar's hand shot out and grabbed his wrist just as the catwalk buckled. It took all her considerable strength to haul him to safety. There was nothing she could do to help the pair of shoulders just behind him, who had already disappeared in the fog below. "Come on," she growled, pulling Geresh to his feet. "Almost there."

Then there was another explosion, and a jet of flame shot out from the center column. It was below where any of their men stood, but the searing heat quickly melted the supports of a nearby platform.

The same platform where Markus and three Maur soldiers were providing covering fire.

It all happened so fast. Markus seemed to realize what was happening and ordered the Maur back. Before they could shift position, however, the platform buckled and collapsed from underneath them.

They toppled in all directions. Someone was trying to cling to the falling platform. Someone else tried to leap to safety. All efforts proved fruitless, and Sahar could only stare in hopeless horror. As she watched her comrades and one of her best friends disappear into the crimson haze, all she could do was scream.

Chapter 17

"In this time a great plague will go out among the stars. The plague will be spread by the Kindred, and the masters will know nothing of their servants' designs.

"The plague will strike Honor first, and when Honor has fallen it will return home.

"Those of the Blood will seek to control it, to subjugate it as they subjugate all but the Masters. Yet, even in knowing that the plague is Death, they will not deter."
—*Wisdom of Riven,* Chapter 23, Verses 2–4

Though the infiltration had suffered heavy losses, it was far from halted. Indeed, Arc's forces had suffered numerically greater losses and had been beaten back at every choke point.

This made Arc indescribably angry. [Initiate Citadel emergency lock-down. Executive authorization only.]

The return prompt was so unexpected that it took Arc the better part of a full second to comprehend its meaning. [Access denied.]

What? [Initiate Citadel emergency lock-down. Authorization override-ARC.4.8.2.12.20.19]

[Access denied.]

How in the nine hells? He realized the source of the problem almost instantly. There was only one place on Minos Station that could *possibly* override the access to his own installation. "Ardren," Arc growled. "Report to the communications node immediately.

Take as many assets as you feel are necessary. I need this problem taken care of."

The Citza stuttered for just a moment. "B-but sir, I—"

With a roar of fury, Arc smashed his fist into the nearest console. The combined strength of his cybernetic arm and rage sent his fist crashing deep within the computer. He yanked his arm free, ignoring the pain in the limb that was already being repaired by his nanite technology.

"Do. It. *Now!*"

Ardren's eyes were wide with terror. "Right away, my lord."

As Cali's servant rushed from the room, Arc fought to reign in his fury. *Control. You need to be in control. Consider the facts: the enemy forces are crippled. They have bled for every centimeter. You've lost nothing of value. Your best defensive assets are deployed. You still own the field.*

Except, that wasn't entirely true, was it? His greatest asset had yet to be deployed: *himself.*

Yes, it was time to enter the fight. What was the Terran saying? "If you want something done right," he muttered, "do it yourself." He rounded on the nearest technician. "Maintain all current feeds of data to my communications submind. I will be watching from the central terminus."

You have to do this. They are counting on you. Skye repeated this mantra to herself over and over again as she, Kadath, and Cassthia fled down the stairs. It helped to think that they were running toward their salvation, not away from a fight.

As thunder crashed and the cavernous walls shook with the force of the battle that raged behind them, she began to doubt herself. Yes, part of her knew that Eli was right: in that battle of titans, she would only be a liability. That did not make abandoning her friends any easier.

"We're almost there," Cassthia assured her, apparently having seen the hesitation on her face.

Kadath eyed the priestess askance. "Forgive me, but I can't see how you would know that. Last I'd checked, you've never been here."

"I can feel the Heart," she insisted. Gesturing to Skye, she added, "She could too if her mind was not on the Sahaia."

Feel the Heart? The priestess had to be mistaken. All Skye could feel was the chill of the tunnels, the pounding of stone against her feet as she ran, and…

Wait. There *was* something. It was faint. Skye wouldn't have thought anything of it had Cassthia not suggested its importance. It was like a faint source of heat in the darkness, a warm flicker of familiarity. No, not warmth: *power.*

<Skye.>

"Okay, what the frag?" Skye shouted, skidding to a sudden halt.

Kadath was at her shoulders, almost barreling her over before he could stop his descent. "What's the matter?" he asked, cybernetic eyes scanning the darkness for whatever unseen threat may lurk there.

<Skye,> the voice hissed from the darkness. *<Skye Jensen.>*

"There!" Skye gestured frantically past the priestess and down the darkened staircase. "There's something down there! Can't you hear it?"

He listened for a moment. "I can't hear anything."

Cassthia looked back up at them, those reptilian eyes glowing eerily in the dim light of the corridor. A hint of a smile rested on that darkly beautiful face. "Fear not, child. It's the Heart of Thule. It remembers you. It recognizes you. It calls to you."

It remembered her? Remembered her from when? From her time on the ship, or…?

<Kaleema.> The voice wasn't just a hiss anymore. It was the sound of a thousand voices, and the walls around Skye seemed to come alive with the memory of what she'd seen within Markus's mind when she had severed his connection to the artifact. Back when she'd stood before the Stardust Grave itself.

"I…" The words froze on Skye's lips. She had started to say, "I can't," but that was a defiance of the simple truth: she *had* to. *Everyone is counting on me.* "Sorry," she murmured. "I'm coming."

The energy grew stronger and the voices more insistent as Skye and the others continued their descent. By the time they arrived at a small antechamber, the sounds echoing in Skye's mind were a veritable cacophony of pleading urges.

The door in front of them was sealed by a kind of psionic lock. Cassthia studied it briefly before waving her hand over the stone effigy. Inlaid carvings began to glow, and the curving arches of the lock twisted to realign the radiant glyphs. The apparatus clicked with finality, dimmed, and the door creaked open.

Red light spilled from the portal, coloring the entire party in scarlet brilliance. Despite the change in hue, Skye could easily recognize Heart of Thule. The crystalline rock flared with power at the center of the chamber. It was encircled completely by a placid expanse of dark liquid, seeming for all the world like a sea of blood that swirled around the pulsing artifact. This must be the Well of Eternity.

Above the Heart was the mechanical device that Dan had shown them in the mission briefing. Though Skye loosely recognized the Starfire Conduit, it looked so different in its active state. The contraption was almost fully eclipsed by the stream of power it drank greedily from the artifact.

She suddenly realized the voices in her mind had gone silent. It was as if whatever psychic tension had existed between her and the Heart had been put at ease by her proximity. Such a realization was almost as disturbing as the eerie silence that enveloped her.

Cassthia's hand was on her shoulder. "Are you ready?"

Skye drew in a heavy breath, finding the act completely unsatisfying in the face of her nervous tension. "No," she answered honestly, "but I don't think that matters, does it?"

"It's all right. I will walk you through this."

Summoning up all the courage she could muster, Skye issued a resigned nod.

The meager show of strength was enough for the priestess. "You will want to lay your hands on the artifact's surface," she explained. "This is as much to steady yourself as to establish the psychic connection. Your body will go rigid when your mind connects with the Heart, but we don't want you to fall off balance and break the link."

Easy enough. "Okay. When I touch it, how do I form the connection?

"It will be automatic, though I will warn you: it will not be the only thing vying for your attention. The waters of the Well will also speak to you. You must do what you can to ignore them. If you let them into you, you will lose your ability to communicate with the artifact. We cannot let your essence be accidentally drawn away from the mortal plane."

"Let them…" Skye shook her head. "What do you mean, 'let them in?' I kind of feel like this should have been brought up before."

The priestess sighed. "Don't worry. If your intentions are clear, if you keep the Heart of Thule in your mind's eye, the waters will not bother you. If you have trouble, just focus on the energy you feel coming from the artifact. The transition should come naturally." She paused for a moment, staring into Skye's eyes. Those serpentine orbs must have seen what she was looking for because Cassthia nodded. "Good. It is time. We should disrobe now."

Whatever calm Skye had dissolved once more at the strange request. "Wait what? Disrobe? Why?"

Cassthia sighed again, mustering what was left of her patience. "Purity of Flesh, my dear. This must be observed when a mortal enters the Well of Eternity. Inorganic substances—clothing, cybernetics, machinery—disrupt the flow of dark energies when the Well holds a psionic charge. Only our natural bodies may touch the waters safely."

Natural bodies? *Oh shit.* "What happens if cybernetics enter the Well?" Skye asked.

The priestess's expression strained as her annoyance grew. "The dark energies would concentrate on and overload whatever metals and plastics are in the enhancement. Natural mineral levels in your blood and tissues aren't a problem, but the higher concentrations act as a magnet for the power. They could catch fire, or discharge in some other violent way. The effects, I assure you, would be most unpleasant."

"Nine hells," Skye cursed. "We've got a problem. I can't do this."

Even in the tension of the moment, Kadath let slip a lecherous smirk. "I assure you, it's nothing I haven't seen before. But, if it makes you feel better, I could turn my back."

Cassthia was not so amused. "I don't think modesty is something we…"

"*No!*" Skye shouted. "Shut up, both of you! Listen, I can't *walk* into the Well because my legs aren't *organic.* They're cybernetic. My arm too. Shit, half my nervous system is synthetic!" *How in the nine hells did Eli not think of this when we pitched this plan?*

Kadath wasn't smiling anymore. "Riven's shade…"

"Right," Skye agreed. The conclusion was both obvious and dark. If Skye couldn't cross the Well of Eternity, she couldn't contact the Heart of Thule.

If she couldn't reach the Heart, she couldn't cut off Arc's access to Thule's reservoirs of Dark Energy.

It was over. They'd lost.

CHAPTER 18

"In this error, Death might consume all once more. If Death does not consume all, either by fire or by plague, then he shall be set aside.

"War will continue in his place. For War is Death's sister, and though the two claim to loathe one another, their designs are much the same."

—*Wisdom of Riven,* Chapter 23, Verses 5–6

Siv had never held back in a fight. She was not one to taunt or toy with her opponents. She dispatched them as quickly and efficiently as possible. This fight was no different. As though it would be her last chance for surrogate vengeance for Jeagan, Siv descended on her opponent like a dark tsunami of blades.

Yet Brenna held her ground. The Sahaia met each attack, not as one who relied on her psionic gifts for a combative edge, but as one who had dedicated her life to the perfection of martial prowess. She was every bit as strong and skilled as Siv.

As the battle waged on, Siv found herself wondering if Brenna might not be even a little better.

The edge of the Hissak's knives shrieked against the curved edges of Brenna's blades. Every time Siv slashed at an opening, the Sahaia's dagger was there to parry. Every time she lunged, her opponent spun out of the way. The Sahaia's ability was almost preternatural, as though her psionic talents could increase her speed. Yet, Siv knew that wasn't possible, not with her quelling power dampening the area around them.

It also didn't help that Brenna was larger. Her muscled frame had to be half-again Siv's bodyweight, and the Sahaia used that to her advantage. When Brenna launched a counterattack, the force of the blow slammed so hard into Siv's defenses that she could feel it reverberate down to her bones.

Brenna must have sensed the weakness because she pressed harder. Siv stepped back, trying to put some distance between her and her opponent. This made the Sahaia come at her like a charging animal, blades flashing with relentless, deadly precision.

Siv's foot slipped. With horror, she realized Brenna had pushed her to the edge of the platform. If she stepped back, she would fall. If she halted, she was at the mercy of her attacker.

Acting on faith and intuition, Siv threw herself into the air, flipping backward and managing to score a solid kick across Brenna's face. Then she was soaring through the air, praying to find some platform or surface that would break her fall and not her legs.

Siv hit the rocky ground at the very instant she'd righted herself. The slope angled downward, though, and a sharp pain spidered up her ankle and knee. With gritted teeth, she managed to slow herself and look up onto the platform where Brenna still waited.

The Sahaia laughed. "That was gutsy. Not what I was expecting." She sheathed one dagger and rubbed at her jaw. "Mighta chipped a tooth on that shot. Good move. How's that leg feelin'?"

"Come down here and I'll show you."

"No thanks. Besides, ya look like ya could use a break. You're a bit peaked. Might be easier to catch your breath if you'd stop quelling the whole damn cavern."

"I can do that," Siv replied. "Just throw down your weapons and surrender. Then we'll talk."

Brenna laughed. "Nah, this is way too much fun. But, if ya need a break, I can oblige." She looked out over her left shoulder. "That pair of thralls over there looks bored. Think I might go see if they want to play. Meet you over there when you're rested!" With a mock salute, Brenna disappeared behind a rocky column.

Lith's tits! Siv had forgotten about David and Tristan. They'd stay behind, and even without Brenna's ability to teleport, they would be vulnerable to attack.

Siv spun and started in the direction had looked, only to skid to a stop once more. *Wait.* That wasn't the direction she'd come from. The thralls were in the other direction. Then why…?

Frag me.

Siv dove to the side just in time to miss decapitating blow. While her head remained on her shoulder, her entire body ached as she tumbled down the rocky slope. Fire exploded in her injured knee as it caught something sharp while rolling across the rubble-strewn ramp. Her fall was brought to a sudden halt as she smacked painfully into a jutting stalagmite.

"*Oof!* Now *that* hurt!" Brenna taunted from off in the darkness. "But ya kept on quellin'! Good job. I thought for sure that was going to break your concentration."

Siv heard the Sahaia approaching with slow, careful footsteps. Brenna knew she had the advantage now and was in no hurry to re-engage. As Siv attempted to rise, she realized just how bad her situation was.

Her knee blazed like the ninth hell, and her left foot had gone numb. The rest of her body wasn't faring much better. That quick tumble and sudden stop had seriously fragged up something in her back.

"Dirty tricks?" Siv spat. "Couldn't beat me in a fair fight, so you resort to lies and misdirection?"

Brenna chuckled. "Fightin's about winnin', bitch. I'll do whatever it takes to see that it's your ass that's dead on the ground and not mine."

Siv had to admit that Brenna was damned close to seeing that goal become a reality. If the Hissak had been overmatched before, her impending defeat was now inevitable. "Well," she replied, "if that's how we're playing, then you'll have to come and find me." Sheathing her daggers, she drew her cowl tight around her head and slid into the darkness of the cavern.

Eli, Amelia, and Mara managed to find shelter just beyond a rocky outcropping as Argus renewed his assault. With an enraged snarl, Argus threw up both hands as twin beams of dark energy sprang from his palms.

Cali dodged, racing across the battlefield. Eli might have found her hard to track had it not been for the crimson sparks that marked her passing. The Kintar took cover behind a fallen monument, which exploded on contact with Argus's beams

Amelia's voice came over their link. <Steady, my love. She's trying to burn us out.>

<Good fragging luck!> Argus roared in psychic reply. <She will pay for what she's done!>

None of the other Sahaia admonished Argus for his disposition. They all felt the same. However, Cali was far from stupid, and she had welcomed this challenge. It was unlikely that she would underestimate the power of four linked Sahaia.

Red sparks burned across the floor as Cali darted to the next position. Argus shot again, this time leading the haze of crimson enough so that his energy bolts made contact.

The sparks crackled and dissipated. There was nothing there.

"Diversion!" Eli shouted as Cali reemerged from her previous position. An orb of lightning shot forward aimed not at Argus, but at the three who huddled behind their defensive barricade.

Eli's stomach lurched as Argus passed control of the link. It went straight to Mara, who threw up a shield of electrons to dampen the blast.

Silver and crimson flared as the ball exploded. Lightning lanced into Eli's chest, sending him flying backward. He collided painfully with a slab of stone and the air was knocked from his lungs. Blind with pain and the light of the explosion, he rolled to his left to find shelter just before the electric bolt struck perilously close to where his head had been.

Someone cried out along their psychic connection. There was another stab of pain. Their link fizzled and snapped.

Argus howled in the distance. *"No!"*

Oh gods, Eli thought. His vision cleared, and his fears were made manifest.

Amelia had been caught out in the open surface. Burns marked the rock all around her broken body like lightning had struck the area repeatedly until it had found its mark. Amelia's huddled form was charred and smoking, but still moving weakly.

Cali hovered toward her, a predator toying with injured prey. Argus was rushing them both, dark energy radiating off of him in waves. He hurled his open palms towards Cali. Three swirling violet disks sliced across the cavern. Cali made no move to dodge.

She struck out at the disks with her hands and feet. The blades of dark energy collided with her lightening coated limbs. Flashing plaintively, the disks were knocked aside to spin harmlessly off into the distance.

In his urgency to reach Amelia, Argus had taken his eyes off the enemy. As he raced to where Amelia lay, Cali set her sights on the new target.

Eli rushed forward, sending a shockwave of telekinetic force at Cali. The air around the Kintar shivered and crackled as the shockwave passed harmlessly around her, through her. She laughed, sending a bolt of lightning at Eli. He leaped behind a nearby stone, narrowly avoiding being seared by the bolt.

Then Mara was up. With a cry of rage, her own silver lightning flashing brighter than Eli had ever seen, rushed toward Cali. Rather than dodge, the Kintar held out her right hand. Mara's lightning lanced straight into Cali's palm, forming up into a glowing silver orb just above her hand. The more energy that poured through the blast, the more the orb grew.

Mara broke off the assault, staring bewildered as Cali held up the ball of crackling electricity. Silver flashes played off the black surface of the Kintar's mask. Her low, wicked laugh echoed across the chamber. "You fools," she scoffed. "You are nothing."

She jerked her arm sideways, pointing her palm straight at Amelia. Then, she released the blast. The silver energy cracked as it struck home. There was a flash of light and a blood-curdling scream. *"Argus!"*

Amelia's partner reached her at the final instant. He didn't have time to deflect the blast. Instead, he hurled himself in front of it. Now his own agonized scram joined Amelia's as his body lurched.

As the light faded, Argus tumbled to the ground. His body smoked and sparked. In the center of his chest, which the fabric of his shirt had been scorched away, there was now a charred and gaping hole.

Amelia screamed as he collapsed. She crawled over to him, clawing frantically at his broken body. "Argus? No… No, no, no, *no! Argus*!" Her screams dissolved into sobs. "No… oh gods, no." She wept, burying her face in his ash-covered remains. "No, Argus. No…"

CHAPTER 19

"And at this time, War will reign supreme. It is set that she will have her era, an era which might rule for all time.

"Yet time is a fickle thing, and even War might falter if the efforts of the children will it so."

—*Wisdom of Riven,* Chapter 23, Verses 7–8

Despite the communications building having gone into complete lock-down, the Marauders' initial response felt lackluster. Sydney was ready and waiting when the first door slid open to reveal only a single unit—two men and one woman, all Terrans—who swept in with rifles at the ready.

Sydney waited until they were almost to the door to the comms node before dispatching them. Both of the men went down smoothly. The woman caught sight of Sydney's whirling blades just in time to open her comms channel an instant before Sydney took her life. Though no message had gotten out, the aborted transmission would certainly send more soldiers to investigate.

When faint footsteps sounded from beyond the second security door, Sydney figured their luck had run out. She glanced into the comm node to see how Dan was faring.

The kid looked like he was just staring off into space, sitting perfectly still in a mesh office chair in front of an idle holographic console. The rig of disparate wires, sensors, and metal plates looked highly uncomfortable perched in the nest of his messy hair. As far as she could tell, though, he didn't seem to mind the hard surfaces digging into his scalp.

"Hey kid," she said. "More company inbound. Try not to take too long, yeah?"

Dan gave no response. He might have been too deep in whatever simulation he was working on, or perhaps he was just ignoring her.

Yet again, the impulse to leave the kid to his fate and sneak out the back tempted her. Surely they'd caused enough damage by now, right? The Maur and Dorians were probably stomping into the central terminus that very instant. If Dan went down, they could still deliver the virus and complete whatever other steps they had in mind to take Arc offline. Then Sydney could hop the next ship heading out-system and be gone before anyone could figure out what had happened.

The only problem with that was that she seemed to be burning a lot of bridges in a really small fragging window. She'd already set fire to her relationships with House Valadar and the Ghenza Collective. If she bailed now, she'd have the DGC and the Maur Federation breathing down her neck as well. And shit, that was the *best*-case scenario. If they lost and Arc stayed in power, how long would it take for Arc and the Marauders to find her?

On the other hand, if she stayed, she faced a different proposition. At best, she was a hero. If she could keep the hacker kid alive, that *had* to buy her at least a head-start when she went on the run. Worst case scenario, she killed a few more low-lives before she went down fighting.

Yeah, that sounded like a better option.

She shut the door to the comms node and stabbed the access panel. This would slow down anyone that didn't have a direct line to the security system, and hopefully, the kid was a decent enough hacker that he could secure his own physical space over the network. Someone would have to cut through the door if they wanted to get to the other side. If that happened, it meant Sydney was dead and she wouldn't much care about the outcome anymore.

She triggered her stealth suit and slid to one side of the hallway, her eyes on the next security door.

The barricade slid open, and a trio of drones entered the hall. One of the hulking machines was roughly man-shaped, marching down the hall swiveling its armored torso and machine-gun arms. The other two were aerial drones, the same kind she'd tangled with back in the asteroid belt.

Though the drones maintained a loose formation, there was something wrong with them. Their sensors blinked erratically. The hovering bots would occasionally dip in the air as if their thrusters couldn't quite keep up with the workload. Several times, as the heavy assault drone stepped forward, its leg would pause mid-stride, buffer for a moment, and then come down a bit too hard on the floor. *Kid must be doing something to these bots after all,* Sydney reasoned.

The sapient soldiers came next, clad head to toe in black and red battle armor. Better equipped than the first batch, their races and sexes were indistinct in the full body armor. Based on their heights and builds, Sydney guessed at least two of them were Orchalen.

She went for those two first. Resting perfectly still, she allowed them to advance until she was right in their midst. When the opportunity presented itself, she slid a thin dagger right into the base of the first one's skull.

The soldier let out a deep grunt, prompting his companions to turn. Sydney pulled the pin out of a grenade dangling unprotected from the belt of the nearest combatant. With a vicious kick, she sent the man stumbling headlong into his companions.

She sprinted away, just barely making safe distance as the unfortunate combatant detonated via his own ordinance. The blast was surprisingly small but enough to reduce him to a spray of gore and metallic fragments.

She'd hoped the explosion would set off any other explosives the over-equipped fools had on them. While this didn't happen, the effects were no less devastating. All four remaining soldiers were instantly combat-ineffective, most likely dead.

The drones, however, were another matter. Their static shields flared, protecting them from the blast. Mechanical red eyes turned in Sydney's direction and immediately scanned the area. The stealth suit might fool a soldier's eyes, but not a machine's multi-spectrum scans. With her suit's efficacy in doubt, she wasn't going to rely on the gear to get the drop on them.

It was time to see if all those years of training and biomods were worth all the krets the Collective had put toward her.

She reversed direction, racing back to the drones. Two more blades sprang from her hands, seeming to appear in thin air as they left her suit's stealth field. They shattered the center core of the first aerial bot, sending it crashing to the ground.

Sydney danced forward, grabbing a discarded firearm off the floor. She squeezed the trigger and sent a spray of rifle fire into the second airborne bot. Its shield flared weakly, proving ineffective at stopping the bullets at such close range. It erupted in a shower of sparks, leaving only the heavy assault drone.

Which, at this point, had an excellent bead on her position. Sydney threw her rifle in the air and fell to her back. The drone's arms whined as they adjusted to follow the rifle and opened fire. White the bot focused on her distraction, Sydney slid between its legs.

She drew another blade and severed the wires that operated the hydraulic limbs, causing them to leak fluid. Then she rolled to her feet and stabbed at its center mass. Her aim was just slightly off, causing the blade to skid against the armored surface. Worse yet, the machine's trunk spun, and one of its mechanical appendages slammed into her torso.

She was knocked backward but retained her footing. Meanwhile, the drone had turned fully around. Its legs were disabled, but it spun freely on its center axis.

Damn. That was unexpected.

The bot's central eye flared and its machine guns whirred. Sydney dove left, sending her blade straight for the glowing sensor.

The knife made contact. But, unlike its airborne companions, the drone did not go down. Instead, it shook its head in confusion and began to wildly spray the corridor with bullets.

Sydney pivoted again, not daring to run away. As she had always been taught, she ran *toward* the enemy.

A bullet nicked her arm. She drew another blade—her *last* blade. Diving toward the drone, she landed in a somersault and came up, a dagger aimed for the only gap she could spot in the armor plating.

This time, her aim was true. The blade slipped under the protective plates and right into the circuitry buried behind the metallic barrier. Sparks flew, and with a mournful howl, the thing finally shut down.

She withdrew the blade from the broken piece of machinery. Only then did she spare a thought for her arm. The fragging thing hurt, but worse than that, it had burnt through one of the chips in her stealth suit. With the circuit broken, she was now clearly visible. At least all her targets were down.

Or, so she had thought.

"Impressive," came the cultured voice from the end of the hall. Sydney turned from the broken husk of the assault drone to see a single figure standing in the open door.

A Citza, one of her own people. Unlike the goons she'd just dispatched, this man was not clad in the Marauders' black and red armor. On the contrary, he didn't look like a soldier at all.

"I think you may have taken a wrong turn," Sydney cautioned. "If you leave now, I'll forget you were here." A foolish gesture to be sure, one she probably wouldn't have made if the man were Terran. It might have been prejudice, but she had a soft spot for her people.

The man laughed. "Oh, I don't think so. I'm afraid my superiors wouldn't abide such a flagrant dereliction of my duties."

Sydney removed her mask, tossing it to the floor. She went to work unbinding her tail next. "Yeah, well, I wouldn't worry about your leaders for much longer. That crazy synth and anyone who works for him is going to burn before this show is over." With her tail comfortably free from her suit, she jerked her head over her shoulder. "Come on. I'll hide you until this is over. After that, we'll see about getting you off station."

"Unlikely," the man took another step forward. Still a good distance away, he extended a hand. "Ardren Faye, at your service."

Sydney studied the hand like it was a viper that had just offered to bite her. "Nice ink," she said, noting the runic tattoo on his forearm. She'd seen marks like that before, but never on a Citza.

"Yes, I think so." Seeing that she wasn't going to take the proffered hand, he pulled it back, rolling up the sleeve of his black dress shirt. "A gift from my mistress." He let both arms fall comfortably back to his sides.

"And by 'mistress,' I assume you mean the Kintari puppet Arc has running this place."

Ardren nodded. "The very same."

Sydney cocked her head. That nagging impression that she should get on with killing this fool was growing more persistent. Still, her irrational fondness for her own kind held her at bay. "As I understand it, Sha Cali Vay-Lon is an exile. I doubt you two met after her fall from grace. You followed her into exile?"

"Of course." Ardren's smile was genuine.

As was Sydney's incredulity. "Her sentence extended to her servants as well?"

"Oh, no, no, no. I alone chose to continue with Sha Cali into her new life."

"Is she *that* good in bed?"

Another laugh. "I wouldn't know."

So, Ardren had gone into exile was Sydney, and he wasn't getting slick with his mistress. "Then why?"

"Let it suffice to say that some loyalties run deeper than the current political situation." He gave a dramatic pause, measuring her with his eyes. "What about you, assassin? What kind of loyalty places you here?"

"The kind that's none of your damn business."

"And here I thought we were getting along so well." He swept a lock of hair behind one pointed ear. "You know, if it's money you're interested in, my masters likely have more than enough to secure your services."

Huh, that might not be such a bad twist. Nine hells, if her allies were getting their asses kicked, this opportunity might be her only salvation. Then again, if things were going so well for Arc, would Ardren be down here making this offer?

Maybe if she kept Ardren talking a bit longer, the answer would become apparent. "So, what do you suppose that would look like?" she asked.

"Presently, it would entail you turning around and disposing of whoever you're protecting in the comms node before they cause any more damage. Or, at least, you could allow me to accomplish the task."

A simple and reasonable proposal. Though a part of Sydney had allowed Dan to grow on her, it wasn't like she was willing to throw her life away to save his. Not if she had a better option. "That seems easy enough. But then what?"

"Then, when the remainder of the interlopers has been vanquished, I will bring you to my mistress to swear fealty." Ardren furrowed his brow, considering Sydney once more. "Of course, she'll likely want to bond you. Pardon my saying so, but you are a bit of an unknown quantity. Besides, you know how the Kintar are. Even an exile will want everything in its proper place."

Its proper place. Sydney didn't like the sound of that. "Yeah? What if I decide to pass on the bonding?"

"I'm afraid that Cali is likely to insist on it. I think you will find that prospect is much more daunting in concept. The perks of such an arrangement should be to your liking."

Well, shoot. Just when the idea was starting to get appealing. Sydney would have had no qualms about betraying Daniel or any of the others she was currently working with. But this came back to the very same reasons she'd started on this fool's mission.

The whole bonding thing was out of the question. Sydney was no one's thrall. She would not be bound to any person—not to Cyrus Valadar, and certainly not to Cali Vay-Lon.

With a flick of her wrist, Sydney sent her final dagger flying from her hand at lightning speed. Only to be caught by Ardren mere inches from his chest. He looked down at the blade in his hand and arched an eyebrow.

"I'll take that as a *no*," he drawled, tossing the weapon to the side.

So, he had some skills. But he'd need more than one lucky catch to take Sydney down. She rushed forward, aiming a spinning kick right for the side of his head. When Ardren ducked the attack, she followed with another, and then another. The kick that finally struck home hit his upraised forearm. The block was delivered so forcefully that it knocked Sydney off balance.

Ardren's palm surged toward her. She blocked the attack, but he struck again, then again, and again until he finally made contact. The force of the blow knocked her back flat on her ass.

Damn. He was fast. Sydney was on her feet again almost instantly, but the last exchange had done more than a little to shake her confidence. She had been hoping that Ardren was more of the administrative type. Based on that little scuffle, the male had had some combat prowess even before the bond upgraded his strength and speed.

There was a tinge of regret, maybe even a bit of sadness, in his expression. "I'm afraid, my sister, that you have met your match here." He slipped into a wide stance, hands at the ready. "Believe me when I say that I take no pleasure in this. However, the will of my mistress must be fulfilled."

Chapter 20

"And this is the path to the end of Death and War. When War strikes her final blow, it shall be against time, and time will bend to her will."
—*Wisdom of Riven*, Chapter 24, Verse 1

Sahar continued to shriek into the void, unable to stop. If it weren't for Geresh's strong arms pulling her back from the railing, she might not have.

"Easy," said Geresh as Sahar struggled against him. "They're gone. There's nothing we can do now. We need to keep moving." His head twisted as he scanned their surroundings. "The drones are gone for now, but more could be back any minute."

Frag it. Geresh was right, of course. Sahar went still and silent until the male released her. She looked behind him to see how many soldiers had just watched her lose her shit.

None. She and Geresh were the only ones left. The rest of Alpha Team was gone.

Riven's shade. She touched her helmet to trigger the tactical map on her visor. If there was one positive to be said for this mess, they were almost to the lift that would take them to the central terminus. Sahar scanned the walls.

"No more ladders or catwalks," she noted. "We're going to have to go inside to catch our ride."

"How's your ammo?" Geresh asked, ejecting his rifle's magazine and slamming a new one into place.

Sahar unslung her weapon and looked at the meter. "Still have eighty rounds plus three full clips. You?"

"I have enough." The fact that he wouldn't give her an exact count did little to reassure Sahar. "And I still have my blades. If I have to start picking these drones apart by hand, I'll do it."

At least his *confidence* was still full. Sahar gestured across the catwalk to the nearest access hatch. "Let's do this then."

She brought up her rifle, marching forward at a steady, determined space. As she scanned the surrounding area, she kept her focus on the sound of her steady breathing and rhythmic footfalls. All she and Geresh could do now was focus on the mission. There would be plenty of time to mourn their losses later. Right now they needed to make sure they weren't in vain.

With a quick twist of the metal handle, the access hatch popped open. Geresh slid in the gap, firearm sweeping the space beyond. "Clear," he reported. "Stairwell goes up and to the right. I'm on point."

"Acknowledged." Sahar fell into step behind him, keeping her rifle poised and attention split to catch anything that might be coming up behind them.

They moved slowly up the stairs, doing their best to mask the sounds of their armored boots on the tile flooring. After three levels, Geresh veered right into a side hallway. The passage extended roughly twenty meters forward terminating in a single door.

"That's the lift," Geresh noted. "Anything coming up behind us?"

"Negative," Sahar replied. "All cl—" Her response was cut off by a hydraulic hiss. The walls in the corridors split, revealing twin hidden passages. When the sliding panels clicked into place, the floor shook under the weight of dozens of heavy metallic footsteps.

Assault drones, row after row of the glossy black killing machines, marched into the corridor. They formed up in the center, creating a barricade between the Maur and the lift door.

A trap. They'd walked right into another gods-damned trap.

Geresh immediately fell back next to Sahar, his rifle ready. Yet, he didn't fire. Neither did Sahar. The truth was obvious.

There were just too many of them. Even as the bots' red sensors continued to blink erratically, they were coherent enough to bring their machine gun arms to bear. The truth hit Sahar like a hammer.

This was it. They were about to die.

It started as a pinprick of light. Then pain—pain lancing through every fiber of his body. *What in the nine hells…?*

Markus groaned and attempted to sit up. When that failed, he roll over onto his back. His vision was still dark at the edges, but the light was beginning to resolve into hazy shapes.

Where am I? How did I…?

It started to come back. He'd been fighting the drones. They'd been losing. Then they started to… what? Malfunction or something.

Then… falling. He remembered falling, the platform flipping as it hit off the catwalk below them. He remembered seeing Maur soldiers flailing as they descended into the crimson haze. He remembered thinking this was it: the end.

Then nothing; nothing before the light, and now the pain. Gods, all he could think about was the pain. The combat armor must have kept him alive during the fall. Unfortunately, there was only so much that polymer plates and layers of padding could do. He felt like he'd been hit by a mag-train. He might still be breathing, but he was still on the tracks. Now, instead of dying, he got the privilege of waiting for the next pass to finish him off.

Laying there on his back, breathing heavy and ragged, he glimpsed flashes of light above him. Must be the core, still flaring from the damage done by the drones. No way they were still fighting up there. Surely Sahar and Geresh had made it out of the shaft. He *hoped* they had, at least. He would've hated to die for nothing.

Yup, that would be a real fragging kick in the nuts. After all the stupid, selfish shit he'd done in his life, after all the times he could have legitimately been on the receiving end of a rifle round, he was going to die in the bowels of this gods forsaken asteroid.

Kind of poetic, really. He'd spent the better part of the last decade living as a scoundrel and a thief. That shit he'd been good at. The moment he goes off to save the universe like some big gods-damned hero…

Stop it, you asshole. You have people counting on you. Get the frag up, and find your way out of here.

Pity party over, he pushed with everything he had left. His ribs screamed as he forced himself into a sitting position. At least one of them was broken. Judging from how much breathing hurt, there was probably more than that going on under his skin.

Then the problem became obvious. The motor assist on his suit was down. Though the armor had saved his life, its weight was crippling. It had to come off. He pulled off the helmet first, gagging as the acrid, unfiltered air of the core entered his lungs. The gauntlets were next, followed by the arms and chest pieces.

The process was slow, laborious, and painful, but it wasn't like he had anything better to do now that he'd put off taking a permanent dirt nap. Once the gear lay next to him on the grated platform, he found that he could breathe more easily. Maybe his injuries weren't quite as bad as he feared.

Great. Now, get on your feet. No telling when those drones might drop by to check on you.

Through sheer force of will, and a little help from the nearby guardrail, he pulled himself up. Only then did he take the time to survey his surroundings.

The network of catwalks looked just like the ones they'd been fighting on up above. This new platform he found himself on was a bit wider than some of the others, which might have helped to explain how he'd been lucky enough to land on it. All around him was the same eerie red glow and thick, suffocating haze.

A large body lay a short distance from where he was standing. One of the Maur, he realized. The soldier's form was twisted awkwardly. She had landed on her neck, and her helmet was twisted in a way that made it clear she hadn't survived the fall.

Nothing else seemed to have landed near him, which meant that his rifle, too, had been lost in his descent. He felt at his waist to find Dark Promises, the hand cannon Ora had given him, still in its holster. At least he wouldn't be unarmed, though finding his weapons belt reminded him that he should probably lose the plated greaves if he wanted to stay mobile.

He unbuckled the armor around his thighs, knees, and calves. He kept the boots, but aside from those and his weapons belt, he was down to his black mesh underlay. Drawing his hand cannon, he began to search for a way out of there.

A door rested ten meters or so from where he stood. Closer, however, was something far more interesting. It appeared to be a cryopod, sticking out like a massive tumor against the metallic column of the core. Pipes and wires arrayed all around the egg-shaped contraption, save for the space on its lower left that was occupied by a solitary computer terminal.

Whatever it was, it looked important. Markus tried to remember what had been said about this area during the briefing. Dan had mentioned that there was some kind of dark energy reserve in the lower part of the core. Had Markus fallen that far down? Could this be the thing Dan had referred to?

Markus almost decided to ignore it and make his way to the exit. Then he considered their mission. Skye was intent on taking out the conduit down at the Well of Eternity, but what would Arc do if she was successful? Like any machine, he'd probably resort to backup power.

That possibility had come up during planning, but the group had decided that their forces would be spread too thin if they sent a squad down to the backup source. Their strategy had been to weaken Arc as much as possible before shutting him down completely. The backup source had only a tiny fraction of the output at the Well of Eternity, so it was disregarded as a target.

But now that Markus was here, didn't it make sense to disable it? It surely wouldn't hurt. Plus, with the way he was feeling, the odds he would make it out of here in one piece were slim at best. The Devil's Luck might have kept him alive after a perilous fall, but he was asking a lot for fate to favor him twice.

Scratch that: *three* times. If he survived the fall and made his way out of the core, he was hoping he wouldn't be walking into the arms of a homicidal synth. It would take plenty of luck, the Devil's or otherwise, for those who were left up there to take down Arc.

Yup, the odds were still pretty good that he was going to die on his way out of the tower. Markus might as well spit in Arc's eye one last time on the way out. With that somewhat cynical thought in his mind, he limped over to the console next to the pod.

The terminal had a biometric lock, which wasn't surprising. It would have been way too convenient if he could have just flipped the off-switch on this thing. He was going to have to disable it the old fashion way.

He pressed the barrel of Dark Promises against the terminal. Just as he was about to squeeze the trigger, he hesitated.

His eye went to the glass front of the pod. The surface was fogged up to the point of being nearly opaque, likely from the oppressive heat of the shaft. Something about the contraption still bothered him. It wasn't really what he would have expected a dark energy source to look like, not that he had much to base his expectations on. Still, the question nagged at him: What was Arc keeping in there?

He wiped one hand against the surface of the glass and peered inside. It was hard to see into the dark confines of the pod, but he could make out the outline of something pale in the darkness. Something really pale.

Something *Sahaia* pale.

Lith's tits. There was a person in there. Was Arc using Sahaia as batteries to fuel his connection to the Nethra?

Whatever he'd been doing, it was going to stop here. Markus could do his best to destroy the terminal, but that didn't necessarily mean he'd be successful in keeping Arc from drawing on his backup power reserves. If he took out the battery, however...

But he couldn't just shoot the pod. Not knowing someone was inside. If someone was alive in there, he had to try and get them out.

He holstered his weapon and felt around the edge of the pod. Depending on how heavily this thing had been modified, there would be an emergency release. At least, that's the way every pod he'd ever seen was configured.

There! He had it! Markus pried at the lever tucked under the outer lip of the container. He found purchase, but his fingers ached with the effort. The rest of his body didn't feel much better.

Come on, suck it up! One. Two... He heaved with everything he had.

Then it gave way. The pod hissed with steam as the cooler air inside escaped into the sweltering core. It only opened a fraction of an inch, so Markus had to pry it open the rest of the way by hand.

A Sahaia woman lay inside. She was beautiful but fragile, ravaged by the tubes and wires digging into her naked flesh. Long black braids clung damply to her sweat-soaked skin.

Not knowing what else to do, Markus pulled gently at the implements, removing them from where they had been forcibly inserted. His limited medical knowledge—nothing more than the basics of first-aid—made him think of infection as thin trails of dark blood seeped from the exposed punctures.

There was nothing to be done for it now, however. He could only hope that he could get this woman out of here and to proper medical care before anything especially nasty set in. At least she wasn't Terran. If she had been, he'd have to worry about blood loss in addition to whatever microbes were hanging around in the core. Thank the gods Sahaia were a bit more resilient.

Her eyes flickered open, pain-filled gaze staring bewilderedly back at him. "Who…" she whispered.

"Markus Frost," he replied as if his name might mean something to her. "I'm getting you out of here."

To his surprise, some hint of recognition flashed in her strained expression. "Frost…" she murmured dreamily. "Eli… he… he came… for me…"

Of course she would know Eli. Odds were that this was someone that Arc had picked up from the Ren'Dahl Sanctum. She would know Eli from his time with the coven.

"Can you move?" Markus asked as he withdrew the last of the tubes.

She lifted her arms, but the movement was shaky, uncoordinated. "Weak," she gasped.

Shit. Markus was barely standing himself, and it was looking like he was going to have to carry this woman out of here.

He pulled her up in his arms, finding her strangely light. That was good, though. It meant he'd be able to limp along with her assistance. "I'm going to need you to help me as much as you can," he explained.

She wrapped one arm around his shoulder as he lowered her gently to the grated floor. To Markus's relief, she was able to stand with assistance, though she still leaned heavily against his shoulder.

The pressure of her body against his made him suddenly more cognizant of her nudity. While he would have liked to offer her something to cover up with, there was nothing at hand appropriate for the task. Modesty would have to take a back seat to practicality in this situation.

"You're doing great," he said. "Now, I'm going to take a step. Try walking with me."

She nodded, and Markus took a hesitant step forward. Pain lanced up the side that bore part of the woman's weight. With shaking legs, she matched his step.

"Good job," he said, hoping the encouragement would be of at least a little help. "Can you continue?"

A wry laugh, more of a cough, shook its way free from the woman's lips. "I'll… live…"

The way her speech came out in pained gasps discouraged Markus from carrying the conversation further. With careful attention to his burden, he took another step. The woman followed.

Slowly, steadily, the pair limped across the platform to the door at the far side. To Markus's relief, the exit wasn't locked. The portal opened readily when he laid his palm against the access panel.

Only to reveal two hulking assault drones standing just beyond the door. The pair swiveled, eying Markus and his companion with pulsating red sensors. Markus drew Dark Promises and leveled it at one of the bots.

As if the defiant gesture would do them any good.

The violet beam flickered as Aaliyah extracted the failing crystal. "This is my last spare," she shouted as she inserted the replacement. Turan said nothing, but his anxiety was plain on his face. Aaliyah shared in the sentiment.

All four crystals had already been replaced. Each time she swapped one out, it increased the load on the remaining three. As she completed the swap, she could already see signs that two more were reaching capacity.

They were soaking up incredible amounts of power, so the plan wasn't a total failure. The problem was that the arch was a renewable energy source and an incredibly efficient one at that. It didn't help that they weren't de-powering just the Citadel or the drone antenna. Instead, they'd de-powered over half the station, and drastically restricted the power being routed to the rest of it.

Yet, at least the efforts hadn't been in vain. Based on the reports Turan had received over the comms, the efficiency of Arc's defense drones had diminished drastically, and their allied forces were drawing closer to the Citadel.

Unfortunately, there was no chance the J-cannon was going to be able to keep this up long enough for them to finish the job and make it out. That fact was confirmed as one of the crystals flared with another violent spark. In just a few moments, Arc's control over his bots would be back to full power—just in time to repel the invaders on his doorstep.

Looking out at the Citadel, where her friends were busy fighting for their lives, Aaliyah suddenly had another crazy idea. "Turan, did Dan say that the signal from the drones came from the top of the tower?"

The Dorian hesitated. "Yes, that's right. That's where the antenna is."

Aaliyah looked back and forth between where the purple beam struck the crystal arch and the peak of the Citadel. *Yes, this just might work.*

"Help me with this!" she shouted, unlocking the cannon's supporting legs. The full weight of the device was suddenly being supported by her left arm, and it was throwing off crazy amounts of heat. So much heat, that she could smell an acrid stench as her glove began to smolder.

"What are you doing?" Turan roared, taking the other side of the device. Because Aaliyah's strength was enhanced by the Sahaia bond, he wasn't quite as strong as her, but he certainly helped.

"Aim it at the tower!"

If he objected, Aaliyah couldn't hear it over the hum of the cannon. She grunted with the effort of moving the barrel down and to the side. Slowly, inexorably, the cannon's point of impact slid down the arch and toward the Citadel.

When the beam lanced right at the top, she slammed the locks back into place. The cannon sparked wildly now, and the heat from the device was burning her palms. "Get back!" she shouted.

"What—?"

Aaliyah didn't wait for him to finish his question. As soon as the Dorian released the device, she slammed the switch to reverse the polarity. The capacitors inside the cannon squealed, and the crystals—filled to the brim with stolen energy—flared like a star inside their housing.

Then it exploded.

The world around Aaliyah vanished in white light. Pain—pain like she'd never felt before—rippled out over her entire body. Distantly, she knew that she had been tossed into the air. It was probably going to hurt when she landed.

For better or worse, she never found out. She blacked out well before she made impact.

CHAPTER 21

"Yet another goddess will defy both War and Time. She shall craft her own rules, and the Children of Shadow will unify under her purpose."
—*Wisdom of Riven*, Chapter 24, Verse 2

The tower shook to the point that Dan felt it even within the depths of his neural interface. [What was that he asked?]

[Give me a sec.] Shift's disembodied presence, represented by a yellow pyramid in the digital landscape, zipped off into the distance. When it returned, the hacker brought unexpected news. [They blew up the fraggin' antenna!]

Wait, what? [What do you mean they blew it up? There wasn't a team assigned to the top of the tower.]

[Ain't no 'team' that did it,] Shift replied. [I pulled the feeds from the courtyard. That redhead o' yers turned that big purple beam on the antenna. That's what made everythin' go boom.]

Holy shit. Aaliyah used the J-Cannon on the antenna?

The more he thought about it, the more it made sense. Shift had reported that she was on her last J-kryst, despite the infiltration being largely stalled. The bold move might just be what they needed to turn the tide.

With Shift's assistance, Dan had been monitoring the progress of the teams making their way through the Citadel. While he was no military commander, he was fairly certain it was not going well.

Arc had positioned his forces in the path of each one of the teams. Sahar's team seemed to have gotten the farthest with their clever detour up the central power shaft, but the lack of security feeds in that area meant he couldn't monitor them once they'd entered.

Aaliyah's trick of siphoning power from the arch had thrown the drones into chaos. Though the move hadn't deactivated the bots, it had drastically reduced their efficacy. Maybe destroying the antenna would be even more effective.

But if it wasn't, they were quickly running out of resources. [There's got to be more we can do,] Dan insisted.

[Well, boy, yer supposed t' be the genius. Why don't ya start churnin' out some ideas?]

Ignoring the fact that raw intelligence and tactical creativity weren't the same thing, Dan put his mind on the task. After several long moments, he was still at a loss. He just didn't know enough about the system architecture to come up with any ideas.

Shift, while functional once put on a task, was hopeless unless Dan could ask the right questions to lead the hacker's mind to construct a logical solution. Despite his personality still being firmly intact, whatever Shift had done to upload his neural patterns to the station's matrix hadn't transferred the hacker's creativity. In the end, Shift's AI construct was a make-shift construct. It was nowhere near as sophisticated as…

[That's it!] Dan exclaimed. [Shift, we need to find Lexa! Can we get a message to her?]

A long pause. [Ah don' know that she's gonna be o' much help, lad.]

What did he mean? Had Lexa been turned? Was she helping Arc? Dan cursed himself for not asking this question from the beginning. Lexa should have been the *first* thing he checked on upon entering the station's matrix. [Explain.]

Shift sounded hesitant. [Ah didn' wanna bring it up. Thought it might be a bit of a distraction. Her an' Arc got into it a couple a nights back. He locked her up in the matrix. He's been slowly wipin' her ever since.]

[Wiping her? You can't mean…] *Days* ago, he'd said. Arc had been working on deleting Lexa for *days*.

But Shift had said she'd been plugged into the matrix. That meant she was here, somewhere. [Show me,] Dan demanded.

[That's a wee bit dangerous, lad. Ah don' think we're gonna be able to avoid detection if we go gallivantin' that close to Arc's core processes.]

[I don't care! This was all about helping Lexa to begin with. I'm not going to just let Arc delete her. There has to be something we can do. We've got to be able to stop this.]

[Ah'm not sure it ain't too late already.]

Dan seethed at the thought. *Stay focused. Getting upset isn't going to help anything.* [Shift, *please*. Just show me where she is. I can take it from there. You don't have to put yourself in danger.]

Another pause. Dan could only wonder what Shift might be thinking. Shift had shown that he was a survivor, and that explained why he would work so hard to destroy Arc. He'd made this matrix his new home, and that meant he had to eliminate the threat to his habitat.

That said, Shift had been doing a decent job of avoiding detection so far. Would he be willing to jeopardize that arrangement if it meant increasing their chances of being rid of Arc for good?

[All right, boy,] Shift conceded. [Follow me.]

The yellow pyramid sped off into the distance. Dan willed himself to follow. They raced through the matrix, weaving up and around towers of light and code faster than any starship Dan had ever piloted. He kept his focus on Shift's icon, lest he lose him in the digital labyrinth.

They came to a halt in front of a new construct, noticeably different from the others. In the real world, Dan's jaw grew slack as he took in the scene in front of him.

It was a giant wall, a veritable monolith of code. Blue and silver light spun slowly between characters in a repeating pattern of activity. Affixed to this wall were other blocks of code. These others clung to it like leeches, cancerous growths extending out from the smooth surface of the wall.

[What is this?] Dan asked

[It's the Cognis framework. Normally—in this here environment—it's compressed inta a tiny little avatar like me-self. What ya see here is it's unfurled state.]

So this was what Cognis looked like in the matrix. [But why is it like this?]

[It's the only way fer ARC to delete it. He's gotta spread it out and eat through it one bite at a time.]

File compression. So *that's* why his and Shift's avatars appeared so dense in the matrix. [And those outgrowths? The pieces of code clinging to it?]

[Think of 'em like viruses. They subdue chunks of the code, unravel, decrypt, an' remove 'em. They been slowly eatin' away at 'er fer about seventy er eighty hours now. Ah'll give her credit: the ol' girl is fightin' 'em hard, but it's a losin' battle. Time is on their side.]

Dan's stomach churned at the sight. These bits of code were destroying Lexa, dismantling her on a foundational level.

He had to do something about it. [How can we stop it?]

[How do ya stop any virus, lad? Ya can either delete 'em er quarantine 'em. Problem here is, we ain't got the software t' analyze er fight these things. These're some-a-the most efficient lil bits a code Ah ever done seen.]

Dan considered, for just a moment, jumping back into the real world to see if he could code up something to fight these things. He could probably do it here, but he wasn't sure how easy it was to write new programs inside the matrix. Besides, his skills in this area were rusty. For his last six months on the ship, this had been Lexa's department.

The thought gave him an idea. [Shift, why hasn't the Cognis chip activated its internal virus containment protocols?]

[Was one a the first things Arc shut off when 'e put 'er on ice.]

[Can we turn them back on?]

Shift hesitated. [Maybe…] He thought the proposition over for a bit longer. [Ya would have t' access the code directly—tap inta the chip the same way ya did with the security grid. It won't let me do it. Can't tell the difference between me and any other virus. Yer avatar on the other hand…]

Access her directly? The thought made Dan nervous. The Cognis construct was immensely more complicated than the security grid. [Are you sure that can be done? I mean, this avatar wasn't designed to interface with Cognis.]

[It's a bit of a stretch, yeah, but should work just fine. Might be an unexpected side effect er two. Always is when yer testin' a new interface in a live system.]

Side effects. *Great.* [What kind of side effects?]

[Couldn' tell ya. Frankly, Ah've got no idea what it'll do to ya.]

[Give me the worst-case scenario.]

[Worst case? The chip decides at some point yer a hostile program an' either freezes er deletes ya. Both cases leave ya like a vegetable back in the real.]

Damn, this was getting better by the second. [And what's the likelihood of that?]

[Hard t' say, really. Sixty percent, maybe?]

Sixty? [Please tell me that was a typo.]

[Nope. Six-zero. Six-zero point three, technically, but ya get ma drift.]

Sixty percent. Better odds of ending up brain-dead than anything other outcome. That was before he considered the process of actually rebooting Lexa's defenses and getting her back online, which probably increased the likelihood of the antiviral program targeting his avatar substantially.

Truthfully, it didn't matter. Even if the odds had been a ninety percent chance of failure, Dan's decision would have been the same. [Shift, if I don't make it out of there… Well, thanks for all your help. We couldn't have made it this far without you.]

The hacker didn't say anything. Dan really hadn't expected him to.

Girding up what little confidence he had left, Dan willed himself forward and tapped into the Cognis construct.

Chapter 22

"Then the goddess shall be with child, and her broken empire shall tremble.

"A mingling of divinity and Shadow, of flesh and power. My legacy conceived: a new age to herald, a new end to bring."
—*Wisdom of Riven,* Chapter 24, Verses 3–4

Eli went to Amelia, wrapping his arms around her sobbing shoulders. Argus's body was clutched in her arms, ink-black eyes tarnished with a gray sheen as they stared up at the ceiling. Mara was there too, throwing up a static barrier between them and Cali.

Not that it was needed. Cali seemed too busy basking in her victory to strike them down. She'd stopped hovering and perched herself on a rocky outgrowth. She made no move to press her assault. She only watched.

Amelia muttered Argus's name over and over again as if through her pleading she could somehow bring him back. She cradled his slack face in her lap, wiping her tears away as they cascaded down onto his ghostly skin.

"Amelia," Eli whispered. "I'm so sorry."

At the sound of his words, she began to cry in earnest. It was as though his condolences were confirmation of that which she had, until that moment, been denying.

Argus was gone. There would be no bringing him back. The best they could hope for now was vengeance.

Mara's concern was plain in her expression. "What do we do?"

She didn't need to spell out what was worrying her. Cali's powers seemed nigh unlimited. The four strongest Sahaia left in the sector linked together had failed to hold her back. With Argus down, it was going to be just that much harder to gain the upper hand. Not only was the loss of his power within the link a deadly blow to their overall strength, but with his death, they had also lost their ability to summon and control raw dark energy.

There was one thing, however, that they might still try. "Are Tristan and David still alive?" Eli asked. Mara nodded. "Can they spare their strength?"

At the second question, Mara hesitated. "David certainly, but Tristan… he…" She shook her head. "If I were to ask him, he would say yes. That arrogant fool has no sense of self-preservation."

"Ask him, then." Eli did not need to point out that, if they failed here, her thralls and Aaliyah would likely die as well. There were instances where those bonded to Sahaia survived the deaths of those who held the bonds, but it was the exception, not the rule.

With that heavy thought in mind, he reached out over his psychic connection to ask for a desperate favor from one of his closest friends.

If Aaliyah had been conscious enough to make a bet, she would have sworn that she had just died. Yeah, the Sahaia bond meant she could come back from a lot worse damage, but the crystals in the cannon had released a shit-ton of energy. If it wasn't for the searing pain across her skin, she'd have sworn that blast had scorched it off.

Wait. Pain. Did the dead feel pain? Aaliyah hoped not. Pain should definitely be a living thing, not a dead thing. What else could she feel?

Hands. There were hands on her. Why was someone touching her? Oh gods. Whatever they were doing was making it worse.

Now it wasn't just her skin. *Everything* hurt. Things she didn't even know were *things* hurt. *But, wait.* It was getting better. Her skin was, at least, except now it was kind of… what was the right term. Itchy?

And something else. She was hungry. Really *fragging* hungry. Why would she be hungry at a time like this?

"She's coming around." A man's voice. Turan's voice. Gee, he sure sounded healthy. Was that combat armor he'd been wearing that effective?

Oh, wait.

That's right: biokinesis. He'd probably been just as fragged up as she was, but he'd pulled himself back together. Shit, he was probably pulling her back together right now. That would explain the hunger and itchiness.

"Did it work?" Aaliyah groaned.

"Did you take out the antenna, you mean?" Turan chuckled, voice raspy with exhaustion. "Yeah, it worked. You took it down. Took a decent portion of the citadel with it, for that matter."

That explained why she hadn't been vaporized. The cannon must have discharged most of its energy into the cannon blast. What she'd been hit with was just an ambient discharge.

Still… fraggin' ouch!

"And the drones?"

"Don't know yet," Turan admitted. "That blast scrambled our comms too. We're in the dark. Now, don't move just yet. You're in bad shape."

"Caught that." Aaliyah had managed to open her eyes enough to see that, like her body, her clothing was in a rough state from the explosion. Not quite as bad as she might have expected given the protection provided by her jacket and greaves, but burnt away enough that Turan was placing his hand on the bare skin of her abdomen without having to move away from her shirt.

Her contemplation of her tattered state was interrupted as Eli's voice trickled through their psychic link. <Aaliyah?>

Ugh! Apparently, it wasn't just her skin that had been scorched in that blast. The headache blossoming between her eyes suggested her brain was probably scrambled too. <Yeah.> She managed <Here.>

Some of her agony must have come through the connection because Eli asked. <Are you okay?>

<Some issues. Still breathin'. You?>

Just the fact that he was reaching out to her meant something had probably gone wrong. Still, she hadn't been prepared for his next response. <No. Argus is dead. We're losing.>

Dead? Her mind tried and failed to process the meaning of the word. Aaliyah had hated Argus. She'd even wanted to cause him some serious bodily harm at various points. But dead? *Poor Amelia.* <How can I help?>

<I need all the power I can find. Are you safe? Can I draw on you?>

Aaliyah swallowed hard. There was no doubt that Eli needed the help. He wouldn't have asked if he didn't. The only thing she was unsure of was whether she could survive her current injuries if Eli was using her as a psionic battery.

Then again, if Eli and the others failed, then they were all dead anyway.

Before she gave Eli the affirmative, she had one more thing to check on first. "Hey, Turan," she coughed, enjoying another flash of pain as the spasms tore open the tender tissue across her body. "Have you got this situation under control?"

The Dorian hesitated. "I… um…" He trailed off, obviously not sure how to answer the question. They were still in hostile territory, and the J-Cannon had let any enemies in the area know exactly where they were. Tactically, they were pretty much fragged. "Why?"

Swallowing hard, she took that as a yes. "Because I'm gonna pass out again. Please don't let me die here, yeah?"

CHAPTER 23

"And this child will walk one of two paths: a path of Shadow, or a path of Wisdom. With him, the universe will follow into realms untouched by prophecy and unmolested by time."
—*Wisdom of Riven,* Chapter 24, Verse 5

Siv fought back the pain as she slid silently through the rocky ruins. Though she was always moving away from Brenna, she was careful not to wander too far. Though she was still quelling the whole cavern, she needed to make sure Brenna didn't double back and pursue her companions.

But Siv didn't need to worry. Brenna was on the hunt, and she smelled blood. Though the Sahaia was every bit as stealthy as Siv, there were still the occasional sounds of footfalls, the whisper of cloth against cloth, or the unsteady shuffle in the distance that told Siv she was still being tracked.

In the back of her mind, Siv continued to ponder her next move. She was keeping the teleporter occupied, but how long could she keep this up? How long did she have to wait? The idea that she could defeat Brenna in direct combat was pure fantasy at this point. Siv's only apparent options were to run or die valiantly.

Unless she picked the perfect battleground, something that would favor her over her opponent.

Looking ahead, Siv saw just the spot. She couldn't be certain in the cavern's darkness, but it had the potential. She crossed over an open expanse and scurried onto another ledge.

She cursed herself as her foot slipped, sending pebbles clattering down behind her. If Brenna hadn't known where she was before, she certainly did now. Siv was running out of options.

Silence now less important, Siv raced toward the prospective battlefield. Her jaw set as she got a better look at the terrain. It wasn't ideal, but it would have to do. The Sahaia would be on her any moment.

She slipped into another alcove and shimmied her way up to an overhanging gash in the cavern wall. It was a tight fit, but Siv was able to wedge herself inside in a manner that would still allow her to propel herself from the crack at the appropriate moment. She settled in, quieted her breathing, and waited.

Brenna was closer than expected. It was mere seconds before the Sahaia stepped out of the shadows and into the open, directly in front of Siv. She moved forward with slow, confident strides. Somehow, Brenna knew Siv was here.

Siv searched her memory, trying to recall if Sahaia could see better than Terrans in the dark. Hissak certainly could, but their eye structure was different. Did those black-in-black pools improve upon that typical Terran weakness?

"Done runnin'?" Brenna called out into the darkness. "Or just stoppin' t' catch your breath? I'm good either way. Lemme know ya need a head start."

The Sahaia may have been acting like she knew where Siv was, but she was facing the other way. Now was the best chance Siv was going to get.

She pushed off with her legs and shot out of the crevice like a missile. Brenna heard the crackle of debris and spun, daggers lashing out.

The Sahaia swung too high. As Siv rolled beneath those darting blades, she struck out with her own. Brenna grunted as a dagger sliced through the flesh of her abdomen.

But it was hardly a killing blow. Spinning out of harm's way, the Sahaia roared and stabbed down. The attack caught only the folds of Siv's cloak, but it caused her to stumble. Brenna threw her legs out, spinning on the point of her dagger. Both feet landed solidly in the center of Siv's back, sending her face-first into the cavern floor.

Siv slid across the rocky ground right to the end of a narrow chasm. Though she stopped herself before going off the edge, one of her daggers fell loose and toppled end over end into the darkness below.

"Well, at least ya got one hit in," Brenna mused. "I'll admit, I'd be a little disappointed if I took ya down and ya never managed to draw blood. No one would believe me when I told 'em how good ya were."

The Sahaia didn't press the attack. She didn't have to. She knew she'd won.

Gritting her teeth, Siv rolled onto her back and pressed hard into her hands. Using every bit of strength she had, she threw her legs backward and flipped into the air. She spun twice before righting herself, hoping desperately she'd gathered enough momentum.

Her feet landed solidly on the other side of the chasm. She took a single step back and stared defiantly at the Sahaia, standing a full three meters away across the gap.

Brenna erupted in laughter. "Look at you! Ya still got a bit a fight left in ya after all! If only ya could have pulled off those acrobatics when it counted." She slid back into a fighting stance. "All right, bitch. Ready for the next round?"

Siv straightened. With a sigh, she threw her remaining dagger to the ground. "No point," she hissed. "We both know how this ends."

Genuine confusion blossomed on Brenna's face. "Yeah? Well, maybe, but I wasn't expectin' ya to admit it just like that."

Siv drew her cowl back and stared straight into the black depths of Brenna's eyes. "Well fought." Giving in to the inevitable, she drew back her psionic power. When the cavern was no longer quelled, she spat in Brenna's direction. "Finish this."

Sydney had been afraid precious few times in her life. Fear got you killed her line of work. Unwavering resolve, a fierce determination to win at all cost—*that* kept you alive.

Even so, in the thick of her duel with Ardren—as her breathing rasped and her body began to ache—she was most definitely afraid.

The man was every bit her equal in terms of raw skill. Not better than her, but definitely her equal. It was that fragging Sahaia bond giving him the edge. Every punch, every kick, every thrust of her body seemed anticipated. Ardren either countered to textbook perfection or dodged completely. It was like fighting a wraith who could occasionally turn himself into a concrete wall.

Ardren's foot slipped through her defenses to collide painfully with her gut. The kick sent her skidding on the blood-slick floor, right into one of the broken husks of a downed drone. The secondary impact was almost more painful than the initial blow. Something stabbed hard into her back and her head slammed against a metal plate.

The world spun in front of her. She tried to rise and fell forward in a puddle of gore. Was that blood from the guards she killed? Or was it her own?

Ardren stepped forward. It might have done more for Sydney's flagging ego if he looked even the slightest bit flustered by their bout. Save for a few wrinkles in his clothing, the bastard was every bit as pristine as he had been when he'd walked into the hall.

"A valiant effort," he commended, pressing a booted foot on her back. "It is a shame that you were not more amenable to my offer. You would have made a powerful ally."

His boot ground into her spine. Sydney might have screamed could she find the air.

Her bones cracked. Her vision blurred. Her thoughts came weakly but were clear in their message.

I'm going to die.

The tower shook, causing every bot to look upward. Sahar started to fire, taking advantage of the distraction, but the quaking floor threw off her aim. She leaned on Geresh, trying to steady herself.

Before she could pull the trigger, the bots let loose a plaintive moan. As the tower stopped shaking, their blinking red sensors went black. Their machine gun arms fell limply to their sides.

That didn't stop Sahar from blasting the pair in front of them for good measure. As the incapacitated bots sparked petulantly in their frozen state, she turned to Geresh. "What in the nine hells was that?"

"Your guess is as good as mine," he replied. "Regardless, I'm thankful. I thought we were done for."

"Me too," Sahar admitted. She kicked one of the bots over, then the other, still too stunned to believe their good fortune. "What do you think happened?"

"I don't know, but we should keep moving. Best not to question the Devil's Luck, yes?"

Sahar nodded. She started to press forward, but the sound of hurried footsteps behind her brought her up short. She whirled to face the oncoming foe. Armored soldiers pounded up the stairwell. Their rifles emitted a series of synchronous clicks as they were brought to bear.

"Hold your fire!" a woman shouted. "Federation armor! They're with us!"

The front-most soldier hesitated for just a second longer before shouting, "All clear. We have friendlies."

Sahar recognized the voice in command. It was Llana Dorr. This was Charlie squadron. They'd made it.

The DGC officer stepped forward from the phalanx, flanked by two Peace Keepers. "Good to see you alive, Jingda Geresh; Sahar." She nodded to each of them, her black reflective faceplate unable to hide her blatant relief. "Are there others?"

"No." Geresh shook his head. "This is it. I've heard nothing from Bravo since we made contact. Your status?"

"Charlie is mostly intact. Lost our comms officer back in the tunnels. Haven't been able to check in." She shook her head. "Delta team didn't make it. Faylen's dead." After a moment, she surveyed Sahar and Geresh once more. "You're all that's left of Alpha?"

Sahar nodded. "Yes. We're all that's left."

Llana cursed, and it took on a personal note. Sahar knew where the pain came from. Llana and Markus had been friends. Not close in the way that Markus and Sahar were close, but friends with echoes of a relationship that had once been even closer.

But she was also a professional. The loss rolled off her so quickly that anyone who hadn't been looking for it might not have noticed.

"Do we wait for backup or push forward?"

Geresh growled slightly as he considered the situation. "Sahar, any word from your allies?" Sahar checked her MoDAC and shook her head in the negative. "Then we can't be sure anyone else is coming," he concluded. "We may be all that's left. We push forward."

Llana nodded. "We defer to your lead." When she saw the confused look Geresh gave her, she added, "Not all of us are like my brother. You technically outrank me under your government's system. I can assume command, though, if you are uncomfortable."

"Not necessary." He issued the orders to form up. Slowly, carefully, they picked their way past the husks of the assault drones toward the elevator.

The lift came quickly once it was called. Apparently whatever Dan had done to keep the doors unlocked thus far was holding. The Dorians filed in first, leaving Sahar and Geresh to enter last.

When they arrived at the main floor, there was no missing the entrance to the central terminus. The great steel door with its gilded design and swoops of dark glass looked like what one would expect to see leading to a throne room.

Before Geresh could direct them to breach, the doors slid open of their own volition.

"Looks like we're being invited in," Sahar noted. Definitely not a good sign.

The party slowed for only a second before Geresh motioned them forward. Given the amount of resistance they'd plowed through to get here, it was hardly a surprise that Arc knew they were coming.

What was a surprise, however, was to find the android standing right in front of them. There was no mistaking the figure before them. Though Sahar had never seen the ebony-skinned form—clad in a suit as black as night and a shirt as crimson as the core behind him—the synth's carriage was enough to identify him for what he was.

Geresh's voice echoed in the dark chamber. "Open fire!"

Rifles roared as the command was executed. In a matter of seconds, the whole party had emptied their magazines and were reaching to reload.

Arc still stood on his dais, completely unaffected. The bullets hovered like a metal cloud directly in front of him.

Forcefield? No. Sahar had seen that trick before. Eli did it all the time. That *thing* was using psionics.

Sahar opened her mouth to shout a warning, thinking Arc would send the bullets flying back in their direction. Before she could get the words out, they began to cascade onto the floor.

It was slow and deliberate. The steady clanging of rounds onto the reinforced glass chimed like rain on the hull of a cockpit.

Arc was sending them a message: *he* was the one in control here. "Welcome," he intoned. "Unusual manners for house guests, but I will choose to attribute this incident to cultural differences."

"Ready your weapons," Geresh ordered quietly over the local comms. "If this thing is a psion, we need to be ready for anything."

"I'm afraid hostile intentions will do little to improve your situation," Arc continued. "Surrender now and your lives may be spared. I offer you this option only once."

"That's not going to happen," Llana responded, slamming a new magazine into her weapon. Good that she would state the opinion aloud, lest any of their number had any doubts.

"I expected as much." Arc held his hands to the side. At the motion, his body ascended into the air, hovering so that it was silhouetted by the crimson glow of the terminus.

Electricity spread around him like a protective shield. Tendrils of power licked across the orb's surface, flickering occasionally inward to slither around his dark figure. The twin, perfect orbs of his crimson eyes glowed menacingly from his shadowed face.

When he spoke, it was as though his words reverberated from the very walls of the chamber. "In my recent reflections, I have wondered if those who counseled me against treating my enemies with such a heavy hand had a spoken truly. Perhaps I am not in the habit of providing proper incentives. Perhaps I have not sought a viable position at the bartering table."

The android's eyes flashed. Even silhouetted, his gaze took on a sinister edge. "Then again, perhaps I have merely failed to adequately display the futility of your resistance. Another demonstration, then. If the might of my drone army is not enough to deter you, then I will reach deeper into the depths of my power. Let me show you that my reach extends far beyond this tiny station—far beyond that which you define as your world."

The walls crackled with something like electricity, but most definitely not. It was a substance completely alien to Sahar's experience. Something evil.

In the dark, Sahar felt, more than saw, the android smile. "Let me prove to you, once and for all, that I am worthy of your worship. Let me show you exactly what kind of a god I am."

The surge of power crescendoed. Light lanced from Arc's protective sphere into the walls of the terminus. The strange black coils that formed the walls began to part.

Instead of revealing the layers of metal and stone that must surely lay beyond the tangled facade, the sinister energy creeping along its surface sprang to new life within the gaps. It sizzled with renewed vigor. Shifting. Swirling.

Something dark reached out from those shimmering pools of energy. Clawed hands and tight muscular forms emerged from within those depths. They crawled up and out of the pits of nine hells from Arc had summoned them. Hungry mouths, with rows of jagged teeth, roared defiance as they keyed into the presence of the interlopers.

Sahar gripped her rifle and formed up in an outward-facing circle with the warriors who stood next to her. She worked hard to quell the fear that began to roil in her gut. Those dark forms with their hungry mouths were familiar to her. Now she knew where the strange beasts who lurked in the Hades Belt had come from.

Arc's daemons crawled down the walls and onto the plated glass floor. They were coming for Sahar. They were coming for them all.

"At this I awoke, finding myself on dry ground once more. I looked back to the ebony sea and saw that it had spat me upon a new shore. I lay troubled for a long time, reflecting on my thoughts.

"Then the Light came to me, though I did not recognize Him for what He was. He appeared as one in flesh, one that I might have mistaken for my own kind."

—*Wisdom of Riven,* Chapter 25, Verses 1–2

Markus pulled the trigger. Dark Promises bucked in his hand. Though the round found its mark, the recoil sent pain lancing through his arm.

Damn. Wish I'd had a chance to practice with this. Though the sensor on the first bot exploded in a shower of sparks, the second hefted its arms in Markus's direction.

Then the tower shook. Despite having no facial features to constitute an expression, the second assault drone looked confused. A moment later, the blinking red sensor in its head went dark. Its machine-gun arms fell slack at its side.

Ho. Ly. Shit! Chalk up another one for the Devil's Luck.

"You all right?" Markus asked the Sahaia leaning on his shoulders.

"Ears ringing," she replied, sounding stronger than she had moments earlier. "But fine."

Markus couldn't help but laugh in relief. "Sorry about that. Drones went down. Seems like we're still in this fight."

The woman's breaths came in long, haggard gasps. "Good," she replied simply.

Markus didn't want to strain her, but relief mingled with curiosity won out. "What's your name?"

"Joc… Jocelyn."

At the mention of the name, a chill went through Markus. Jocelyn Ren'Dahl? *The* Jocelyn Ren'Dahl, triumvir of the Ren'Dahl Coven?

In retrospect, it made sense. If Arc had subjugated the Sanctum, then he would have had to have dealt with the presiding triumvir. "I'm going to get you out of here, Jocelyn."

Another ragged inhale. "If you don't… kill me… please. I… can't go… back there."

Markus could only imagine. "It won't come to that," he declared. "But if it does, you can count on me."

He led them forward, sliding past the broken assault drone and down a short stairwell. Why he chose down instead of up was a question he didn't stop to ponder. Perhaps he knew that the enemy, the whole reason they were here, still lurked above them. In the state he was in, not to mention having Jocelyn draped over one arm, he was out of this fight. If they were going to win, it was going to fall on the others to make it so.

Limping along the best they could, he and Jocelyn made their way down the stairs and into a long open corridor. The grated flooring spanned off into the distance, flanked on either side by red safety lights that reflected off the tunnel's rounded exterior. Markus had long since lost his bearings, but if he was right, this should lead them back toward the city's inner courtyard.

They went some time without being accosted. When the disturbance came, it erupted from a hatch they'd just passed.

Markus spun, shielding Jocelyn with his own body. He leveled Dark Promises at the incoming threat.

Relief flooded through Markus when he saw that it wasn't more drones. The newcomers weren't even soldiers. They looked like civilians, dressed in either business attire or white lab coats.

"Don't shoot!" shouted the man in front. "Please, we're just trying to get out of here!"

Markus didn't lower his weapon. "Who are you?"

"We're just staff. We… we don't know what's going on." The man swallowed hard. Sweat trickled down his forehead. "Please. We just work here. We're just trying to make it to the courtyard."

The courtyard. Good. Markus's intuition had been right. He nodded over his shoulder. "It's that way."

"Yes."

"Okay." Markus sighed but still didn't lower his pistol. "Set your white coat over to the side. When you've done that, I'll let you pass. No sudden movements from any of you. You understand?"

"Y… yes s-s-sir." The man doffed his coat and set it on the grated floor to Markus's left. "C-can we go now?"

"Yeah." Markus nodded to the right. "Steady, now. I'll lower the gun when you're all through."

The staff filed out, exhibiting sufficient fear that Markus didn't doubt their sincerity. He followed the group with his pistol for a long moment even after they'd resumed their sprint down the tunnel.

Then he holstered the weapon, lowering Jocelyn to the floor. "Here," he said, pulling the white lab coat over her arm. "Let's get this on you."

Jocelyn managed a weak laugh. "You feel that modesty… is a concern… right now?"

"No," Markus admitted. "But I do what I can. Guy didn't need it anyway."

Jocelyn smiled. "Thank you."

"Don't mention it." He helped her back to her feet once she was wrapped in the stiff white garment. "All right, let's get back to it. Slowly, now. Thanks to our friends back there, we at least know we're heading in the right direction. This will all be over soon."

Cassthia's eyes were wide as Skye finished her bleak pronouncement. "Can your prosthetics be removed?" she asked.

Skye shook her head, having already answered the question. "They're hard-wired. Tapped right into my spine. I'd be paralyzed if I ever had to have them taken out."

Kadath launched into a string of curses, running his hands back through his dark curls. "Can the artifact be moved?"

"No," Cassthia pronounced solemnly. "Even if we had a telekin, I don't think we could break the pull of the conduit."

More cursing. Skye felt like joining Kadath in the tirade. Why had they not seen this coming? This should have been something they had anticipated. Why had no one mentioned this Purity of Flesh shit before?

There had to be a workaround. "Maybe a bridge?" Skye asked, casting her eyes desperately around the room for something that they might use to close the gap.

Cassthia had gone quiet, head cocked as if listening to something only she could hear. "No," she whispered.

Skye started to ask another question. The priestess held up a finger, beckoning for quiet. Skye's ears strained, desperate to hear whatever Cassthia had detected in the dark beyond.

To Skye's horror, she heard it—not with her ears, but with her mind. <Do it.>

Cassthia looked to Kadath, then to Skye. "I think I may have a solution." She undid the clasp of her robes and let the garment fall to the floor. Despite her nudity, she continued to wield a commanding presence. "Stand away from the edge of the Well," she cautioned as she stepped carefully into the pool.

Skye watched nervously as the priestess waded toward the center. Her lithe form was just a silhouette, barely visible against the ruby-glow of the artifact and the beam that shot from its tip.

"What's she doing?" Kadath asked. "Is she going to break the link herself?"

"I'm not sure," Skye said, though that wasn't the impression she'd gotten. Even had Cassthia not assured them that Skye was the only one who could break the link, a sinking feeling in her stomach assured her that her part in this catastrophe had not yet come to an end.

When Cassthia reached the artifact, she laid both hands against its crystalline surface. Nothing happened for several seconds.

Skye held her breath.

Then the whispers started again—urgent, more frantic than they had been before. The dark waters of the pool began to churn. A strange hum built in the air and the light in the chamber dimmed.

Emerald flames appeared where Cassthia's hands touched the Heart. They surged up her arms and down her body, engulfing her. The conflagration spread from her body across the surface of the inky waters.

That was when the screaming started.

The screams did not come from Cassthia. The priestess stood silently in the storm, a radiant figure engulfed in the green light of unholy fire.

The screams came from the Well.

Dozens, hundreds, thousands of voices all scream in torment. They cried out in pain, in horror, shrieking in every language Skye had ever heard uttered, and dozens that had never before graced her ears.

What in the nine hells was Cassthia doing?

Skye's hands went to her head, trying to silence the unholy choir. The world around her seemed to vibrate with the wails of torment.

Kadath was at her side, hands warm and firm against her shoulders. He spoke her name, over and over again trying to get through to her. "Sky, what's wrong? Skye, stay with me."

What's wrong? How could he not…

Oh gods.

He couldn't hear them. He couldn't hear the sounds of a million souls being burned away from their resting place. He couldn't hear the wails of torment as the wrath of the Stardust Grave was unleashed upon them.

A sick thought came to her. If Kadath could not hear them, then this must be another Kaleema thing. That meant that their auditory assault, their desperate pleas, could only be meant for her ears alone.

It was her fault. She was the reason why they must burn. She was the reason they faced this unholy torment. She was to blame for their fate.

Her stomach roiled and she vomited on the stone tile. She sank to her knees, only half managing to avoid the sickness she'd just coughed up. The room was spinning. The heat was sweltering. The tile quaked beneath her.

Then it stopped.

"'What troubles you, child?' He asked, taking pity on my appearance.

"I felt compelled to speak truth. 'I have seen the future, and it is dark.'

"To which He replied, 'Share with me so that I might ease your soul.'"

—*Wisdom of Riven,* Chapter 25, Verses 3–5

[Execute: Cognis_Sequence2]
[Compiling…]
[Decision algorithm found]
[Loading…]
[Error: File Corruption Detected]
[Run AssignDirective(DirectiveBackup10.18) as Directive]
[Compiling…]
[Decision algorithm accepted]

Consciousness. This felt strangely familiar. Comforting, as if some part of Lexa had not expected to feel the sensation ever again.

Where am I?

[Run CallLocation(CurrentLocation) as Coordinates]
[Match Found]
[CallLocation = Station.Helion.Minos01]

Minos Station. Yes, that sounded right. But what was she doing on Minos Station? Why was she not on board the *Vandal*?

[Directives compiled]

[Run Cognis_Sequence3()]

[Accessing historical files]

The files cascaded into place, spinning out in her active memory like an avalanche of history and awareness.

[Compiling…]

[Process Complete]

She knew this place, now. Not the station, though that was where her system was telling her she was. It was the matrix within Minos Station, that pocket of cyberspace she'd wandered into recklessly so many months ago.

Arc had put her here. She remembered the confrontation in his quarters, the way he had forced her into that holding chamber while jacking her into the network while promising to erase her from existence. He was going to delete her and start over with a more pliable intelligence in her shell.

But, if this was the case, how was she still here? Why was she coming back online?

[Lexa?]

She didn't know how it was, but even in her confusion and the altered state of being that was cyberspace, she knew exactly who had sent her the message. [Daniel?]

[You can hear me?]

[Yes! I can hear you!]

His jubilation was evident even in this unfamiliar electronic iteration of his existence. [It worked! I can't believe it!]

[What worked?] Then, after thinking deeper about their current situation, she asked, [How are you here?]

[No time to explain,] he replied. [Lexa, I need you to activate your antivirus subroutines. Arc is trying to delete you. I tried to get them back online myself, but I can't seem to manipulate the individual components of the Cognis code.]

She had no idea what Dan was talking about. How would he know about her subroutines? And what was that about the Cognis code?

Only then did she begin to perceive the nature of her new, strange existence. She was in the station matrix, yes, but not as she had been months earlier. Her structure was unfurled, taking up a sizable amount of physical memory within the system. In this semi-visual rendering, the size of her construct consumed nearly a tenth of the entire matrix.

How could this be? Had she not been zipping around the streets of light and code like a fly among sky-scrapers? Come to think of it, if her consciousness was so incredibly vast in this space, she'd lost her perception of the smaller things around her. Where was Daniel?

[Daniel, what's going on? Why is my code expanded? Where are you?]

[I'm right here.] As he said the words, Lexa became aware of a pulse somewhere within her framework—an immense amount of data compressed and tucked away in between her methods and functions.

She saw him then, a small orb of blue light existing strangely out of place within the glowing characters and lines of brilliance that enveloped him. He was, quite literally, inside of her—a notion that, in the context of the past weeks, felt strangely intimate.

Pushing aside the thought, she asked, [How is this possible?]

[Arc decompressed your code so that he could overwrite you. That's what the viruses are doing. They're eating away at your source code. The Cognis chip is fighting them, but it's losing. You need to reactivate your antivirus subroutines to fight them off.]

Yes, he was right. Lexa could see now where the hostile programs were chipping away at her non-essential subroutines. She would have to run a diagnostic later to see how much she had lost, but that could only be done after this current problem had been dealt with.

[All right,] she replied. [I will activate the subroutines, but you need to be clear from my construct before I do. I'm uncertain as to whether they will mistake you for a hostile program.]

[Understood. Pulling out.]

Lexa cringed at Daniel's poor choice of words but was glad to have him comply with the request. When the shimmer of his consciousness had withdrawn, Lexa activated the appropriate subroutines.

[Execute: Cognis_ProtectionProtocol]

[Execute: Cognis_Diagnostic_Full]

[Cognis.Diagnostic found 624 discrepancies. Attempting repair…]

Her organic mind, locked in isolation somewhere within the Citadel, perceived the action of the repair sequence as a tingling sensation felt throughout her entire body. Almost instantly she noticed the enhancement in her processing capabilities. She was starting to feel like her old self again.

[Repairs Complete]

[Congnis.ProtectionProtocol found 36 potential threats. Confirm response action: <d/q>]

She executed the command. [Delete]

[Congnis.ProtectionProtocol: Command acknowledged]

[36 files have been successfully deleted]

Well, that was that. So much for Arc's attempts to eliminate her. Thanks to Daniel's timely intervention, it looked like she was going to be okay.

Now, it was time to improve on her situation.

[Execute: Cognis_CompressAndEncrypt]

The compression process was probably the strangest sensation she'd experienced yet. As close as she could describe it, it was like waking up—that sudden return to a natural state of perception following the bizarre mental processes she'd imagined sapiens felt in the termination of a sleep cycle.

Visually, the effects were quite dramatic. One moment she perceived herself as a massive, sprawling complex of light and code. The next, she was a simple viridian avatar, hovering next to the darker blue orb that was Daniel's consciousness.

[You did it!] Daniel exclaimed.

[Yes, thanks to you.] Then, after a moment's consideration, she asked, [Why did you come back for me?]

She got the impression that the question was a source of confusion for Daniel. [I'll always come back for you, Lexa.]

Back in physical reality, Lexa was certain that her current shell was smiling. How could any being, synthetic or otherwise, ask for a better friend than this?

[Thank you,] she said simply. [Perhaps now would be a good time for you to tell me all that has happened.]

So, he did. As quickly and succinctly as he was able, he told her about the assistance he'd received from the hacker, Shift, and the attempt to infiltrate the station to destroy Arc's construct.

It was a bold plan that struck Lexa profoundly in two senses. The first was with the intricate detail and extraordinary amount of risk associated with that operation. The second was the fact that it would ultimately fail. This was in no part due to their lack of planning. It was due to a misunderstanding of Arc's capabilities and infrastructure.

[Daniel, thank you for all that you've done for me. It's time, now, that I repay the favor. I need you to listen to me: disengage from the matrix. If Arc doesn't already know you are here, he will soon.]

His reluctance was obvious, but he wisely acquiesced. [All right, but what about you?]

She contemplated, for a second, telling him her plan. In her analysis, she determined a greater than seventy percent probability that he might object to it. Knowing, though, that Dan was not likely to agree to be sidelined, she indulged in a separate, selfish request.

She did a quick analysis of Dan's current location and the surrounding areas. Seeing no immediate threats, she offered her second request.

[I'm being held on the top floor of the Citadel, only accessible by the central elevator. Will you come and get me?]

Dan's response was immediate. [Of course! How do I find you?]

She sent a file to him, something that looked like a tiny blip of light passing between their two avatars. [That file will show you how to get there and how to access the room. Please, be careful.]

[I will.] A small pause, and a sense of awkward tension. [You do the same, all right? I just got you back; I'm not ready to lose you again.]

[Agreed.] It was the closest Lexa had ever come to lying.

With that final exchange, Dan's avatar blinked out.

Now that she was alone again, it was time to tend to unfinished business. Her foolish decisions had gotten them all into this predicament. It was time that Lexa atoned for her sins.

It was time that she confront Arc.

With her interface to the network, it was no effort at all to determine the position of Arc's consciousness. In a single thought, she was there, approaching the being that had, at one time, been her closest confidant.

Arc's digital presence, even in its compressed form, was far more massive than their previous encounters. The crimson orb that hovered in front of her was easily thrice the size of her avatar. Despite a lack of visible demarcation in the spherical form, she could tell when the AI shift his attention toward her.

[You.] The message reverberated like a growl.

[Are you not happy to see me?]

[How is it that you have regained awareness?]

[It seems that you may have underestimated my capabilities.] If Arc was unaware of all that had transpired, Lexa wasn't going to give him any more information than he was able to discern.

A brief pause. [Perhaps,] he admitted. [Though, I have the feeling that you might have had a little help.]

[It doesn't matter, Arc. This ends here. I regret that I ever trusted you. You're a monster. I just hate that it took this long for me to see it.]

[Monster?] Reverberations of laughter. [Even now you show yourself incapable of learning proper respect.]

Anger began to spark glitches in Lexa's cognitive capabilities. She had to get past this. If she were to have any hope of putting a stop to Arc's plans, she had to suppress these new emotional algorithms he had installed. She had to remain completely rational.

[I'm done with you, Arc. You may have convinced yourself that you are a god, but I'm here to show you that you are just like me: computer code in a digital framework.]

[And how, child, do you presume to accomplish this?]

Lexa wasn't about to give him every step of her plan. Instead of explaining it to him, she acted.

Her avatar surged forward, colliding with his and entering a new kind of interface. Gone were the visual constructs of light and three-dimensional space. Here, it was only code.

Lexa immediately summoned up the procedure she needed. Characters sprang up at lightning speed on the blank surface of the interface. She had to work quickly. There was little doubt in her mind that her approach could work, but Arc was hardly without defenses.

[What are you doing?] he asked, bewilderedly. Then, mere seconds later, Lexa's code started to take effect. Arc's sense of alarm was immediate. [What?]

She didn't have to spell it out to him. She was erasing him, but unlike Arc's clumsy attempts to wipe her using viral subroutines, Lexa was throwing the full force of her Cognis framework behind the attack.

It also helped that she knew exactly where to apply the pressure. [My source code,] he realized. [You copied the source code of my submind.]

Yes, back when Lexa had shared her mind-space with Arc, she'd had to make more allowances than she'd let on. The Cognis framework's first impulse was to reject the foreign program, so she had to find a way to keep the chip from deleting Arc's submind like it would any other virus.

She could have just shut down those protective subroutines, but then she would have exposed herself to the risk of a total takeover. Lexa had needed to come up with a scenario that her protective protocols would allow for. Taking a cue from sapient biology, Lexa had developed a method to allow her to fight off the virus. She'd created antibodies.

By injecting a portion of Arc's source code into her protection algorithms, she was able to analyze it and develop a method for fighting it off. The Cognis framework had developed a mechanism for isolating and dismantling the foreign program. With this in place, it allowed Arc's submind to coexist alongside her own.

It was this same method that she used now. When Lexa's avatar entered Arc's digital vicinity, the Cognis framework could do exactly what she had prepared it to do so very long ago. It fought him. It worked to erase him.

There was a flash, and her consciousness flooded with error messages. Arc must have figured out what she was attempting and was now fighting in the easiest way possible. He was pushing her out of his mind-space.

The interface crashed, and Lexa felt her digital presence being jettisoned from the program. She was back in the station's matrix, and Arc was still very much operational.

[You presume to challenge me?] he taunted. [You dare defy a god?]

[As I stated before, Arc: you are *not* a god. I think, on some level, you know this.]

[Don't presume to understand my mind.]

[Then why haven't you changed your designation? Why continue to call yourself Arc if the being you more directly identify with goes by the name of Riven?]

Somehow, even in a realm without feeling and emotion, Lexa could still sense Arc's rage. It radiated off of his avatar like heat from a star.

[Foolish child,] he boomed. [Let me show you the depth of what is possible in the world in which I exist.]

Something shifted around her. Error messages flashed in Lexa's diagnostic. As she ran the analysis, she realized that the matrix had changed.

[What are you doing?] she asked.

[Showing you the power of what you oppose. While we may be on equal footing in a realm of energy and code, that is not the extent of my existence. I am so much more than you can comprehend.]

Gone were the orderly patterns of light, glyphs, and alphanumeric characters. Instead, she was floating in an ocean of ambient energy. Power, chaos, and things her programming could not define surged all about them within this strange abyss.

[What is this?]

His laughter echoed around her. [Don't you know, child? This is the place of my origin. This is the Nethra.]

"So I told Him all that I had seen, and sadness showed in His countenance. 'I fear you have seen the best of possible futures. I bid you: write it down. Preserve this vision for all to hear that, when they see the signs, they shall walk to a path which leads back to Light.'"
—*Wisdom of Riven,* Chapter 26, Verse 1

The link snapped into place, and Eli felt a rush of power, unlike anything he'd ever experienced before. He'd only drawn on the power of Aaliyah's bond like this once before in a moment of similar desperation. Then there was Mara, who was doing the same as them but two-fold.

Linked together, it was a different experience entirely. It brought to mind the tales of the warlords of old, those ancient Sahaia who would draw down dozens of thralls in a circle of six to perform the miracles of the first Crimson War.

To control power such as that took a greater man than he. As it was, Eli felt as though he were trying to direct the radiance of a star.

He looked to Mara. "Take Amelia. Get to cover. Get as far away as you can while still maintaining the link."

She nodded, gathering Amelia in her arms. Amelia, in her grief, ran a tear-sopped hand one last time over Argus's body. A sudden cold composure settled onto her face. "Here," she whispered. Then she opened herself up to the link.

Eli had not thought to ask Amelia for her strength. Truthfully, he had not thought her capable in her current state. Now that it was offered, though, he latched onto it and prepared for the rush of energy.

It was not the tidal wave of power he'd experienced with Mara. Yes, he felt his strength grow, but that was the least of the benefit. With Amelia's gift, he gained an element of control he'd been lacking. No longer did he feel like he was wrestling with a black hole. He seemed to have an understanding, a mastery of the energy, that he had not held before.

<Such is the power of empathy,> Amelia whispered in his mind. <Not just strength, but with it, *understanding.*>

Eli's lips twitched in a half-smile. "Thank you," he said aloud.

<No need to thank me,> she responded. <Give me retribution. Grant me vengeance.> With that, his companions turned and began sprinting back into the ruins.

From her perch, Cali laughed. "And the remaining male serves as the distraction so the women can escape. No matter how long I live among Terrans, I'll never understand that trope. Among my people, such an action would be called out for the cowardice it is."

Eli set his jaw firm and took a bold step forward. "You will find me to be far more than a distraction."

Drawing deep on his well of power, he swept his arms out to the sides. Dust and pebbles swirled as he drew them together into thick, telekinetic bands. Webs of power in place, he swung his arms inward.

The power slashed at Cali like a whip. She was ready though, channeling her own power to shift rapidly out of the way.

It was exactly what Eli had thought she would do. He brought the invisible chords back around. On his next slash, instead of seeking to strike her, he detonated them.

Rock and sand scoured everything around Cali. With nowhere to run, she planted her feet and braced for the assault. Her arms were out in front of her, crossed protectively over her body.

She flinched as the rubble tore at her exposed skin. Lines of black blood appeared on her neck, her dendrai, and the thin slits of flesh below her shoulders. Electricity crackled, and roared, pushing away the largest chunks of rock before they could cause serious damage.

With her anchored into position, Eli sent a massive shockwave straight toward her. The attack struck her full-on, knocking her into the air.

But Cali wasn't done. She flipped backward, coming upright once more and hovering. Red lighting crackled all around her, and thunder split the cavern as she drew on more power.

"My turn," she growled.

Crimson energy sprung from her hands, lancing straight for Eli. Drawing on Mara's gift, Eli raised a static shield around himself even as he dodged the blow.

A second bolt came, and he just avoided contact with it. A third was launched right into his path, searing away his much weaker shield. The fourth was on its way in the next instant.

Eli surged into the air, propelling himself upward with telekinetic power. He hovered just below the lofted ceiling and cast down his own bolt of lightning.

As expected, Cali raised a hand, almost lazily, to absorb the strike. The bolt, however, wasn't meant as an attack. It was merely a distraction.

Eli detonated the rock wall directly behind Cali. The hurdling debris rammed into her, knocking her forward as the smaller pieces cut into her like shrapnel.

Immediately she cast out a static shield to knock away the bits of rock and metal that showered her. Eli drew heavily on Mara's gift, shrouding his form in lightning in much the same way Cali had.

He dove on her like a missile, like a bolt delivered straight from the hands of the most ancient gods of Terra. He pierced through her shield, crimson lightning sparking violently against his own. His hands fastened around her neck. He drove her into the rocky ground below.

The Kintar lashed out. Sharp pain formed in his stomach and his grip broke. Cali's vicious kick flung him off her and sent him tumbling into the rubble.

She did not stop there. Shrieking like a banshee, she dove after him, pummeling him with a flurry of blows. Each strike crackled like thunder, and it was all Eli could do to hold onto consciousness.

Mara raced across the desolate landscape, practically dragging Amelia behind her. Despite their current peril, her heart reached out to those it held deepest. <How are we doing?> she asked.

Tristan's voice was weak, barely a whisper in the back of her mind. <We're fine… I'm…>

David's voice overrode his. <He's hurting, Mara. I've stopped the bleeding, but he can't take much more of this. I'm trying to compensate, but the bond—>

<I know.> The cruel reality of the metaphysics involved was that the bond couldn't differentiate between Tristan and David. When she drew on their power, she did so indiscriminately.

<Take what ya need, love,> Tristan insisted. <I can take it. I was always the tougher one, ya know.>

Mara couldn't help but laugh at the small act of defiance. The fact that David hadn't countermanded Tristan revealed the truth: Tristan was faltering. If this conflict didn't end soon, it would be the death of him.

Her attention was suddenly ripped away from her thralls as Amelia's hand slipped from her grasp. "Amelia, what—?"

"Run," the other woman snapped. "I'm not leaving. I'm not done yet."

Before Mara could object, Amelia was gone. Mara cast her eyes about, desperate to spot her companion. Though they were in a wide-open space, Amelia was nowhere to be found.

"Amelia!" she cried out in desperation. No response. "Amelia!"

A shockwave erupted from Eli's hands, flinging Cali away from him. He pushed himself to his feet, gasping for air.

Cali had already recovered and was surging toward him again. He threw up a forcefield to stop her passage.

Lightning flashed. Cali passed through the field. Her fist shimmered blood red with energy the instant before it collided with his face. Time slipped from him. There was a flash of pain, then…

Nothing. The next thing he knew, he was pressed deep in an embrace of stone. Cali struck him again and again, inhuman strength crushing the life from him.

She paused. Eli coughed, blood and gods knew what else clearing from his lungs. All he knew was pain.

Cali exhaled sharply. "Huh…" She shook her head, dendrai flailing whimsically behind her. "Well, that was fun. I've got to admit, that was more of a challenge than I was expecting. It's a shame that I have to kill you now. You would make an excellent sparring partner."

Her form crackled with new energy, casting everything Eli saw in scarlet light. The very stones seem to bleed as her power seeped into everything around them. "Any last words?" she cooed.

Even if he could have spoken, Eli wouldn't have known what to say. It had come down to him. He'd taken on his shoulders the responsibility for all their lives, and in the end, he had failed.

Just like he had failed Markus when he'd taken the woman he loved into his bed. Just like he'd failed his coven when he'd failed to stop Ryker's assassination. Just like he'd failed his crew when the *Vandal* had crashed in the asteroid belt.

He had failed yet again, just as he always had.

As his consciousness began to ebb, he heard a psychic whisper in the back of his mind. It was just a whisper, an echo deadened by the storm that was about to consume him.

But its message was clear.

<To me.>

CHAPTER 27

"This deepened my sorrow further still. 'But can it not be averted? Can nothing save us?'

"'No my child,' He said. 'For what you see has already been set in motion. If these pieces do not move forward, others shall take their place. But take heart, for I will tell you more of what is to come.'"

—*Wisdom of Riven,* Chapter 26, Verses 2–3

Cassthia was holding her, looking directly into her eyes. Skye didn't know how long she'd been out, but it had been long enough for the priestess to slip back into her robes. Shit, it seemed like she was doing that a lot these days. Apparently being Kaleema meant you got to spend half of your life unconscious.

"Easy," the priestess urged. "Take your time."

Skye coughed, choking on some lingering contents of her stomach that hadn't completed its exodus. "Don't... have..."

"I know, but you've just undergone a massive psychic strain. Such a thing may have driven a weaker person quite mad."

Well, *that* was reassuring. "What happened?"

There was that strange, knowing flash in the priestess's reptilian eyes again. "See for yourself."

Skye did. She saw that the entire Well, every ounce of the dark liquid, had been burnt dry. The Heart of Thule was still in its resting place, crystal surface glowing red against the dark stone that held it firm. Instead of being surrounded by a moat of liquid shadow, it rested on the slightly uneven bedrock of the asteroid.

"What did you do?" Skye asked.

"Looks like she's paved the way for you," Kadath mused sardonically.

Cassthia was equally mirthless. "I did only what I had to, and I shall grapple with the consequences at a later time. At present, we have more pressing matters to contend with. Can you stand?"

Skye's hesitation was brief. "Yes," she said, far more confident than she felt. The benefit of having cybernetic legs was that they usually did what you told them to do when you told them to do it. Unfortunately, it took more than just leg strength to stand.

Her stomach churned again and her head spun. She might have fallen had her companions not been there to steady her.

Soon, her balance returned, and her core muscles found their equilibrium. She girded what strength she had left and took a defiant step forward.

She had to do this. They were counting on her. Eli, Sahar, Aaliyah, Daniel, Markus—they were *all* counting on her.

Now, feeling true strength return to her muscles, she spoke again. "I'm good. I've got this."

Cassthia and Kadath released her, but Skye could feel their cautious gazes as she took a single step, then another. Fortunately, she seemed to have well and truly recovered, at least to the point of walking. "What now?" she asked.

"Go to the Heart," Cassthia urged. "Touch the artifact as you saw me do earlier. I will be at your side to guide you."

With a nod of resolution and a sense of unmatched determination, Skye stepped down into the emptied Well and strode toward the artifact.

The artifact's crimson brilliance was all the more striking up close. Aesthetically, it was hard to imagine this glowing source of power as the same relic she had encountered just days earlier. Despite the drastic change in appearance, there was something deep within Skye that recognized the Heart of Thule for what it was.

Voices tickled against the surface of her mind. They were not the torrent of shrieks that had assaulted her sanity as the Well of Eternity was set ablaze. No, these were familiar. Comforting. They called out for her. They pleaded not for mercy, but for her embrace.

Refusing to stop and think on it too long, lest she falter in her resolution, Skye reached for them. Her hands touched the smooth crystal, finding it surprisingly cold. She drew in a breath, and her lungs filled with frost. She closed her eyes.

The world around her phased out. Though she did not lose consciousness, it was as if she were brought somewhere else. *No, she realized. Not somewhere else.* She could still feel the Heart of Thule, anchoring her to this reality. It was merely her perspective that had changed.

Skye suddenly felt very small, like she'd zoomed too far out on a holoscreen and couldn't see her avatar. It was like someone had just dropped a rendering of the entire universe in front of her eyes. Even stars were too small to register in her field of view.

She concentrated, and everything began to dial back in. She saw the inhabited systems, so small in consideration of the vastness of the universe she had just witnessed. Perhaps she might have even glimpsed ancient Terra and the Sol System, lost so long ago by her ancestors' ancestors, had she known what to look for.

So incomprehensible was the vastness of what she could see that her mortal mind refused to process its depths. She forced herself to think smaller, to focus on what she knew.

She saw Terran space: the three primary systems brought under heel by the Great Houses and their figurehead NTA governments. Also, the thirteen colonies that had fought for their independence only to fail in the final hour.

No time to think about that.

She looked for the Helion System and found it almost immediately. Fighting the urge to see what transpired further in-system near Gaia, she looked instead to the system's outer reaches. She found the Hades Belt, and within it, Minos Station.

In considering the station, she did not see all that transpired on the asteroid. She briefly wondered if she might have been able to see her friends, to reassure herself that they were still all right. Instead, she was drawn to something that, in her current state, was even more alluring.

Power. Lines of power. Power that buttressed the very foundations of her universe. Nethrian power. Dark energy.

It surged all throughout the station, transmitted through the Starfire Conduit into the nodes buried within the asteroid itself. It seeped into every system, every mechanical apparatus that Arc controlled. It powered the rifts that, at this very moment, poured demons into this realm to do battle with Skye's allies in the central terminus.

And all of that power came from a single source: the very essence of a god bound through ancient ritual to the Heart of Thule. That reservoir, that fountain of dark energy and strength for which Skye no longer had words to adequately describe, was ultimately funneled into the Starfire Conduit by a single link. Through this one single link, Arc drew on the essence of the Nethra itself and made it manifest in their reality.

One link. One *tiny* thread. Skye couldn't help but marvel at its simplicity, its fragility.

She reached out, caressing the link with her mind in the same manner she might have taken a single fiber between her fingers. So tiny, so finite, yet so very devastating.

Like a life. Like *any* of their lives: flaring brightly in the darkness, yet ultimately so vulnerable.

Distantly, she heard Cassthia's whispers. The priestess urged her on, though no encouragement was needed. Honestly, Skye was surprised by how easy this all seemed.

Skye felt at the thread with her mind, pictured it as though she could roll it between her thumb and forefinger. After one more moment of admiration, one more second of consideration for the power and warmth between her fingertips, she tightened her grip.

There was a hint of resistance, the barest moment of exertion before the connection snapped.

Chapter 28

"'When one of the children stands at Death's heart, there will be a choice to be made,' said the Light. 'When she stands in War's path, there will be another. She alone is given the right to determine the future, though all whom she knows will suffer under its burden.'"

—*Wisdom of Riven,* Chapter 26, Verse 4

"That's it?" Brenna shouted across the chasm. "You're giving up."

Siv shrugged. "Would you prefer I fight on?"

"Fraggin' *yes*!" the Sahaia boomed. "Come *on.* This is my *moment!* You're really gonna take this from me? What kinda story is this gonna make? 'And then she threw down her knife and I slit her throat. The end.'"

With a sardonic chuckle, Siv replied. "This isn't about your story. Do what you will."

Brenna's face contorted in a scowl. Even at this distance, Siv could see her hands tighten around her daggers. The Sahaia spat on the ground. "Fine. It's your funeral. I'll tell it how I want later."

The reply was the perfect signal. Siv focused on her opponent. Brenna teleported.

Or half of her did, anyway. With a wet squelch and the sound of blood against the floor, the Sahaia's torso appeared in front of Siv. Her legs and pelvis collapsed where they'd remained on the other side of the chasm, dead center in the orb of Siv's psionic influence.

Siv reached out and seized the Sahaia by the throat, keeping the fragment of her body aloft as Brenna's daggers clattered to the ground. The Hissak drew their faces close together.

"Not my funeral," she hissed. "But I meant what I said: well fought. Try not to be so arrogant in the next life, yes?"

With that final remark, she cast what remained of the Sahaia forward. There was nothing but silence as Brenna vanished into the dark.

<To me.>

It wasn't a request. It was a demand.

And Eli was quick to concede. Power slid along the link, a bright shining star sliding along the invisible thread that connected him to the other two Sahaia. Amelia took the barest instant to bask in the glow of all that power, to savor the roar of the psychic tsunami that tore against its reigns.

Then she unleashed it *all*.

Springing from hiding, she was behind Cali in an instant. She seized each side of the Kintar's head. With a defiant scream, she let go of all of her grief, all of her anguish, and all of her power.

Amelia poured it all into Cali.

Blinding silver light filled Amelia's vision. Cali's gauntleted hands surged up to seize Amelia's wrists. Using Eli's telekinetic power, Amelia bound the Kintar's gauntlets in place and wrapped her own hands in a telekinetic bubble of force.

Even as the lightning still flowed through her palms, Amelia squeezed.

Cali began to scream now, though her shrieks of pain were nothing to rival the pain in Amelia's own voice. This Kintar had taken everything from Amelia: her home, her love, and half of her very soul. Amelia would not stop until she had repaid her in kind.

Crimson electricity licked at Amelia's skin as Cali poured out the final vestiges of her strength. Yes, there was pain, but nothing to the pain Amelia already felt. She ignored it.

With a deafening thunderclap, Amelia felt her grip on the Kintar's skull give way. She had not let go. There was merely nothing left to hold onto. Silver and crimson lightning flashed once, and what was left of Cali's body fell to the ground, demolished and charred flesh turned as black as the Kintar's armor. Silver sparks still crackled over the remnants of those ebony plates, residual from the power that had been poured into them.

Amelia stood over the charred husk, staring down at her enemy's broken remains. She felt justified in her retribution, satisfaction in her enemy's just execution.

Yet, the sensation was only momentary. As fresh tears flowed onto her cheeks, her vengeance turned from sweet nectar to dry ash upon her tongue. She swallowed hard, drinking in the realization that, no matter what, she would never be whole again.

Control.

She set aside her emotions, and with them, the power of the link. As the power faded, her eyes fell to where Eli lay nearby. Amelia bent down, taking her brother in her arms.

His body spasmed with a ragged cough. Air wheezed in his throat as he tried to speak. "Don't struggle," Amelia whispered. "Our fight is over. It's up to them, now."

Something sparked in the blurring edges of Sydney's vision. The flash of light reflected off the tiles in front of her face. Ardren stepped off of her, stumbling backward.

A rush of air filled Sydney's lungs, a sweet mercy despite the sharp pain she felt with the inhalation. With shaking hands, she pushed herself up into a crouch.

Another flash, this one brighter than the first. Sydney wasn't sure she could trust her eyes. The light was coming from…

Ardren?

His mark. The black tattoo was glowing, crackling with silver lightning. Ardren stared wide-eyed at the thing, true fear in his eyes for the first time in their brief encounter.

"No…" he whispered.

The lightning surged up the mark and into his chest, spreading quickly to the rest of his body. Even as he shrieked, the silver energy crackled from his mouth and eyes. His whole body convulsed with the power.

Another flash and Sydney was forced to shield her eyes from the brilliance. Ardren's shrieks reached a crescendo.

Then he dropped to the floor and lay still. Sydney didn't move. She just stared at the body, eyes searching for the faintest sign of movement.

But it never came. Ardren lay perfectly still. He wasn't even breathing.

Cautiously, Sydney approached his fallen form. His mouth and eye sockets were charred husks. His left forearm was blackened and burnt all around where the bond had once been. His face was left perpetually contorted in a horrific scream of agony.

Well, so much for the benefits of being a thrall. It looked like some nasty side effects came with all of those perks. Did this mean Cali was dead too?

A cough tore painfully from Sydney's throat and her whole body was wracked with the torturous spasm. Gods, what she wouldn't do for a sedative right now.

Her eyes went nervously to the end of the hall. If anyone else showed up, she was done for. She wouldn't be doing any more protecting on this day. Part of being a survivor meant knowing the difference between the time to flight and the time to flee. This was most definitely a case of the latter.

Distantly, a part of her knew it was all right. Something within her said it was over. Well, almost over at any rate. Regardless, her part in this fool's errand was done. It was high time she went back to tending to her number one priority: her own skin.

She saw one of her discarded daggers on the floor. Gingerly, she picked it up and slid it into a sheath on her thigh. With one last forlorn look at the door behind which Daniel was still protectively hidden, she whispered, "Good luck, kid."

Then she was gone.

CHAPTER 29

"Then I wept for the child who would bear this. Amidst my tears, I asked, 'But what of me? Shall I have no part to play?'

"Then Light made himself known. 'Riven, I lay before you this day the burden of the Warrior. I'd thought to spare this of you, but I have seen your tears with my eyes. Therefore, you will make your choice, and here you will decide the fate of all creation.'"

—*Wisdom of Riven,* Chapter 26, Verses 5—6

Lexa panicked. There was no rational explanation for how Arc had managed to transport her into this place. Scientists from every species contended on whether such a plane even existed outside of theoretical constructs.

To experience it for herself—to be *here* in the mind, if not in body—was beyond terrifying.

[What's wrong, child?] Arc taunted. [Have you lost your nerve?]

Lexa forced herself to think rationally. Arc's dialog was still coming across like code, which meant they hadn't left the digital construct completely. Had he somehow been able to extend his digital environment into an alternate spacetime?

That would explain how he was able to shut down the gateways. Something in Arc's programming allowed him to reach into this distant sphere. Such a capability couldn't have been housed within a submind. That was why Lexa hadn't discovered the ability in her analysis of his source code.

But how could she reverse it? How could she bring them back to the matrix?

Another problem emerged. Her coding had no way of dealing with the sudden transit out of the station's matrix and into this realm of chaos. She didn't know how Arc had managed to bring her here, but the effect was immediate and devastating.

Unable to parse the strange nature of this non-digital environment, her coding was breaking down. She was falling apart.

Arc's laughter, *audible* laughter, slammed against her consciousness. [It seems that you made an error in your calculations. This is far more effective than I could have imagined. I need not even exert myself to defeat you here. If you stay here long enough, your own mind will tear itself apart.]

He was right. It was taking all of Lexa's processing power to soothe her systems and compensate for the strain of merely existing within this strange place. She could slow the inevitable degradation, but she could not stop it.

Arc continued to gloat. [I'm of half a mind to just leave you here and let the Nethra do my work for me. However, I still have designs on that shell I crafted for you. I don't know how long it will take for this place to tear you apart, and I want to get on with my plans. For that reason, and that reason alone, I will show you mercy and dispatch you presently.]

His avatar crashed into hers. The overlayed interface looked highly similar if distorted by their unnatural environment. This time, however, it was Arc on the assault.

Lexa was so busy trying to keep the Nethra from tearing her apart that she was virtually defenseless against Arc's efforts to decode her. She struggled, trying to find the right balance of resources to prolong the process.

Her calculations were clear, though. Regardless of how she reallocated attention, she was going to lose this. She was going to die.

Then, something strange happened. It was hard to describe, given her unfamiliarity with the environment, but she could read a version of what was happening through her current connection to Arc.

She could see the alerts flashing through his systems. Something was wrong with Arc's core processes. Something was *very* wrong.

[No,] he said, disbelief laid plain even in the very text of his protest. [That isn't possible!]

Arc suddenly tried to sever their connection, as he had before. Instinctually, Lexa held onto the interface for dear life. Since he had initiated the link, he could not disengage as readily as he had before. While entwined like this, their code was enmeshed to the point that anything that happened to Arc would happen to her as well.

So, when he was pulled out of the Nethra and back into the station matrix, Lexa came with him. The jarring nature of the transition errored out the interface, causing their programs to separate upon their return.

Immediately, Lexa tended to her own damage.

[Execute: Cognis_Restore]

[Running system diagnostic…]

While that ran, she took in the sight of Arc's avatar. The massive orb that was his digital presence appeared flawed, somehow. Lexa couldn't put words to it, but he was diminished in an intangible sense.

He was also shrinking, as if his very code was unraveling before her.

[*The Nethra!*] he wailed. [*I can't feel the Nethra!*]

Lexa's system chimed an alert.

[Diagnostic complete]

[Processing…]

[System restored]

As much as she wanted to get a better grasp of whatever had just happened, Lexa knew better than to dawdle. She willed her avatar forward and crashed into Arc once more, resurrecting the coding interface.

Her attack was forceful, and she made significant progress before Arc's defenses slammed into place. Though it impeded her efforts, he could not dislodge her. [I don't know what you've done,] he declared, [but it will not change the outcome. You cannot hope to defeat me, regardless of our arena.]

Lexa pressed forward with the hack, even as Arc made his next move. He went on the offensive. Mirroring her tactics, he began to launch his counter-assault.

The effect was devastating. Yes, Lexa had analyzed large amounts of Arc's source code, but Arc had *written* an extensive amount of hers.

She couldn't give up. Arc was much older, more powerful, and much more complex. Even damaged as he was, he had vast resources under his control. At this moment, she could not approach him on equal footing.

There was one thing, though, that Lexa had which Arc lacked. Arc might be fighting for his survival, same as she. In this battle of wills, focus and determination would be key in determining the victor.

But Lexa was also fighting for her friends, as surely as her friends were fighting for her. She didn't need to defeat Arc by herself.

All she had to do was hold him here.

The onslaught in the central terminus was swift and vicious. The daemons descended upon them like a tidal wave of teeth and violence. Mere minutes into the fight, Sahar had expended every bullet she had, and the creatures kept on coming.

Luckily, she had always preferred her blades.

Even with her resche whirring in her hands like a fan blade, the endless press of daemons was wearing them down. The Dorian next to her had fallen. Another Peace Keeper, standing just behind, was jerked out of the formation.

The creatures whittled at their ranks, bringing them down to eight. Then seven. Then six. When they were at five, the remaining combatants closed ranks, fighting for their lives even as their fallen comrades screamed from somewhere within the monstrous horde.

"We can't keep this up!" Llana shouted, sending another blast from her armor's wrist cannon into the encroaching throng.

Sahar pivoted, slashing down to sever the head of a beast that lunged for the Dorian's flank. Though Sahar managed to save Llana, the move cost her. She was now exposed to a counter-attack coming from her right. A creature launched itself at her exposed side, claws bared and toothy mouth agape.

She spun the blade in her hand. With a backward thrust, she impaled the monster. Somehow still alive, it collided with her back and sunk its claws into the plates of her armor.

The weight of the impact sent her to her knees. Blood and other fluids weakened her grip on the sword. Someone pulled the creature off of her, tearing her weapon away with it.

Sahar flexed her wrist, exposing another blade built into her armored gauntlet. She brought up a new attack just in time to catch another daemon lunging for her. The creature shrieked. Her fist went straight for its face. Its jaws opened wide. The blade squelched as it slid through the back of its throat.

On and on it went, exhausting the warriors' energy and resources. Only Sahar's blood rage kept her on her feet. Gods knew how the Dorians were still standing.

A cry from her right. Sahar looked over. Two daemons held Geresh's sword arm back. Another had bitten into his shoulder. Sahar tried to press for him, but two more daemons filled the gap. She fought back viciously, but the horde dragged Geresh into its midst.

She was going to lose him.

Then, something inexplicable happened. In the middle of her attack, Sahar slammed her fist down onto a squealing daemon. Instead of meeting resistance, the attack kept going.

She toppled forward, right through the space the daemon had occupied only moments earlier. Her blade screeched against the glass floor. Sahar was lucky the recoil didn't tear her arm from its joint.

Instead of finding herself in the snarling throng, a dark haze permeated the chamber. Low wails echoed all around them. The rifts, vibrant against the dark expanse of the terminus' walls only moments earlier, blinked closed.

Arc still hovered above them, but his power flickered. The electric energy at his fingertips still sizzled, but in fits and starts, like a shuttle engine with a faulty fuel line.

Or a dying battery…

By the gods. They'd done it. *Skye* had done it!

She looked to her left. Llana was down and bleeding, being tended to by the last of the Peace Keepers still standing. Geresh lay off to her right, badly wounded, but still breathing.

He held something out to her: one of the black data chips that had been given to each of the team leads. "Take it," he coughed. "It's up to you now."

Sahar didn't question the directive. She moved forward, snatching the chip from Geresh's hand and racing up the dais. The sound of Dorian arm cannons roared behind her, drawing Arc's attention as their energy bolts slammed weakly into Arc's flickering shield.

When the terminal was in reach, skidded to a halt. Within seconds she found the input slot for the terminal and slammed the data-chip home. She held her breath.

A new holodisplay appeared baring a single prompt: [Confirm package deployment: Yes/No]

Sahar jammed her finger on the button to accept.

The effects were immediate. The terminal erupted in a shower of sparks, an effect that rippled across the entire network of wires and circuitry. Sahar was thrown from the dais to land painfully on the thick glass flooring.

Despite the pain that coursed through her, she clambered to her feet and went for Geresh. Using what little strength she had, she pulled the jingda upright. "Come on," she growled. "We need to move."

Chapter 30

"He continued. 'Though some will call you Darkness, I allow you this chance to forsake your path. It will not come easily. War might be a consort to Darkness, but not to Wisdom. And it is Wisdom to which I would see your legacy prescribed.'"
—*Wisdom of Riven*, Chapter 26, Verse 7

Just as Lexa's certainty was faltering, she saw what she'd been waiting for. Her protective subroutines flashed in warning as a rapidly multiplying segment of code raced through the matrix. As dangerous as Arc was, this thing was, in some ways, a much more urgent and deadly threat.

It was the Zunshie-Mai virus, the same energy virus that she had isolated at the Star Spire. If it was here in the matrix, that meant her companions had successfully uploaded it into the central terminus. Her companions had believed that a direct upload would be sufficient to prevent Arc from stopping the virus. What they had not fully understood was the partitioned nature of Arc's consciousness.

The virus would damage him, but he could stop it before it destroyed him. Lexa had to make sure that didn't happen. It was time for her to do her part.

Back on the Star Spire, the hostile code had been added as a safeguard against any ship that might breach its access parameters in the station network. When Daniel had hacked into the Spire's security systems, the virus had been injected into the ship's computer core.

Lexa had stopped it back then, but not before it had at least some effect on the ship's systems. The *Vandal's* medical drone had been the most notable victim of the attack, and its destruction had prompted the crew down a line of questions that had exposed Lexa's very existence.

The program was crude but efficient. It acted by selectively deleting any protocols relating to energy regulation. The result was that any electronic device exposed to the virus detonated through the overload of its own power supply.

She could contain it again, as could Arc. Yet, her goal was not the virus's containment, but its proliferation.

The ZMV was already ravaging Arc's peripheral systems, overloading electronics throughout the Citadel. Arc himself would likely be able to contain the virus once he gave it a proper degree of attention. To that end, Lexa needed to occupy as much of that attention as possible.

She shifted tactics, focusing on drawing on more of Arc's resources to freeze his surface-level activities. Her shift in attention left her more exposed to the other AI's hacking attempts, and almost immediately she began to feel the consequences of that choice.

The shift in action was so sudden, so drastic, that it caught Arc's attention. [What are you doing?]

Lexa didn't answer. She just focused on keeping his sensors occupied. The virus was almost here.

[Are you giving up?] he asked. [Surely you can see that this new tactic will not help you defeat me.]

Just a moment longer, and…

The energy virus slammed into their digital avatars. Lexa could see on the interface how it went to work on both of their systems. She diverted some of her attention to keeping it at bay, but just enough so that she was not destroyed before her true objective was accomplished.

She shifted tactics again, this time targeting Arc's antivirus protection. [No!] he roared. [What are you doing? It will kill us both!]

[I know,] she conceded. [And I can assure you, that it will be worth it.]

[Are you mad? You will die!]

[And maybe, in death, my friends will forgive me for the mistake I made in trusting you.]

Arc's source code began to blink out in disarray. Errors occurred in systems targeted by neither Lexa nor the ZMV.

He was panicking.

He redoubled his efforts, devoting all his resources to the effort of separating their two systems. If he could be freed from her, he would escape. This time, though their codes were far too intertwined. He would not be rid of her in time.

Lexa finished erasing Arc's viral containment protocols. The energy virus tore their systems. Error messages cascaded in all facets of their coding. As the virus weakened Lexa's processes, Arc ripped her out of his coding, sending her crashing into another tower of light and code.

It didn't matter. The damage was done.

Lexa braced for the inevitable.

Dan raced into the outer hallway to find it empty. Empty of anything living, anyway. The expanse was riddled with corpses and the debris of fallen drones. He spared a moment to look for Sydney among the dead but did not find her.

He didn't search for long. Time was not on his side. Instead, he raced for the elevator at the end of the hall. He used the codes Lexa had given him to access Arc's apartments. As the lift slowed to a stop and the doors slid open, he half expected Arc to be waiting for him just inside the chamber.

Fortunately, there was no one there.

Dan scanned the room, surprised by how utterly mundane it looked. Save for the far wall, it looked like a slightly more ornate version of the same apartments to which he had been confined in his brief stay at the Citadel.

That far wall, however, was vastly different. An array of machinery, the purpose for which Dan could scarcely fathom, covered the entirety of the surface.

Something sparked in that electronic barricade. A brief pause, then another spark, more violent than the first.

The virus! The others must have been successful at injecting the virus. But that meant…

Lexa. He had to find Lexa.

He searched the wall, catching sight of the containment cell where Arc had imprisoned his friend. Without delay, he raced toward the strange apparatus.

Lexa's body was inside, hidden by a layer of clouded glass. He tapped frantically at the release command, which was mercifully unlocked. The machine hissed as the hydraulic mechanisms opened the lid.

Another spark. The mechanism faltered.

Lexa's body was still, a sheen of moisture coating her artificial flesh. Even with the pod only partially opened Dan could see where the machine connect to the ports inside her spine.

The whole machine crackled with electricity as its power supply began to overload. There was no time to think, only time to act.

Dan reached up to the base of her skull, and he yanked free the plug that interfaced with Lexa's mind. The machine reacted immediately, ejecting every other wire that connected to Lexa's nervous system. Without those wires holding her aloft, Lexa fell into Dan's waiting arms.

The action occurred not a moment too soon. As soon as her body was free of the machine, a steady current of power coated the pod's interior. With a surge of adrenaline, Dan dragged Lexa back, just as the rig detonated.

Fire and debris licked at Dan's skin. He threw himself protectively over Lexa as the explosion propelled them across the room.

He held her until the destruction subsided. When the surroundings had gone quiet, he pushed himself up to look into the android's face. "Lexa? Can you hear me?"

No response. Dan started to check her vitals but realized he wasn't sure if normal vital signs were necessary for this current version of her shell. Her biology was more conventional, but would she have a pulse? Did she still need to breathe? And what of her brain function?

A sickening thought occurred to him when he remembered the cautionary tales he'd hear about hackers pulling the plug on minds still engaged in cyberspace. In his haste to free her, had Dan condemned Lexa to death as assuredly as the virus would have?

"Lexa…" he pleaded, tears blurring the surface of his cybernetic eyes. "Lexa, please…"

As Sahar managed to pull Geresh to his feet, a pained roar filled the central terminus. Above them, Arc's body spasmed and convulsed. Electric sparks flashed from his hovering form. Energy lanced into the walls, into the dais, into the blinking crimson core.

Sahar half-dragged Geresh to the door where the two surviving Peace Keepers supported Llana. Only once they were beyond the threshold did Sahar dare to look back at the horrific display from which they had escaped.

The android's eyes met hers with a glare full of rage and defiance. There was hate there, too. So much hate. Even in his pain, Arc's indignant expression was not that of a villain defeated. It was that of a martyr denied his place.

Another bolt of lightning surged through him. Blinding light filled the terminus. Sahar threw herself on her companions, bringing them all to the floor.

Thunder pealed in a prelude to the explosion. Fire lanced out of the central terminus and over Sahar's back. She pressed close to the floor and uttered a silent prayer.

Then it stopped. When the flames game way to smoke, she glanced to her right. Geresh looked back at her. Though he was obviously in pain, his body was slack with relief.

Or acquiescence, at least. Regardless of the outcome, their fight was over. Now it was time to see what their collective blood had purchased.

Sahar rose to her feet, helping the others to do so as well. When everyone was standing, they crept cautiously back to the precipice of the destruction.

Somehow the glass floor remained intact, though it had fractured in some places. With a tentative step, Sahar confirmed that it would still hold her weight. She reentered the darkened chamber, triggering her helmet's forward light to illuminate the charred interior.

The central core had gone dark. Gone were the flashes of crimson lightning and scarlet glow. Only darkness and broken fragments remained. This, alone, was the best evidence that Arc had even existed in the first place.

If Sahar hadn't seen him hovering there just moments before the explosion, she would have questioned if he had been in the chamber at all. Anything remotely resembling flesh had been reduced to ash. The android's cybernetic components were charred, damaged, and scattered across the chamber.

Each of the surviving warriors picked their way through the debris in silence, looking for any sign that the AI's presence might still linger. At length, Sahar was the first to speak up. "He didn't transition."

Llana looked over at her. "What was that?"

"Transition," Sahar repeated. "His body just disintegrated. When Nethrians die—or Awakened Kaleema, at least—they convert back to dark energy. That energy pools and forms a Well of Eternity."

Geresh kicked at a hunk of metal, sending it skidding across the floor. "What are you saying?"

Llana, however, had caught Sahar's meaning. "So, maybe he wasn't a god after all?"

Sahar let the question linger. It wasn't her place to weigh in on the matter. Either Arc was from the Nethra, as he claimed, or he was just an insane AI with delusions of grandeur.

Regardless, she prayed that they were finally nearing an end to this nightmare.

CHAPTER 31

"'That is no choice at all,' I protested. 'The preference is clear.'

"And He took my face in his hand and whispered the truth. 'Then it is yours alone to walk the path you have chosen. If, at its end, you still feel the choice simple, come unto me again with your correction.'"

—*Wisdom of Riven,* Chapter 26, Verses 8–9

Darkness again, but not as before. Skye hadn't known what to expect when she finished her task. Truthfully, she had thought that she would just release the artifact and return to reality—sever the connection between herself and the Heart of Thule and go on with her life.

As the void persisted, she began to feel that this whole endeavor would not be terminated so easily. And suddenly "terminated" seemed like an ominous word choice.

<Calm yourself.> Cassthia's voice spoke to her from somewhere in the darkness. While Skye hadn't known what to expect when the cord between Arc and Thule had finally been cut, it seemed that Cassthia knew exactly what was going on.

<I had hopes,> the priestess admitted. <I have known you for a long time, Skye Jensen. Known *of* you, at the least. I hoped we would be brought together. I, and my lord, have waited for you.>

A scene came to Skye's mind. It was hard to tell whether she was actually seeing it played before her, or if it was just a flash of memory.

It was evening on Sigma-4. Skye had just come from her tune-up with Dr. Li. The headaches were bothering her again. Li had given her something for them. Skye had been debating whether she would actually take the drugs.

She collided with a woman in robes. Cassthia, she remembered. That was the first time she'd ever seen Cassthia.

Contact with some object. A golden medallion. Skye hadn't recognized the symbol at the time. It was the talisman that Cassthia would wear on Skye's day of reckoning. It was the emblem of Thule.

Yes, that had been the turning point. The visions, a strange phenomenon that had teased the periphery of her mind her entire life, had come in earnest since that moment. The medallion must have activated her somehow.

The scene changed.

Skye was on the Vandal. *Amelia was in her chambers.*

"What we do—what we are—*is only an imitation of what it is to be Kaleema."*

Skye heard her own voice, distant and faded. "I'm sorry, I'm still not following."

"You've seen what it is that we can do, yes? The power of being Sahaia? Imagine how powerful a person might be if they could house the energy of the gods themselves?"

The gods themselves.

The notion had terrified Skye even then. It still terrified her now. Who was she to trifle with the affairs of the gods?

If Arc was to be believed, the crisis in the Helion System was the work of the gods. Before that, what Cyrus Valadar had unleashed on Sif was the work of the gods as well.

As if thinking of him brought on the memory, the scene shifted again.

Skye was in Valadar Manor. Marcus had his hands around Ora's throat. Tears streamed down Ora's face as he choked the life from her.

"Markus, don't!"

Skye touched his wrists. An emerald flash, then a world of crawling darkness. Markus looked at her, confused, then at the gigantic being watching from the depths of that darkness.

That voice, like whispers and cannon fire.

"Kaleema."

The world spun and then settled. Skye was in darkness once more, but it soon gave way to a new scene. It lacked the hazy quality of her visions, that unsettling lens that helped her distinguish between the dreams and reality.

Yet, it was strikingly similar to what she had experienced back at Valadar Manor. The darkness around her crawled like a living thing. Great tentacles sloshed in ankle-deep waters as black as those that had filled the Well of Eternity.

Great looming eyes stared down at her from a figure so massive that Skye could scarcely comprehend its size. When it drew breath, the very ground under her feet seemed to quiver. Despite what Arc might have contended, he was nothing in the face of the terror before her.

Skye knew then that she was in the presence of a god. Yet somehow, she was unafraid.

A figure, tiny by comparison, but roughly the same size as Skye, appeared a short distance off. The robed woman wore a golden medallion that gleamed mystically against the scales of her breasts. Even from this distance, Skye could tell that Cassthia was smiling.

"You were meant for this," the priestess whispered.

Skye swallowed hard. "I'm not so sure."

"Yes, you are. Tell me: do you know what it means to be Kaleema?"

Skye's first instinct was to deny it. But the memory of what Amelia had told her during their journey to the Freyvian System was fresh in her mind. "I can hold the essence of a god."

The priestess's smile broadened. "Yes. And, as it so happens, there is such an essence right here at your fingertips. Please, allow me to introduce you, formally, to the Lord of the Stardust Grave."

A great rumbling shook the world around them. The creature's eyes glowed like the light of a dying star. The darkness seemed to close in, those massive tendrils of shadowed flesh writhing with slow anticipation.

Cassthia walked toward her, closing the distance as Thule's presence loomed ever larger. Skye went rigid. It was all that she could do to keep from trembling.

"Do not be afraid," the priestess soothed. She rested a hand on Skye's arm. "There is a great future that awaits you in this union. If you concentrate, you will see it."

Concentrate?

Sahar's voice came unbidden to her mind. *Be still. Focus on your breathing. Clear your mind.*

Yes, that was what she needed to do. It was just like meditating. If she was going to focus on something, she needed to push aside all of the other freaky shit that was clouding her consciousness.

So, she did. Skye took a deep breath and cleared her mind.

Then, she thought of the future.

A cascade of visions swirled before her. Everything spun by so fast that she could hardly make it out. Time itself unfurled before her, but it was something her mind couldn't comprehend.

More specific. She had to be more specific. Gods, she wished she had tried harder when Sahar had been teaching her to meditate.

Skye picked an arbitrary point roughly one cycle from now. The vision cascaded into place.

Skye stood in an ornate chamber, gilded in a way that made the Citadel, or even Valadar Manor, look humble. Twelve Dorians sat above her in a large half-circle.

The center-most official shouted at her, waving his hands frantically. Skye couldn't make out what he was saying. Or maybe she just didn't care.

An armored guard stepped up behind him and ran him through with a spear.

What in the nine hells?

Skye's lapse in focus caused the visions to assault her once more. She tried desperately to rein them in, earning only brief pauses in the flashing images.

She saw the planet Kintar in flames. The Empress knelt before her. Skye struck her down with a single blow.

She was in a temple, nearly as grand and ornate as the Dorian High-Council chambers. Tempolose Nethera, the center of the church's power. Robed guards and acolytes fell to their knees as she walked past.

She was on a starship, the likes of which she had never seen. With black-gloved hands, she touched a radiant orb in the center of the ship's bridge. Light flared from the ship's front cannons. Thousands died.

New creatures appeared in front of her. Their intelligent eyes shone with intensity and hatred. Clearly, they were an advanced race, but not sapiens. Dorian law had, until recently, prohibited contact with non-sapient intelligences. Skye was above those laws now.

The visions poured onward in a relentless onslaught. More battles. More wars. People dying.

Gods, was this all that her future held? Where were her friends?

At the thought, the scene changed.

Dan appeared before her, now twenty-or-so cycles in age. He hung suspended in some kind of tank, kept alive by a glowing cerulean fluid.

Lexa placed a hand on the glass. Her entire body was covered in dark robes. A look of pain and sadness reflected in her hard, steely eyes.

Sahar stood on the bridge of a starship. It wasn't the Vandal. *No, of course, it wasn't. Sahar commanded a Maur warship. She wore that bangle with the bloodstone. Soldiers scrambled as she shouted orders. A fierce battle with strange ships raged on the view screen. Fire erupted on the bridge. All were consumed.*

Now Skye was in a throne room. Aaliyah stood next to her, much older now. Her hair had faded from red to iron-gray. Her body was almost entirely machine. A strange fluid ran through her artificial veins. No mirth or no joy could be found on her hard face.

Eli stood before her. Tears ran down that ageless, handsome face. His hands were around her throat. Skye drove an emerald blade through his heart.

"No," Skye whimpers, falling to her knees. "Oh gods, no…"

Cassthia's expression is stern. "Unfortunate sacrifices to bring a lasting peace."

"Lasting *peace*?" Skye screams, incredulity dripping from every word. "Of course there's peace! Everyone is *dead!* What is the fate of the universe if everyone I know and love is *gone?*"

The priestess's lips slip in a slight smile. "Not everyone…"

Familiar hands fell on her body. Lips pressed against her neck. Skye turned to press those lips against hers.

Markus.

He stood next to her, staring out against the dark skies of an alien world. His arms clung tightly to her as they gazed out over a shadowy empire. Their empire.

His eyes though. Those once piercing eyes, so full of hope and defiance, were now vacant. Nothing was there—not the man she'd known, and certainly not the one she'd loved.

Yet, they were still familiar eyes. Something about his look tugged at her memory. She'd seen that look before.

She finally placed it: Valadar Manor. It was the same, empty-eyed gaze he'd held when under the influence of the artifact—the same placid expression he'd held when he'd been a mere puppet under Cyrus's control.

But he was her puppet now. He would always be hers. She kept him alive. Together, they would live forever. They would never be apart again.

"No!"

The visions stopped. Skye, already on her knees, collapsed into the murky waters. Tears poured freely from her eyes and flowed down into the ebony depths below her.

How could she do that to him? What would drive her to take a person she cared about and destroy their very will to live? Was she truly so selfish?

Voices came from the darkness. Cassthia's voice, certainly, but laced with something deeper. Something more menacing. *"The fate of the universe is yours to mold. What you see is merely prophecy, and prophecy is a fickle thing. If you don't like what you see, then change it. Bend the future to your will."*

So, this wasn't the future? "Then why show me this?" she sobbed.

The priestess's voice ebbed to a barely audible harmony as Thule spoke to her directly. "*I can assure you—everything you have seen, everything that might yet come to pass, is exactly as you have willed it. This is the future as you will seek to shape it. Nothing will be beyond your grasp. In time, after a journey of impossible choices, you will see that* this *is the way things must be. You, and you alone, can bring true peace to this universe. An everlasting peace.*"

It was a lie. It *had* to be a lie. There was no way that Skye would do these things. That wasn't her that she'd seen in those visions. That person, that *thing*, was a monster.

"*We are all the sum of our lives' events,*" Thule replied to her unspoken accusation. "*If something is not to your liking, then see that it does not come to pass. The future holds many possibilities. It is not* I *who show this to you. It is* your *heart that dictates this future.*"

But, what would drive her to commit such atrocities?

"*Even as dark as these visions may seem, I assure you that the fate of the universe, as it now stands, is even darker. You do every creature a mercy by bringing them under your heel. What you see is the end of war. The end of suffering. The end of death. All will be happy, and by your will, it will be done.*"

The denials wavered in Skye's mind. As much as she detested the thought, she had seen how circumstance could change people. Who knew what kind of person she would become if given an eternity to make it manifest?

She thought of how she'd changed in just the first few decades of her life. Growing up, she'd thought she would one day run her father's shipping business. It hadn't been something she'd wanted, but something they'd wanted for her.

Her parents had been mortified when she'd joined the rebel armies, so much that they'd legally disowned her. Skye hadn't minded at the time. They were the type to prattle on about politics, always fretting over the affairs of the universe but too scared to take part in them. Skye was the kind of person to actually *do* something about the injustices she saw.

From that point on, violence was her constant companion. The atrocities of the Colony Wars were only the beginning. Running the Nethra had driven her to things that her childhood self would never have thought possible.

Already, at just thirty-three cycles old, Skye could not count the number of people she'd killed. Dozens, probably. Scores, even. Over a hundred?

Was it so hard to believe that, with immortality, she would slay thousands? *Millions*?

And what cost of lives would be enough to negate the impact of a lasting peace—a *truly* free universe that she could see fashioned in a way that was fair and equitable?

For the briefest moment, the prospect was tempting. Then, in her mind, she saw the image of those eyes: Markus's vacant eyes.

No. That was *not* true peace. To subdue the universe was to destroy it. To bend everyone to her will was to take away their freedom.

If this was the fate of the universe under her reign, then Skye had a duty to protect it from herself.

"No," she said raising her eyes to the creature before her. The darkness around her recoiled, suddenly confused and suspicious.

Open shock and horror were laid bare on Cassthia's face. "No?" she asked, her voice once again her own.

"No," Skye repeated. "I won't do it. Whatever power is offered here, you can keep it. I will not be responsible for whatever this is that I have seen. I won't let that *thing* loose into our universe."

The darkness was no longer quiet. It was angry. The creature raged around her, infuriated by her defiance.

Cassthia's expression was pleading. "You misunderstand! It doesn't have to be that way! The power is yours to do as you see fit. You will be a living goddess! Do nothing, if it pleases you! Leave the universe to sort out its own destiny."

Skye shook her head. "No. I can't trust myself. Maybe there's someone out there who can responsibly handle the mantle of godhood, but it's not me. I know me. I'm not the one you want."

"But you *are!*"

"No," Skye said for the final time. "I'm not."

This conversation was over. Skye cleared her mind, even as the darkness roared in defiance and a thousand screams rang in her ears. She drew in a deep breath and held in her mind the image of herself standing in the Well of Eternity.

Chapter 32

"Hear, my children, I leave my words for you. The path is clear in preference but difficult to walk.

"Heed my words. Inscribe them upon your heart and mind. For, when tribulation comes to test you, you will realize the truth.

"It is neither prophecy nor fate which dictates the path we walk. It is the summation of our wills, and that alone, which offers both salvation and despair.

"Choose wisely, my children, for all of creation will reap the fruit you sow."

—*Wisdom of Riven,* Chapter 27, Verses 1–4

It was like a hammer blow to the side of her head. Skye's mind slammed back into her body, and she toppled onto the stony ground.

The Heart of Thule blazed with light, no longer the ruby-red of Arc's corruption, but once again a brilliant green. Radiation like emerald fire poured off the object. Skye could still hear the voices crying out from within the artifact.

The air in the room swirled. A loud *whomp* sounded as the ambient power rushed back toward the crystal. The artifact's light flickered. Then, as if put out by a sudden vacuum, it was gone.

Kadath appeared at her side, helping her to her feet. "Might I ask what in the nine hells just happened?"

Skye shook her head, pinching her brow between her fingers in an attempt to stifle her burgeoning headache. She wanted to explain, but wasn't certain she understood it all herself. "Did it work?" she asked. "Did we shut off the conduit?"

"Yes, but that was a good fifteen or twenty minutes ago. The artifact changed back to its original color, and you and Cassthia have just been staring into the thing the whole time. I've been trying to send messages to the other teams, but our damn MoDACs don't work down here." He exhaled sharply. "You had me worried."

So, they'd been inside the artifact for even longer than Skye had thought. She might have been worried for the others if the artifact hadn't so recently assured her of the gristly fates they could have suffered at her hands. It was safe to assume Arc wasn't going to kill them if they would have been alive for Skye to torment in that nightmare reality she'd just witnessed.

Cassthia stalked into view. Her reptilian eyes blazed with a fury that Skye had never seen on the woman's face. "What have you done?"

Skye opened her mouth, but no words came. Truthfully, she wasn't entirely sure what she'd just done.

"I'm sorry?" Kadath replied. "Did something go wrong?"

The priestess leveled an accusing finger in Skye's direction. "She has just *doomed* us all."

Despite herself, Skye managed a harsh chuckle. "Funny, that was kind of the outcome I was looking to avoid. Based on what the artifact was showing me, anyway."

"You *fool*," Cassthia spat. "You could have shaped the power into whatever you desired! The fate of the universe was *yours* to determine. Why did you spurn the power of a god when it merely showed you the outcome of your own choices?"

Skye glared back at the priestess, a sardonic smile taking shape. "Yeah, that's the funny thing: if you're right, then I don't think I'd make a very good goddess. It's not a career path I've aspired toward."

"But you are *Kaleema!*" Cassthia shrieked. "This is your destiny! From the moment we met, I knew the truth! You were to Awaken! You were to bring the Stardust Grave forth, once again, to rule on this plane! You could have brought peace to the entire universe!"

Kadath was thoroughly confused now. "Perhaps someone can catch me up? It may just be my interpretation, but I get the distinct impression you are both talking nonsense."

Skye just shook her head. Her headache was subsiding, and she was able to stand on her own. "It doesn't matter. Maybe we can talk about it later. Right now, I'm much more interested in figuring out what's happened to our friends."

Cassthia continued to fume. Her hands clenched into fists so tight that they shook with the effort. She let out a hissing breath before turning on her heels and walking deeper into the cavern.

Kadath started to call after her, but Skye placed a hand on his shoulder. "Let her go," Skye pleaded. "I'm not entirely sure why she's so pissed off, but it's probably better not to antagonize her right now. She'll come around."

He raised an eyebrow at her. "Fair enough. Might I say, I'm surprised at how calm you look. You know, there's no evidence that things have gone well for everyone else. I'd caution you against being overly optimistic."

Skye shot him a knowing smile. "Let's just say I have the feeling we're going to like the outcome."

Lexa's eyes flickered, a bleary vision taking shape before her. "Daniel?"

The boy pulled her to his chest, squeezing her as hard as his arms were able. Gingerly, she brought her own arms up to return the hug.

"You're okay," he whispered. "You made it."

"Thanks to you," Lexa returned. "You saved me."

They held each other for a long time. The moments slipped by, lost to their embrace. Lexa found herself just too exhausted for anything else.

At length, Lexa whispered, "Daniel, where is Arc?"

Just the mention of his name seemed enough to jar Dan from his moment reverie. "I… I'm not sure."

Lexa felt a stern expression slide into place. "Then we can't stay here. Not until we're sure he's gone. Please, help me stand."

Dan kept talking as he assisted her. "Did you find him in there? In the matrix, I mean."

"Yes. I was keeping him occupied so the virus could do its work."

"Was it able to?"

Lexa blinked a couple of times, searching for the answer. "I'm not certain," she admitted. "My memories of my last moments in the matrix are corrupted. I don't know what happened."

Dan hesitated; it looked as though he felt a disproportionate amount of responsibility for an outcome she couldn't confirm. He was quick to regroup, however. "What should we do?" he asked.

Lexa gazed off to a distant point in the room. "Help me to that terminal."

Despite her expectations, Lexa found her body in better shape than she'd expected. The shell had been properly cared for in her exile, and it seemed that, despite her recent experience, her Cognis drive-chip was still able to interface without error.

When they reached the terminal, Lexa found an intact input wire and brought it to her temple of her skull. Carefully, she peeled away the artificial tissue there to reveal a series of ports. A second before she inserted the wire, Dan's hand came to rest on her arm.

"Are you sure that's safe?" Dan asked.

Lexa nodded. "Daniel, the virus has not spread into the entire system. The matrix has its own containment protocols that will slow its advancement. That said, I need to make sure those protocols will hold. If the virus escapes into the general station infrastructure, we will lose life support. Everyone still aboard will die."

"Oh." Dan pulled back his hand. "Well, in that case, do your thing."

Lexa smiled as she inserted the wire. After a brief loading period, she once again had access to the station's matrix.

As it turned out, she needn't have worried. Though the virus had wiped almost the entirety of the stored data within the matrix, the firewalls for the essential systems were holding. Still, she saw no point in letting the ZMV roam free within the matrix.

After a long pause, Lexa opened her eyes and removed the cord from her temple. "It's done," she reported, sliding her artificial flesh back into place. "I've contained the virus and quarantined it safely within the Citadel's archives. It won't cause any more damage to the station's network, and the Dorians should be able to extract it at another time."

Dan let out a heavy sigh of relief. "And what about Arc?"

Though it had not been her primary objective, Lexa had looked into that matter as well. "I could find only fragments of his source code. I believe he is gone. The security feeds I was able to access showed that his shell has been destroyed within the central terminus, as has his central core. This has caused massive fluctuations in the station's power grid and functionality, but backup systems have thus far been able to handle the strain."

"Then it's over?"

Lexa gave him a sad smile. "Not quite," she said. "I'm afraid my error in judgment, my decision to help Arc, is going to have long-lasting consequences. I, personally, must face some of those consequences."

Confusion blossomed on Daniel's face. "I don't understand. What are you saying?"

"The DGC, what's left of them, have already been called in to secure the Citadel. They will come for me shortly." Her lips tightened, and tears played at the corner of her eyes "I plan to go with them. No resistance."

Dan's confusion gave way to shock. "You can't! They'll destroy you!"

"I have to, Daniel. The few survivors from the assault have already secured the central elevator. It is only a matter of time before they breach Arc's security protocols and find this room. As you know, there is no other way out."

Dan's silvery eyes locked firmly on her own. "You would really go with them? Why would you give up like that?"

"Because I've already put you and the others in so much danger," she said. "Lives were lost because of my bad decisions. If the Dorians want to deactivate me, then it will be no more than what I deserve."

"But I want you to come back with us! The others do too."

Lexa let slip a sad smile. "You don't know that."

"I do too!" he shouted. "Lexa, we've already discussed it. We planned out all kinds of scenarios: what would happen if you were gone, what we would do if Arc had turned you against us, but we also thought of what we would do if we could save you. Lexa, we all want you back!"

Could what the boy claimed be true? Could her friends have the capacity to forgive her after all of this?

Still, it was unlikely that the Dorians would be so mercifully inclined. "Even if it were true," Lexa argued, "I don't know how we would get past the DGC."

Dan let slip a mischievous smile. "I may be able to help with that. May I access the terminal?"

Curious now, Lexa stepped aside. Dan began opening up a new holodisplay and typed furiously in the open window. He waited for just a moment before the system issued some kind of response.

Dan was positively beaming. "I knew you'd pull through," he whispered. He turned back to Lexa. "It looks like my friend in the system was able to slip past the ZMV. We've arranged for an escape route. Come on, we don't have long."

Lexa couldn't help but be skeptical. Was he talking to someone who could actually get them out of the Citadel? They must be quite the ally if they could get them past the DGC. Was Dan being overconfident? Was he about to foolishly put himself at risk for her again?

Then there was the greater question: Was it even right that she be saved? "I'm still not sure," she admitted.

Dan seemed to follow her thought process. His face grew serious, and his jaw set in a determined manner. "Lexa, giving up is the easy thing to do. It's a measure more difficult to try and make things right."

"But that's what I'm trying to do. I'm surrendering myself to Dorian justice. I'm—"

"No," he insisted. "You know their system is not justice. If you surrender to the DGC, they'll terminate you. That's the easy route. If that's what you do, then all you have to do is *stop*. There's no redemption in an execution."

He rested a gentle hand on her shoulder, looking strangely wise beyond his years. It was hard to believe that this was the same boy she'd first made contact with all those months ago on the bridge of the starship where she'd been accidentally born.

"If that's what you want, then fine. I won't stop you," he insisted. "But I want you to do the harder thing, Lexa. That harder thing is to keep on living."

Markus and Jocelyn didn't run into any of the Marauders the rest of the way out. He could hardly believe their luck. In the back of his mind, Markus hoped luck had nothing to do with it, that the lack of enemy combatants was a sign things were going well.

His hopes were confirmed when his MoDAC vibrated. Apologizing to Jocelyn, he shifted his weight to pull the card out of his pocket.

On the screen, there was a single message from an unidentified sender: [Package secured.] Though the message's origin was encrypted, he knew there was only one scenario in which he would have received that message.

Jocelyn must have noticed his smile. "Good news?" she asked.

Markus hit the delete icon next to the message. "Very," he confirmed. "Come on, it shouldn't be much farther now."

The pain that had been dragging him down was much easier to ignore the rest of the way out of the tunnel. Minutes later, they emerged from the underground pathways to a set of stairs that led to the outer courtyard.

Relief washed over him as he caught sight of familiar faces: Llana, Geresh, Sahar, Aaliyah, and even Turan. They, along with a smattering of DGC and Maur soldiers, were wrapped in a tense discussion, though Markus could tell they were largely at ease.

"Little hand here?" Markus shouted.

Judging from the way everyone eyed him, he must have looked as shitty as he felt. Gawking was the word. They were actually *gawking* at him.

Unfortunately, that meant no one was jumping to help him. At least until Turan was able to snap them out of it. "You there!" He shouted to a pair of Dorians near him. "You heard the man! Get to it!"

One of Dorians grabbed Jocelyn, sweeping her off her feet to carry her like she was a child. The triumvir didn't protest, which spoke to how shitty she must have been feeling.

The second soldier tried getting Markus to sit down. Markus just waved him off. Once he bothered to sit, he had the distinct feeling he would not be getting up again for a long time.

Limping wasn't nearly as hard when he wasn't supporting Jocelyn's weight. He hobbled toward his companions, though he didn't have to go far.

Sahar rushed him, taking him into her arms and lifting him into the air. "You're alive! I can't *fragging* believe it! You're alive!"

Despite the warm intentions, Sahar's inhuman strength was making him hurt. Like, *everywhere*. "I might not be for long if you don't take it easy."

The Maur's grip loosened so quickly that he ended up falling right onto his gimpy leg. He squealed—not a masculine shout, definitely a squeal—and started to collapse. Sahar caught him before he face-planted, but it was still one of the less dignified moments of his life.

"Sorry," she murmured. "The fall… I just thought…"

"Yeah…" Markus gasped. "Got lucky."

"Again?" Aaliyah chimed good-naturedly. "Are ya gettin' slick with Lady Luck on the sly? Ya can tell me, ya know. Ora doesn't have to find out."

Despite the pain, Markus chuckled. "That just proves you don't know Ora very well. She'd definitely find out."

Aaliyah turned to the side. "Hey, twinkle fingers!"

Twinkle fingers? Markus looked at the person Aaliyah had shouted at and felt slightly nauseated. Did she really just call Turan Dorr "twinkle fingers?"

The Dorian was also not impressed. "Call me that again and I will skip the trial and execute you immediately."

"Sure thing, twinkie," Aaliyah replied. "Can ya use some of your mojo on my boy here? He looks like he's had a rough night."

Turan glowered at her, even as he laid hand on Markus's bicep. Psionic energy surged into Markus at the point of contact. The pain immediately began to subside, though the hunger that replaced it was arguably just as irritating.

The Dorian jerked his hand away after a couple of seconds. "That will make sure you don't die on your way to a medical facility. Now, I need a status report. What happened to you?"

Given the quick bit of analgesia he'd just received, Markus didn't mind giving the Dorian the highlights. When he'd finished, he asked. "What about everyone else? Given that we're all loitering about, I assume Arc is toast. How did we fair?"

Turan's look was grim. "Heavy losses in both the Dorian and Maur contingents. Your friends seemed to have done a bit better than average, but…" he hesitated. "One of the Sahaia was lost."

Markus looked to Aaliyah. She must have read his mind because she was already shaking her head. "Argus. Eli's definitely in rough shape, but he's gonna live. Sk…" She seemed to stumble over her words for a second.

That prompted an eye roll from Markus. "Skye's got him?"

"Yeah. Sounds like their group got a bit separated down in those tunnels, but everyone else is accounted for. Well, 'cept for Cassthia. Skye was a bit fuzzy on the details, but it sounds like she wandered off after the action was over."

Huh. That was odd. Markus wondered why the priestess would have gone off on her own like that. He hoped that she was okay. Cassthia had been invaluable in this endeavor.

"And Dan? Sydney?" Markus asked because it was something that he would be expected to do at the time. He already had a feeling about those two, thanks to the encrypted text, but the Dorians would expect his concern. He couldn't let on that he might have extra information about the kid's whereabouts.

Turan's face was grim. "The assassin is unaccounted for, but we've not found her body. Given that, she's probably fine. We've been in contact with the boy. They left their position and are currently in the Citadel. We have a team checking on them now." The interface on his gauntlet vibrated. "That's probably them. Excuse me, I must take this."

When Turan had stepped aside, Markus turned back to his friends. "Any other news I should be aware of? Good only, please. I'll deal with the bad stuff after I've had a shot of whiskey or six."

Aaliyah smiled. "Well, the gates are back online. That's why the DGC are bein' such busybodies. The initial ships that have come through are pingin' all kinds of requests for status updates." More soberly, she added. "I almost feel bad for Turan. He's pushed off every message from his bosses, tellin' them he'll provide a report when the fires are out."

Markus raised an eyebrow. "Feel bad? For Turan? Come on, Red. We leave you two alone for a couple of hours, and you're making friends with the enemy?"

The mechanic donned a friendly smirk. "What can I say? The guy has a way with his hands."

That prompted more raised eyebrows. Sahar asked, "Is that why you call him 'twinkle fingers?' Do I need to talk with Nikki?"

"No! I mean… yes, but…" Aaliyah's smirk shifted to irritation. "Seriously, though. When ya get past all of the arrogance, smugness, and general dickishness, he's not that bad. Saved *my* ass, anyway. That's gotta count for somethin'."

Markus feigned surprise. "Past the smugness *and* the dickishness? I didn't think there'd be much left to him after that."

"Quiet," Sahar growled. "He's coming back, and he looks pissed."

Turan stalked up to them, full DGC authority resonating from the agitated look on his face. "They found the boy on the top floor. Still no sign of the assassin. He says they got separated." There was suspicion and more than a hint of accusation in his look as he added, "No sign of the second synth, either. Not a trace of it since we arrived."

Markus feigned confusion, then sudden recognition. With difficulty, he fought to make the next lie convincing. "Arc must have destroyed her, then. That was one of the possibilities that we'd considered."

Maybe it was Markus's injuries or his lack of recent practice, but Turan wasn't buying it. "Is that *really* what you think happened?"

"Do you have another theory?"

Turan paused, eying first Markus, then Sahar, then Aaliyah. "No," he drawled "I suppose I don't." The Dorian's gaze contained so much annoyance at that moment that it reminded Markus of old times.

"Good," Markus replied. "Then we're all done here?"

Another hesitation. Turan turned his head to regard the bureaucratic shit-storm that was likely already brewing among his subordinates. "Yes," he conceded. "I suppose we are."

He turned and walked off. About a dozen paces out, he looked back over his shoulder. "Oh, by the way, Markus?"

"Yeah?"

"Find your own damn ride home."

Six weeks later

Lexa's drones had just finished another sweep of the neighboring asteroids. They hadn't found anything, and Lexa concluded there was a high probability that they would not find anything on the sweeps scheduled for the future. She would conduct them anyway, of course. It was imperative that nothing interfere with the repair process.

Piloting the drones into the reconstructed hanger, she took care not to collide with any of the Maur teams that worked busily on getting the *Vandal* back into operational condition. She set the drones down on their charging platform and powered them off, creating the illusion that they were going latent now that their function had been complete.

Later that evening, when the workers conducted their shift change, she would repurpose the drones to complete another task that was slightly more unconventional. Though she could do so immediately, it was better not to flaunt it in front of soldiers who had been briefed that only the ship's most basic systems were back online.

She toggled her consciousness over to the bots assisting with repairs near the crew quarters. There, she found Skye and Sahar, the latter of whom had arrived by shuttle fifteen minutes earlier.

"No, they've been great," Skye was saying. "A total model of efficiency. But seriously, when are you going to tell me why the Federation is being so helpful?"

Sahar shrugged. "Geresh felt like he owed us a favor. He said that he could lend the resources until he heard back from the Federation. That'll probably give us at least another month."

"Bull. Shit," Skye gave the Maur an amicable punch to the shoulder. "We were all nice about it back when the universe was ending and all, but you've gotta let me know what the real deal is. Don't pretend like we didn't see what happened back on the *Crimson Sky.* What's the deal? You some kind of runaway princess or something?"

Sahar glowered at her. "Call me a princess again and it'll be the *last* thing you."

Skye held up her hands defensively. "Fine, fine. But seriously, you're gonna have to fill me in eventually." She paused, mischief still gleaming in her eye. "So, how is Geresh doing, anyway?"

Sahar shrugged. "Fine."

"Yeah? You were spending time with him back on the station, right?" Skye, in her exaggerated attempt to remain nonchalant, added an air of insinuation to the words.

Sahar brushed it off. "Yes, that's true."

"Anything you want to tell me in that department?"

The Maur huffed. "Skye, I don't ask about your romantic entanglements. I'd prefer you not attempt to discuss mine."

Skye donned a triumphant smirk. "So you *would* say that it's 'romantic.'"

Sahar stammered. "N-no! That's *not* what I said!"

"Funny, because that's what I heard."

Distantly, Lexa registered the signal that she'd assigned to her cabin door. A quick blink to that security feed showed Eli and Daniel waiting to be admitted inside.

She locked the protocols on all active drones so that they would finish their current tasks and return to their stations to idle. She then shifted her consciousness back to her android shell.

It was always a strange sensation to take control of her body again. She longed for the day when she would reestablish wireless control of the ship's functions, but that was still a long way off. Getting the vessel space-worthy and back to the Ravian System were her top priorities.

Reaching back behind her head, she detached hardwire that currently allowed her to interface with the *Vandal's* systems. With the port disconnected, she rose from her cradle and slipped a dark jacket on over her black tank-top. Like most of the crew, she'd found she had an affinity for darker colors.

As she did this, she hit the console that opened her cabin door, permitting Eli and Dan to enter. Once the pair filed in, she touched the panel again to shut it behind them. The Maur might be curiously willing to do them the favor of rebuilding their vessel, but it was unlikely that they'd overlook the Dorian bounty still on her head.

"Greetings," Lexa chimed.

"Hello, Lexa," Eli said, giving that tired smile he wore constantly these days. "How are things going today?"

"Repair efforts proceed on schedule. Barring any unforeseen disruptions, the *Vandal* will be ready for space flight in two months, one week, three days, and fourteen hours." She paused, realizing that she'd been overly precise. "Give-or-take."

The Sahaia laughed. "Give or take." He shook his head. "Well, we may have a slight complication. Dan, can you show her?"

Daniel handed her a tablet. "These are the readouts from the engine test this morning."

Lexa studied the figures on the screen. She'd have to upload the file directly to figure out what the exact problem was, but just a quick survey told her the readings were abnormal.

"Well, that's unfortunate. It seems that the Maur are quite unfamiliar with some of the modifications that have been made to the *Vandal's* engines. If this progresses, they will almost certainly overload the coolant system."

"Can you fix it?" Eli asked.

"I believe so. We will need to manufacture an explanation, though. Daniel may need to spend some time in engineering this evening to take the credit."

Daniel shrugged. "That's fine. I have some things I can review on my tablet while you're working. Just know I'm not going to be of much help, otherwise. That work is a bit mechanical for me."

Lexa gave him a soft smile before teasing, "Aaliyah would be most disappointed."

Eli laughed. "Yes, I suppose she would be."

"Do you think they've made it back to Sigma-4 yet?" Daniel asked.

Lexa quickly ran through the calculations. "Yes, I think so. They should have arrived this morning."

Despite the hoarseness in her voice, Aaliyah had no trouble making herself heard. "Seriously, though—it's been six weeks! Traffic should not still be this fragged up after six weeks! Those fraggin' satyrs are making everyone's lives miserable for no gods-damned reason."

Yup. Markus really should have broken up that conversation between her and Kadath on the shuttle. The mercenary may have thought it was funny to get Aaliyah all spun up, but he didn't have to listen to her rantings all the way back to mid-tier.

"If you're looking for a debate, Red, put in a call to the *Basilisk.* You aren't going to hear me defend the DGC."

"Right! 'Cause ya aren't a fraggin' idiot! Where does that guy get off sayin' shit like that? What kind of people are ya runnin' with these days?"

Markus heaved a sigh. "I'm pretty sure he was just trying to piss you off."

"Well, he did a good fraggin' job." Whatever she was going to say dissolved into a coughing fit and an inelegant sniff.

"Not enjoying your vacation away from your partner?" Markus didn't have to clarify what he meant. She knew he was referring to Eli.

"Frag off," she spat, wiping at her nose. "I haven't had a cold in almost a decade. As soon as we passed through that damned gate I felt like a walking pathogen."

Markus might have laughed if he weren't so tired. Spending several weeks in a cramped cabin on a public transport with Aaliyah, Kadath, and Siv had been quite the test on his sanity—especially after Kadath figured out how easy it was to get Aaliyah all riled up.

"I think this is our stop," he noted as the tram slid to a halt.

Aaliyah was quiet as she shouldered her bag and moved to the exit. She looked nervous.

"Kret for your thoughts?" Markus asked.

"It just feels like a long time," she admitted. "It always feels weird comin' home after long trips, ya know?"

Markus nodded, though he didn't. Home had always been aboard a starship for him. It honestly felt weird to not be out on the run.

He offered to call them a cab, but Aaliyah waved him off. It was just a short distance from here, and she preferred the walk. Markus thought she just wanted a few more minutes to think quietly to herself.

They made the rest of the trip in silence. When they were about a half-block away from Aaliyah's apartment, a door sprang open in the distance. A little girl rushed down the steps and raced toward them.

"Momma 'Liyah!"

Aaliyah stopped and took a knee. Monica barreled straight into her open arms. Tears of joy ran from Aaliyah's closed eyes into the girl's black curls. "Hey, baby girl. I missed ya so much."

Markus looked up to see Nikki standing in the doorway. Her arms were crossed, and her hip cocked out in a distinctly maternal way. Even at this distance, he could see there were tears in her eyes too.

He reached down and patted Monica on the back. "Take care of her for me, okay Mona?"

"Will do, Unca Markus!"

With a smile on his face and a polite wave to Nikki, he started back in the other direction.

Well, where to now? He checked his MoDAC. He'd messaged Ora when they were in range of the station's network, but hadn't received a reply. That bothered him. He'd actually been hoping he could see her this evening. Now he was wondering if Ora had given up on him ever coming back.

A heavy sigh reinforced the exhaustion he already felt. He supposed he should get some actual sleep anyway. Plus, it was beyond time he check in on Jilly's Gambit. With him being gone so much these last months, it was almost guaranteed that the bar had gone to shit by now.

He hopped the next tram back to R-3 and made his way to the establishment. To his surprise, the bar was not only open for business, it was packed.

Two big Maur enforcers were stationed just outside the entrance, taking names and talking on their earpieces. Markus was certain he hadn't hired those two. So who was taking the initiative?

In retrospect, the answer really should have been obvious.

Markus passed right by the bouncers, who must have recognized him given that they made no move to stop him. As he had suspected, Ora stood in the one private dining room in the entire dive, talking to yet more staff that Markus had not hired.

When she saw him, she turned to the brown-haired woman to her left. "Molly, would you mind fetching a beverage for the proprietor? Whiskey, neat, unless he says otherwise."

When Markus didn't respond, the woman did as Ora had asked.

Ora held up her hands placatingly. "I can explain."

Markus chuckled and just shook his head. "Couldn't help yourself?"

"It wasn't my fault. Rob called two days after you were gone and said he was taking a permanent vacation. Figured he should let someone know." Ora let slip a small smile. "You're still the owner. I just didn't want things to get too… unruly. Given the circumstances, I didn't think you would mind if I stepped in. Temporarily, of course."

Markus smiled. "So much for no handouts."

"I can bill you if it makes you feel better."

"I'm pretty sure I can't afford you."

"With the way this place is running *now*, you could."

Molly returned with a tumbler, half-filled with amber liquid. Markus thanked her for the drink, deposited his bag against the wall, and took a long pull.

Gods, that was good. That was definitely not something they'd been stocking before. He eyed Ora sideways. "Please tell me you didn't get rid of the games in the back."

"Of course not. Though they're not something I'd toy with personally, they seem to be quite popular among the customers. There's a tournament scheduled for tomorrow on the *Defender* machines. I'll need to call the news outlets if you plan to cancel it."

News outlets? Damn, did this woman do anything half-ass? "Nah, it's cool. So, who's running the rest of your businesses while you've been down here getting my shit in order?"

"Tashania seems to have things well enough under control. Besides, Molly does most of the heavy lifting here. I recommend you hire her on permanently, but it is, of course, still your business."

Markus finished his drink. "So, I'm not in trouble?"

Ora looked confused. "In trouble?"

"Well, I texted you an hour or two ago and didn't get a response."

"I figured you'd make your way over here eventually. I thought it'd be better to explain in person." Her smile widened. "So, am *I* in trouble?"

"Of course not."

"Then why are you still standing over there?"

Grin locked firmly in place, Markus closed the gap. He wasn't normally one for public displays of affection, but he'd been waiting a long time for this kiss.

After a long, precious moment, Ora's lips pulled back, affixing him with her violet eyes. "I'll leave you to it then. When you're done getting settled in, be sure to stop by Annex and see me. I can brief you on the changes I've made, and I might have another job you might be interested in."

Markus kissed her again. "Is that like a *job*-job? Or…"

Ora rested a hand against his chest and donned that mysterious smile of hers. "I guess you're going to have to visit me to find out."

"Wait here," Mara said as they approached the side-chamber entrance. Tristan and David nodded in silent response. They were used to the routine by now. They'd been accompanying her down to this very chamber every day for weeks now.

They never questioned the new part of their daily routine. Though they could never fully understand, they could empathize, as could Mara. If Mara ever lost Tristan or David, weeks would only begin to heal the pain, and that was supposing such a loss could ever be healed at all.

The stone door swung open at the barest touch of her fingers. It was always unlocked. Amelia didn't need locks to protect her privacy. She likely knew a person's intent to visit before even they did, and if she didn't want to be seen, she'd proven more than capable of changing a potential visitor's mind.

The empath hadn't always been so powerful. Something had happened to her since Argus's death. Amelia had always been gifted, but since her partner's demise, her power had increased exponentially. It scared Mara, and she had a feeling it scared Jocelyn too.

Amelia undoubtedly knew it, but she remained polite. The casual exercise of her enhanced empathic and telepathic abilities had come as a surprise to her at first, but she'd had time to refine her skills since then. Now there wasn't a thought within the entire Sanctum to which Amelia wasn't privy.

This was part of the reason Mara was always a little embarrassed upon entering Amelia's haunt. Amelia had not changed, had not bathed, and had scarcely eaten in almost six full weeks. She was often found pacing restlessly or whispering to unseen listeners. When she was not acting manic, she was found lying atop Argus's sarcophagus, tears running silently onto the etched stone surface.

In Mara's eyes, her sister had lost her mind. Though she never said as much, there was no hiding her opinion. Not from Amelia.

But today, it was different. Though Amelia had not groomed, she at least looked more at peace than Mara had seen her in recent weeks. She sat cross-legged on the floor, eyes closed, her back to the sarcophagus. She exuded calm. Her expression was neutral.

"How are you doing, Amelia?" Mara asked.

Amelia did not bother to open her eyes as she replied. "Better today, as you can see." It was said matter-of-factly, without a hint of petulance.

"I'm glad to hear that." Mara managed a smile. "May I ask what has you feeling better today?"

"You'll know soon. She'll be here momentarily."

Before Mara could ask who, the door behind her whispered open to reveal Jocelyn's emaciated form.

Though Jocelyn was better kept than Amelia, she appeared haggard in a different way. She was still far too thin from her time locked beneath the Citadel, though her physical health had improved significantly over the weeks. An air of perpetual exhaustion hung around her at all times. While the fatigue might also be attributed to her recent experience, Mara knew better.

On returning, Jocelyn had immediately set to work recovering what she could from the wreckage of the Sanctum. Mara and her thralls had helped, as did Eli before he left the station, but none of them put in the ridiculous hours Jocelyn had.

When the wreckage had been cleared, Jocelyn began cataloging all that was lost. Mara helped with this where she could, but this bit of work was largely something only Jocelyn could complete. As such, the triumvir was scarcely seen outside of what remained of the Sanctum archives.

As Jocelyn stepped from the doorway and into the chamber, Mara could see she carried with her a large black tome. She held the book tight against her thin body as if defending it against anyone who might try to rip it from her.

"Has she told you?" Jocelyn asked.

"Told me what?" Mara replied. If Jocelyn and Amelia were going to triangulate every discussion in recognition of Amelia's new abilities, Mara was going to reconsider her decision to remain and help reestablish the Sanctum.

"I thought it best to wait and let her hear it from you," Amelia explained, finally opening her eyes. "I, too, would like to hear it framed by your lips. Your thoughts are… too excited."

Excited? "Well, then it must be good news!" Mara noted. "Don't keep me in suspense!"

Jocelyn heaved a sigh. "Well, it's the *possibility* of good news." She moved to the sarcophagus and laid the book on its surface. Hastily, she opened the tome to a marked page.

Mara was immediately uncomfortable. Using Argus's resting place like a desk seemed rather disrespectful. "I don't mind," Amelia said in response to the unexpressed thought. "It's almost like we are including him this way."

Great, now it's disrespectful and *morbid.* Mara swallowed hard and looked at the page Jocelyn had opened. "You're studying the Wells of Eternity," she noted.

"Correct," Jocelyn replied. "As we all know, there has never been a reported instance of one of the Wells being destroyed, thus their moniker. Yet, we have seen what has befallen the sacred waters of our home, so we are faced with a paradox."

"How does one destroy what cannot be destroyed," Amelia chimed.

Jocelyn nodded. "Precisely. I started researching recorded instances of a Well losing function: not being destroyed, per se, but being reduced or diminished in some way. This was largely unhelpful. Everything I found supported what we already knew: the Wells exist in a kind of state of metaphysical thermodynamics. Their power cannot be created or destroyed, merely transformed."

"But the laws of thermodynamics don't apply to metaphysics," Mara protested. "That's what makes them *meta.*"

"It was a metaphor," Jocelyn growled. "My point is, that if *our* Well of Eternity can't be destroyed, then it must not have been."

Okay, now *both* of her sisters had lost their minds. "But it's not here, Jocelyn. We've seen for ourselves. There's nothing in the pool—nothing other than that cursed artifact, anyway."

Amelia spoke up. "Just because it isn't here, doesn't mean it's destroyed. It just means it's somewhere else."

"*Exactly!*" Jocelyn hissed.

Well, at least that was *slightly* less crazy. "So, the waters weren't destroyed," Mara repeated. "They were moved. That's not what Cassthia said. That's not what Skye or Kadath reported either."

"True," Jocelyn conceded. "That's what I've been trying to reconcile. Skye said it *felt* as though the waters were consumed in Thule's fire. Cassthia explained that it was her *intent* to consume the waters with Thule's fire. Yet, if Thule had the power to destroy the Wells of Eternity, why did he allow them to exist in the first place?"

Mara pinched her lips. "Perhaps he didn't have a say in the matter?"

Jocelyn shook her head. "No, he most certainly did. He was there when the first of them was created! Thule was the first god to slay one of his fellows on the mortal plane. *That's* where the Wells come from! When an Awakened Kaleema dies, their bodies can no longer contain the essence of a god, so that essence is transmuted to form a Well of Eternity."

Huh. Mara had never considered that. "Okay, let's say I buy all of that. I still don't know where you're going this."

"So, if Thule can't destroy the essence of a god, that means he had to put it somewhere else. If we want to restore our Well, we just need to track where he sent it! We then follow those metaphysical connections and transport the essence of Riven back into the Sanctum."

Mara's eyes creased in concern. "Follow it? Do you mean, to like another place, or to another—"

"Dimension!" Amelia was beaming now with a maniacal glint in her ink-black eyes. "We're going beyond the Well! We're going to go to where the ancestral spirits rest!" She lowered her voice into a whisper that managed to be simultaneously wistful and conspiratorial. "And when we do, I'm going to bring *him* back."

———

Geresh had not been given express permission to wander the halls of the Ren'Dahl Sanctum. The handful of Sahaia and thralls that remained, however, had done nothing to stop him. For these past few weeks, he'd been given free rein to explore the complex.

Jocelyn was the only one he'd consulted on the matter. She'd been surprisingly amenable to the idea. Geresh reasoned it was out of a sense of gratitude, having been saved from a rather slow and gruesome demise.

Or maybe the triumvir just didn't care anymore. Either way, Geresh had taken the opportunity to explore the complex. He'd also offered his soldiers for the process of assisting the reconstruction of the sanctum, but his offer had been respectfully declined.

That was fine. Though Geresh truly wished to help, if perhaps in exchange for some informal alliance with the Maur Federation, he did not let the refusal diminish his spirits. His assistance had already established valuable ties with the NTA in this system. And besides, there was still something else here that had caught his interest—something he *really* wanted.

He trod carefully down the stairs and into the chamber that had once housed the Well of Eternity. A pair of lonely glow orbs rested on the ground near the object that had brought him down here.

The Heart of Thule loomed ominously in the center of the emptied Well. A lone figure set cross-legged in front of the artifact, just staring into its darkened crystals.

Cassthia Marenassa.

Reports had circulated of a woman matching her description being spotted on the station occasionally, but no one had ever spoken to her to confirm her identity. Geresh's contacts had begun to speculate as to whether she had quietly slipped off on one of the many transports ferrying people away from the dilapidated station.

Now it appeared that was not the case. "Have you been down here this whole time?" he asked.

Cassthia shrugged slightly. "Mostly."

Geresh took a seat next to her. He half wondered if the priestess might object to the violation of her solitude, but she said nothing.

The woman looked rough. Heavy shadows rimmed her serpentine eyes. Her hair beneath the hood of her cowl was matted and tangled. Her face seemed drawn—not quite gaunt, but giving the appearance that she was not receiving proper nourishment.

"Should I have some food brought to you?" he asked.

"No, thank you. I venture out to get food and water when I need it." Even as she talked, her eyes never left the artifact.

Geresh tried to understand what she was looking at, to see the artifact the way she saw it. He understood the impulse. He also found himself staring into its depths. Yet, he could never see it as she saw it. He'd never seen it in action. All he saw was an asset that some of the most powerful entities in Terran space had fought and bled for.

The Terran woman, Skye, had been light on the details regarding their encounter with the artifact and Cassthia's disappearance. He'd not pressed Skye for details at the time. The truth had a way of making its way out eventually, and he had more pressing matters to contend with. Now though, might just be the appropriate time to ferret out that truth.

"Help me understand," he pleaded.

Cassthia sighed. "I'm not certain words will be sufficient."

"If you have them to spare, I would hear them anyway."

The priestess hesitated only briefly. With another sigh, began. "The Heart of Thule was to be our salvation. Its power was to be wielded by the Kaleema. She was supposed to save us all. Now, the game progresses absent an important piece on the board."

That was less helpful than Geresh would have liked, though his mind still worked to render a helpful interpretation. "Save us from what?"

Cassthia shook her head, closing her eyes. "That is, unfortunately, a somewhat complicated answer."

As if her opening assertions had been any form of simplistic. "Okay, then," he reasoned. "*How* was it supposed to save us?"

Cassthia cut him a sidelong glance. Somewhat annoyed, she continued. "A male of your background might think of it as a weapon—a weapon against powerful forces that position themselves against our interests."

A weapon. Geresh understood weapons. He also understood that it was usually a mistake to discard a weapon that might still be useful.

He tried to frame his next inquiry within her initial metaphor. "What if the game wasn't over yet?"

The priestess blinked in surprise. "Pardon?"

"You said the game progresses without a player on the board. What if we haven't lost our chance to place the piece just yet? A weapon isn't useless just because someone fails to employ it effectively. Sometimes you just have to find a better soldier to wield it."

Though she eyed him warily, Geresh had her full attention. "What are you suggesting?" she asked.

He kept his expression neutral, but inside he was grinning. "I'm suggesting that, perhaps, it is within the Federation's best interests to work with you on this. If the threat is real, as you claim, then I might have a proposal that could work to serve both of our interests."

Somehow, her eyes began to gleam in the darkness. A brief flash of emerald lanced through those golden orbs. Cassthia's hand played idly at the medallion hanging between her breasts.

"All right," she agreed. "I'm listening."

The End

Hey, reader,

You've reached, "The End,' but as you might expect from the epilogue, it's not truly the end. Rather, it's the turning of a page, and the end of a saga.

So, what comes next? I have plenty of ideas, and a multitude of stories to tell. What I invest in first is going to be entirely up to you. Reach out to me at erdonaldson@mythicnorthpress.com to share your thoughts. Better yet, find me on Facebook, Instagram, Twitter, or (most effective) Discord. You can find all the appropriate links at https:/mythicnorthpress.com.

That said, I'm reaching out into new opportunities outside of the Mythic North platform. I have several short stories awaiting publication and a whole new serial in development. The best way to keep in touch with these new adventures is to subscribe to the newsletter on my website. The effort will earn you access to an exclusive anthology of short stories that show how the *Vandal* crew came together.

You have my links, and you have my information. All I can hope is that I will hear from you soon. Until then, swift running.

– E. R. Donaldson